SOLDIERS OF FORTUNE

A *Just Cause Universe* Novel

IAN THOMAS HEALY

Local Hero Press Edition

Soldiers of Fortune
Published by Local Hero Press, LLC
http://localheropress.com

1st Printing
Local Hero Press: trade paperback, June 15, 2020
Printed in the United States of America

All rights reserved worldwide.
Copyright ©2020 Ian Thomas Healy

ISBN-13: 9781971445182

Cover art by Nathaniel Dickson
Book design by Local Hero Press, LLC

Books by Local Hero Press

The *Just Cause Universe*

Just Cause
The Archmage
Day of the Destroyer
Deep Six
Jackrabbit
Champion
Castles
The Lion and the Five Deadly Serpents
Tusks
The Neighborhood Watch
Jackrabbit: Big In Japan
Arena
Hero Academy
The Path
Cinco de Mayo
Search and Rescue
Rooftops
Plague
Soldiers of Fortune
Just Cause Universe Compendium
Destroyer of Earth
Flint and Steel
The Club
Jackrabbit: Rinse and Repeat
Posse
Extinction Event
Rain Must Fall

Pariah of Verigo

Pariah's Moon
Pariah's War

Three Flavors of Tacos

The Guitarist
Making the Cut
The Scene Stealers

Collections

Airship Lies
High Contrast
The Good Fight
The Good Fight 3: Sidekicks
The Good Fight 4: Homefront
The Good Fight 5: The Golden Age
Muddy Creek Tales
Caped

Other Novels

Assassin
Blood on the Ice
Funeral Games
Hope and Undead Elvis
Horde
The Murder Squad (2026)
Roast Wyvern (and Other Recipes)
*Starf*cker*
Strings
The Oilman's Daughter
Troubleshooters

Nonfiction

Action! Writing Better Action Using Cinematic Techniques

Author Notes

The '90s were a crazy time, as I recall.

It's now thirty years since I graduated from high school, and the past has become a generalized haze with notable high and low points. The decade of grunge brought about a number of changes in my life. Friendships began, friendships ended. I went to college. I worked a series of unfulfilling jobs. I got married. My first child was born. The internet exploded.

In general, the Nineties were a time of transition, as the world began to take its first steps into cooperation and communication instead of conflict. People of my generation (Generation X, in case you're a Boomer or a Millennial and didn't know we existed), occupied a vast landscape of confusion and uncertainty. We became Content Creators in the form of angry, dirty music wrapped in flannel and bearing a squalling guitar.

Action movies really hit their stride in the '90s. Keanu Reeves transformed from a teenage stoner to the hero of *Speed*, *The Matrix*, and *Point Break*. Chow Yun Fat introduced us to *Hard Boiled* and *The Replacement Killers*. Arnold Schwarzenegger brought us *True Lies* and *Terminator 2*. Bruce Willis gave us another *Die Hard* and a ridiculous sci-fi extravaganza in *The Fifth Element*. Women became heroes as well, with Linda Hamilton, also in *Terminator 2*, and Geena Davis in *The Long Kiss Goodnight*.

I **loved** these movies. Action films from this era were less about CG effects and more about spectacle, with many practical effects and choreography. The '90s also brought an era of ultra-violent, nihilistic characters in comics, drawn in over-the-top styles. Giant guns. Swords. Pouches (*so many pouches!*). This was the look of comics in the '90s, wrapped up in collectible, chromium covers.

I wanted to recreate that feel in this book, and thus bring you this tale of Jingshen, *aka* the Chinatown Ghost, a three-hundred-year-old warrior who just can't stop fighting. Like every good action hero, he's going to take his lumps and keep coming back for more.

* * *

As always, I have a list of people without whom this book would never have come to pass. As a good portion of this book was written during the COVID-19 pandemic, my team has been smaller and tighter than ever. Ira did a bang-up job with editing and proofreading. Nathaniel brought me a superb cover. My friend AJ, who is somewhat obsessed with the Just Cause Universe, kept my toes to the fire on getting this book finished so he can read it.

I'm especially grateful to my family for giving me time and space to write when we're all crammed into the same tiny house to avoid catching the plague. And last, thank you to all my fans around the world who inspire me to tell new stories. Stay safe!

-Ian Thomas Healy
May, 2020

Chapter One

September, 1993
Los Angeles, California

It was a beautiful late summer night in the Los Angeles Basin—at least, Jingshen thought it probably was as he roared up the highway on the Harley-Davidson. He'd always associated beautiful nights with clear, starlit skies, neither of which were applicable to the City of Angels. Once, the air hadn't been congested with smog, trapping and reflecting a million lights back upon the city's denizens. Once, he remembered, he'd stood atop one of the San Gabriel Mountains to look out across the valley in the light of a full moon, and even though he knew there were campfires far below, the brilliance of the heavens drowned them out in a symphony of starlight.

That had been a long time ago, before cities, before railroads, before the omnipresent constellation of brake lights forcing him to bypass them by swinging the big bike into the breakdown lane. The exit ramp was mercifully free of backed-up traffic, for no commuter in their right mind would risk the crime-ridden neighborhood below. The only kinds of people who sought it out were those for whom the lure of dark business was greater than the fear for personal safety.

People like Jingshen.

The smog seemed to have settled onto everything along the road, giving parked cars, storefronts, and people loitering under streetlights a dingy grittiness that might not wash off even with a fire hose. The Harley's engine thrummed. Exhaust echoed off the glass panes of bodegas, video stores, and taquerías. The blatting report made hookers and dealers look up from their business before returning to the transactions at hand. Jingshen kept his eyes forward. He didn't care what anyone else on the streets was doing. A brief thump of bass overpowered his bike's engine as a primer-brown Buick rolled the other way down the street on tiny gold-spoke wheels, leaving a cloud of blue oil smoke tinged with marijuana in its wake.

Jingshen made a right turn, barely nudging the bike's throttle, and cruised away from the main strip along a narrow boulevard with fenced-off yards and shuttered storefronts decorated with decades of graffiti. The streetlights were sporadically placed, isolated pools of light along the otherwise darkened street. The people he saw here were more furtive, stepping into shadows at his approach. Still, he kept his eyes forward. Nothing here was his business, except in the bar with the blue and red neon sign at the end of the block. It was called *Johnny Danger's*, except the *er's* was burned out, naming the establishment *Johnny Dang*. A couple other bikes and a half dozen beater cars were parked haphazardly along the front of the bar. Several Latino toughs smoked out front, wearing bandannas over their shaved heads and showing off their tattoos.

Their conversation died as they watched Jingshen roll up to the bar and swing the bike around to back it into the last spot. He ignored them as he switched off the ignition and lowered the kickstand.

The whispers began, behind his back. Some of them were in Spanish, which he spoke fluently after a decade-long mercenary stint in northern Mexico. He heard the men joking about his size and the size of the bike, and about the two sticks sitting in sheaths across his back, strapped over the dusty leather jacket. He unhooked the clasp on the bike's saddlebag and withdrew a battered black fedora he'd taken a liking to in Chicago. When he set it upon his head and straightened the brim, the men behind him laughed, as if it were the funniest thing they'd seen in days. He swung his leg over the bike and found a tall Hispanic man with a goatee and a teardrop tattoo by his left eye confronting him.

"Yo, what's the deal, Homes? You steal that fuckin' bike or what?"

"No. Excuse me." Jingshen kept his voice quiet and sidestepped the tall man.

The man trotted back to stand before him once again. "Hey, Homes, I was talkin' to you. Where'd you get the bike?"

"Look at him, Timo, he's Asian. Maybe he don't understand you so good," one of the other men catcalled, eliciting laughter from the group.

"Lemme try again," said the man called Timo. He grinned, showing a gold tooth, and spoke in slow, exaggerated English. "*I said . . . where'd . . . you . . . get . . . the . . . bike?*" He pointed at Jingshen then at the motorcycle and then made a "*vroom vroom*" sound that made the others burst out in giggles.

"I bought it. Excuse me," Jingshen said.

"Oh, you *bought* it. Well excuse me, Mr. Rich Fucking Asian. So sorry to be in your way and all." Timo made no move to get out of Jingshen's way. "So since it's yours, maybe you'll sell it to me, Homes. I always wanted a Harley. And it looks like it's way too big for your tiny little ass."

"It is not for sale," Jingshen said. He raised his head enough for Timo to see his face in the light from the bar's neon sign.

Timo blinked as he took in the network of fine white scars crisscrossing his face. "Goddamn, Homes, the fuck happened to you?"

It was a question that had no simple answer, and Jingshen was in no mood to tell stories. "Excuse me. I will not ask again." He stepped to the side and Timo made his mistake, reaching out to grab Jingshen by the shoulder.

Jingshen reached up and locked Timo's wrist by twisting it up and outside. Timo's bravado vanished and he yelped as Jingshen forced him to his knees by the simple efficacy of a painful joint lock. He made a halfhearted attempt to punch at Jingshen with his other hand, but another twist of the wrist and the blow stopped before crossing half the distance between them. Tears of pain ran over the tattooed tear.

"One more move and I break it," Jingshen said softly.

"Hey . . . hey, man . . . oh, shit . . . I didn't mean nothin'."

"I know you didn't." Jingshen heard someone else approaching. Without releasing Timo's wrist, he pulled a knife from its sheath in the small of his back and hurled it. The Damascus steel blade bit into the soft asphalt in front of the other man's feet.

"Oh, shit!" the man cried. "What the hell, man?"

"Tell them to back off," Jingshen said to Timo.

"Back off, you fuckers!" Timo cried. "He's gonna break my fuckin' arm."

"He threw a goddamn knife at me!" the other man shouted, hand straying toward the small of his back where he undoubtedly had a weapon.

"I threw it near you. The *next* one will be at you." Jingshen pulled his backup knife from his ankle sheath.

"Goddammit, back off already!" Timo shouted.

"Okay, okay," said the other man, and the others grumbled and cursed under their breaths.

Jingshen released Timo. "Make sure they leave the bike alone."

Timo winced, rubbing his wrist. "Hey, how come I'm in charge of it? It's your goddamn bike, Homes!"

Jingshen straightened his hat and said nothing, but he took a single step toward Timo.

Timo blanched, his skin going a sickly yellow under the red and blue of the neon glow. "Yeah, okay, nobody touches the goddamn bike. Shit."

Jingshen walked to where the knife stuck out of the pavement. The group of men tensed, hands reaching beneath shirts and into pockets. Then he stepped over it, leaving it where it stuck as a reminder, and entered Johnny Danger's.

Over the course of his life, Jingshen had spent time in thousands of taverns. Perhaps tens of thousands. None of them stood out in his mind, for he'd never visited any frequently enough to become a habit. But certain things never changed, transcending years and cultures and continents. He'd never been in Johnny Danger's before, but of course, he recognized it.

A long bar spread along one wall with a pair of disheveled but bright-eyed bartenders slung pitchers of beer as fast as the raucous crowd could down them, and still found time to mix drinks for their more discerning patrons. Most of those in the bar were shouting at the TVs mounted high in the corners, showing a heavyweight boxing match. The shouting ringside announcers competed with Los Lobos blasting from the jukebox at the end of the bar. A couple working girls negotiated terms with their johns. A heavyset man with greasy hair and a stained t-shirt swayed into Jingshen on his way to the door. "S-sorry, man," he slurred, and patted Jingshen by way of apology.

A chorus of yells came from the boxing fans as one of the fighters delivered a solid blow that rocked his opponent back. Jingshen didn't know who either of the boxers were, and didn't care. He dug in the pocket of his jeans for his marker from the Source, a white plastic token the size and shape of a credit card with a stylized *S* printed in red on one side and a magnetic strip on the other. He shouldered up to the bar. One of the women behind it, bosoms barely contained in her blue button-down top, set a paper napkin in front of him. "What'll it be, *señor*?" She had a fine sheen of sweat on her forehead.

Jingshen slid his token across the bar to her, along with a twenty dollar bill. She tucked the cash into her bra without missing a beat, then spun around to swipe the token through an innocuous box on the back counter. A green light illuminated atop it. If his token had been bad, the red light would have lit instead. In that case, the bartender certainly had orders to kill him where he stood.

"Members Only door, past the restrooms. I'll buzz you in," the bartender said. She handed Jingshen's card back with a tight smile.

"Hey, how about some service here?" A man in mechanic's coveralls banged his fist on the bar.

"Talk to the hand, asshole. Wait your turn." The bartender held up her palm toward the impatient customer while nodding Jingshen in the direction of the door toward the restrooms.

"Thank you," Jingshen said. He shouldered past a man holding a low conversation on the bar's pay phone and went into the hall. The wall across from the men's room door had a round crater in it, about the size and height to suggest someone had been thrown headfirst into it. A single bare overhead bulb lit the hall in a sickly yellow. Someone was being noisily sick in the women's room. A camera was mounted over the *Members Only* door at the end of the hall. Jingshen stared up at it until the door lock buzzed and he let himself through.

Dark business, as always.

* * *

The Members Only room wasn't much more than a glorified storage room. Shelves along one wall held various cleaning supplies and stacks of cheap disposable coasters. Stacks of kegs filled the corners, along with crates of mismatched bottles of tequila, gin, and rum. A round table dominated the center of the room, marked with cigarette burns and ring-shaped stains from the bottoms of glasses and bottles.

Three other people waited in the room, two of whom Jingshen recognized. The huge man with arms bulging out of his Soundgarden t-shirt was a brutal combat monster known in the industry as Rook. His dirty blonde hair stuck up and out on top, as if he'd stuck his finger in a socket and waited. His stubbly face seemed to be all chin. He would have been good-looking if not for the perpetual sneer wrinkling his nose. "Well, I'll be. You're a hella long way from Chinatown, Ghost."

"A job's a job, dear brother," said the woman lounging beside Rook. She wore too much eye makeup and her platinum hair was plaited into two long braids with silver ribbons wound through them. She raised a glass to her lips, marking it with lip-prints from her crimson lipstick. Her movements flowed with a lithe, inhuman grace. "We can't be the only ones with expensive tastes."

Jingshen nodded at them. "Rook. Bishop. Small world."

Rook pressed his thumbnail against the cap of a bottle and popped the piece across the room before raising it to his lips. "What's it been, Ghost, three years? Miami, wasn't it?"

Bishop smiled and arched her back, thrusting her small breasts forward in a provocative gesture. "Oh, it was definitely Miami. I heard you got blown up in that boat."

Jingshen shrugged. "I got better."

"No hard feelings? It was just business," Bishop said, preening for his benefit.

Rook snickered. "Yeah, wasn't like we were making cheddar on you."

"What is this, Mercenaries Reunion Week?" asked the third man. "You guys got unfinished business to take care of? Because I'll wait." He examined a bottle of Boone's Farm wine before setting it back in its crate. He had the sort of face that would be instantly forgettable seconds after looking at it.

"Nah, we're cool," Rook said. "Past is the past."

"Who're you, anyway?" the third man asked. "He called you Ghost. Don't think I've heard of you."

Bishop gave the man a radiant, predatory smile. "You've never heard of the Ghost? He's a legend. Real O.G. Damn near impossible to kill. God knows, enough people have tried."

"I have been lucky," Jingshen said, feeling his cheeks grow hot. He didn't like talking about himself, and liked other people talking about him even less. "I know the siblings here and what they do. Who are you?"

"Nobody Special," said the man. "Shapeshifting's my game. Any idea what's the gig?"

Jingshen shook his head. "As Bishop said, a job is just a job."

"I heard you just did a job up in Sacramento," Rook said, like he was driving splinters under fingernails. "Heard it didn't go so smooth."

Jingshen shrugged again. The truth was that the Sacramento job had gone poorly. A couple people died who weren't supposed to, and someone who was supposed to wind up in the ground was now in the Federal Witness Protection Program. That hadn't been a Source job. If it had been, he would have been blacklisted. The Source had a reputation to maintain, and it wouldn't accept failure.

It was the sort of thing that left him questioning why he was doing work-for-hire at all. It wasn't like he needed the money; he was a wise and patient investor, and lived modestly within his means. He could have done any of a thousand jobs to keep himself busy, but making war was simple, and he was good at it. He'd spent much of his life in one military or another, often fighting for leaders he didn't respect and causes he detested. At least when one was a soldier of fortune, one could pick and choose one's battles.

"We just came in from Laredo," Bishop said, finishing her drink. "Shot a man there just to watch him die."

"Like the song?" Nobody Special asked.

"No, I actually did that. Gut shot." Bishop grinned. "It took him *hours*."

Jingshen grimaced beneath his fedora. With Rook and Bishop involved, the job would be . . . messy.

"So, uh, anybody know about this job?" Nobody Special asked into the silence after Bishop's admission.

Rook shrugged. "Who cares? We're here, so wetwork's involved." He cracked his knuckles. "That's our specialty."

Bishop laughed, although Jingshen wasn't sure if it was at her brother's bloodthirstiness or the idea of getting to spill a little blood herself.

The door buzzed and someone unlatched it. Jingshen moved out of the way quickly and dropped into one of the chairs around the table. A slender Japanese woman entered, leaning on a silver-headed ebony cane. She wore a suit that would have seemed out of place in an establishment like Johnny Danger's if she didn't carry the attitude of being in charge no matter where she was. The suit was all black with a dove-gray button down blouse beneath it. The only splash of color came from a golden silk scarf loosely knotted about her throat. Jingshen guessed she might be forty, still carrying her youthful beauty and majesty.

"Please be seated," she said in a rough voice. As she moved to the head of the table, her scarf dislodged just enough for Jingshen to see the end of a ragged scar along her throat. Despite her quiet demeanor, Jingshen could see the secret she hid in her movements. Whatever else she might have been, she was a killer.

Nobody Special sat beside Jingshen and clasped his hands atop the table. The woman stared pointedly at Bishop until she sighed and slid off the table to sit next to her brother. She grinned and held out her hands as if to grant permission to continue.

"My name is Kobura. I represent a group of interested investors who are financing this operation. A research firm called DuraGen is transferring an asset from a peripheral group to their main facility. You are being employed to intercept that asset at the transfer and deliver it undamaged to me. You will be paid in full at the successful delivery of said asset. If you fail to do so, or the asset is harmed in any way, your retainer is forfeit. The investors may then choose to recoup their losses with your suffering. You may opt at this time to back out with no penalties and a simple return of the retainer. Do any of you wish to do so?"

Nobody Special shifted in his seat and for a moment, Jingshen thought perhaps he was going to take Kobura up on her offer to leave. Instead, he merely crossed his legs and smiled. Rook and Bishop glared across the table at Jingshen but he returned an emotionless stare back at them. "I think we're all good to continue," Bishop said.

Kobura laid out a straightforward plan, based upon intelligence she'd received from a mole within the DuraGen organization. The team would intercept the *asset*, which Jingshen figured was a person, at the transfer location. It was a basic smash-and-grab operation, with Rook and Bishop handling the *smash* and Jingshen and Nobody Special on *grab* duty. Once they secured the asset, they would meet at either the first prearranged time and location or, if they couldn't get there in time, the second. The asset would be handed over to Kobura, the team would get paid upon delivery, and that would constitute the completion of their contract.

"Piece of cake," Rook said with a chuckle. "Why the hell you need four of us? Me and Bishop could handle this on our own."

"Bishop and *I*," Bishop said, correcting her brother's poor grammar.

Rook's brow furrowed. "What the hell you talking about? *You're* Bishop."

"And that is why there are four of us," Nobody Special said.

"You looking to get your ass beat, shapeshifter?" Rook flexed, making throbbing veins stand out on his bare arms.

"Oh, snap," Bishop said. "Take a chill pill, brother. I still want to get paid today."

"My bad," Nobody Special said, raising his hands in supplication. "I didn't mean nothing by it."

Kobura waited until the three finished their squabbling. Jingshen watched her, noting her indulgence and patience, both rare traits. He didn't remember everyone he'd met in his life—a practical impossibility over more than three centuries—but he was certain he'd never forget Kobura. She met his gaze with an unreadable expression of her own. He wondered what secrets it held. When the interruption finished, she set a briefcase upon the table and unsnapped the clasps. The mercenaries grew silent as she removed four neat stacks of cash, bound with paper ribbons, and set them before her on the table. "Ten percent retainer's fee," Kobura said.

Each stack had a business card atop it with an unidentified phone number. Jingshen looked at the number, committed it to memory, and then handed the card back to Kobura. The others did the same. She followed up the cash with four clipboards, each bearing a Source contract. One contract went to each of the mercenaries for their review.

Jingshen flipped through his, checking the boilerplate and scanning for any unexpected clauses. He'd seen hundreds of Source contracts since the organization's inception after World War II. Very little had changed in fifty years.

Kobura held out bloodspikes to Bishop and Nobody Special. A bloodspike was a fancy name for a spring-loaded needle. It would pierce the pads of their thumbs so they could sign the contracts in blood. Jingshen knew the documents were treated with a special chemical that would instantly set and preserve blood. He also knew a bloodspike wouldn't work upon Rook, whose resistance to harm was in direct proportion to the force exerted upon him until exhaustion made him vulnerable. It also wouldn't work on Jingshen, who would heal from such a small injury almost instantly, before he could set his blood to the contract.

"Not really playing to the room, are you, Kobura?" Bishop said. "Not everybody can bleed on command."

Kobura's face remained impassive. "Let us say I am gauging your ability to improvise in the face of the unexpected. After all, it is well-documented that no battle plan survives contact with the enemy."

Rook grinned. "I came prepared," he said, and drew a wicked-looking knife from his belt. It had a swirling pattern within the metal, suggesting it was made from Damascus steel. Jingshen nodded his approval; he'd owned several Damascus steel blades over his life, and every one had been an exceptional weapon. The big man made a slice along the side of his thumb and squeezed it so blood welled onto his pad. Then he pressed it upon the contract, creating a small puff of mist as the chemical-laden paper instantly preserved the blood. Bishop and Nobody Special used their bloodspikes to accomplish the same task.

Jingshen removed a cigar cutter from his pocket. He, too, had come prepared. While the others watched with a mixture of sick fascination and disgust, he stuck the end of his pinky into the cutter and snipped it off.

"Du-u-ude . . ." Nobody Special sat down suddenly, as if his legs had just failed.

Before the wound could heal, Jingshen rubbed the stump of his fingertip against his thumb, painting it with his own blood. He pressed the thumb to the page and watched the tiny curlicue of mist rise into the air.

"Goddamn, Ghost, doesn't that hurt?" Bishop asked.

"Yes." Jingshen watched as the flesh reformed at the end of his finger, pink and new like a baby's. Wounds hurt; they always had. He'd just grown used to the pain over the centuries. The piece of his flesh he'd snipped off rapidly decomposed into dust.

Kobura retrieved the four clipboards and tucked them into her briefcase. "I thank you," she said in her soft, hoarse tone. "I shall meet you at the rendezvous point. Deliver the asset to me and you shall receive the balance of your payment at that time." She spun on her heel, briefcase in one hand and cane in the other. Instead of shuffling her items to free up one hand to open the door, she stepped into the shadow of the room's corner and was gone as if she'd never been there.

Rook jumped to his feet. "Holy shit!"

Bishop punched him in the arm. "Dumbass. You'd think you never saw a parahuman before."

Rook rubbed his arm. "No, it just surprised me. She's so . . . *old*."

Jingshen snorted in spite of himself. Rook really had no idea.

"What, old people can't be parahumans?" Nobody Special asked as he sucked on his thumb where he'd pierced it for his blood signature.

"I assure you they can," Jingshen said.

Chapter Two

September, 1993
Los Angeles, California

The mercenaries emerged from Johnny Danger's, walking single file like the Beatles crossing Abbey Road. That would have made Jingshen barefoot Paul McCartney. Rook, leading the others, stopped as he saw Jingshen's knife sticking out of the pavement. "What the shit is this?"

"That's mine," Jingshen said. "I must have . . . dropped it."

"You always drop stuff this hard?" Rook bent to pry the knife from the asphalt. He brushed crumbs off the blade, looked at it for a moment in the sulfurous glow of the streetlight, then handed it to Jingshen.

Jingshen shrugged. "It was careless of me."

"We brought our van," Bishop said. "You boys riding with us?"

Nobody Special nodded. "I came by cab."

"How about you, Chinatown?"

Jingshen didn't answer Bishop immediately. He looked toward his bike, expecting it to be gone, or tipped over, or otherwise defaced. Instead, Timo stood in front of it, arms crossed and head lowered with his eyes shadowed. The other men paid him no attention, carrying on with the same jocularity and machismo they'd displayed upon Jingshen's arrival.

Jingshen walked toward him with an unhurried, nonthreatening pace.

"Hey! Hey, Chinatown, you coming or what?" Bishop called.

Jingshen turned his head slightly. "In a minute."

Timo stiffened as Jingshen approached. "Hey, Homes. I done stood watch here. Didn't nobody mess with your ride. See?" He stood aside so Jingshen would have a clear view of the bike. The larger man dropped his voice to a whisper. "Please don't fuck me up again in front of my boys, Homes. They ain't never gonna let that go."

"Hold out your hand." Jingshen reached into his pocket. Timo's eyes widened and his muscles tensed as if he were expecting a knife to get flung into his belly. Instead, Jingshen withdrew the bike's key and dropped it into Timo's palm. "Keep it."

"Huh?" Timo looked down at the key in his hand, then back up to Jingshen's face, shadowed beneath the brim of his hat.

"You said you always wanted one." Jingshen turned away and walked toward the van where Bishop was impatiently drumming her fingers on the steering wheel.

"Wait a minute, Homes. Are you giving it to me? Seriously?" Timo called after him.

"You just give that asshole a Harley?" Rook hung his head out the passenger window. "I ought to kill his ass just on general principles."

"Leave it. I don't need the bike." Jingshen gave Rook a tight smile. "Because you have a van."

Rook slapped the door, denting it. "Goddamn right we do."

"Can we please get going?" Bishop said. "We're on a tight schedule and I want to scope out the transfer point before the place gets crowded."

The van peeled out of the parking lot, leaving behind a group of confused *vatos* and one proud new owner of a Harley Davidson.

* * *

The transfer location, as Kobura had defined it, was a nameless factory fallen victim to the recession of the past couple years. Southern California's loss was the underworld's gain, as abandoned industrial and commercial facilities made excellent locations for transacting business on the wrong side of the law. Bishop parked the van behind an adjacent building and the four mercenaries geared up for the action to come.

Rook and Bishop both wore suits heavy on the black leather and burnished armor plate over the most vulnerable areas. Straps covered with myriad pouches crossed their chests, waists, and thighs. Bishop kept a pistol strapped to one leg, but her weapon of choice was a *naginata* taller than she was. Essentially a serrated sword blade atop a six-foot staff, the weapon crackled with electricity when she triggered a thumb switch.

"Dope weapon," Nobody Special said as he shrugged into a shoulder holster and checked the clip of his pistol.

"Damn skippy." Bishop deactivated the arcing blade and looked at her brother. "You think you brought enough?"

Rook looked down at himself, with pistols strapped to each leg, under each arm, and a bandoleer of clips running down from one shoulder and grenades down the other. In his arms, he cradled a rifle that looked more like an antitank gun. Jingshen imagined it must have weighed a couple hundred pounds easy, but Rook handled it like it wasn't any more massive than a toy. "What, you think I should have brought Bertha?"

"No, you shouldn't have brought fucking Bertha," Bishop said with a snort. "We'd need a bigger van. Who names a gun *Bertha*?"

"The Germans did," Jingshen said.

Rook pointed at Jingshen as if to illustrate his point. "Exactly. The krauts did. Seriously, you think I might need her? What kind of firepower you think these DuraGen losers are carrying?"

Bishop snorted. "Whatever it is, I'm pretty sure we can handle it. You, me, and your goddamn howitzer."

Nobody Special asked, "How long do we have?"

"Why, you got a date, pretty boy?" Rook sneered.

Nobody Special's face and clothing flowed like claymation, rearranging him to mirror Rook's appearance. "No. I find them distracting when I'm trying to look more like a specific asshole."

Rook recoiled from the unexpected change, while Bishop burst out laughing.

Nobody Special had perfectly matched Rook's face, body, and armor. He leered at Rook.

"Take that shit off," Bishop said, wiping her eyes. "It's bad enough to have one dumbass brother."

Nobody Special transformed again before their eyes, becoming a slender young black man with a short fade hairstyle.

"That is . . . fascinating," Jingshen said. "You can change your skin tone and mass? And . . . clothing?"

"Skin and hair tone, body shape, yeah. Can't change my mass. When I'm bigger, I'm lighter. Skinny cuss like this, I'm dense. As far as clothing goes, well, I can't change that. Only myself."

"Wait, are you *naked?*" Bishop was aghast.

Nobody Special looked at his hands and smiled. "This kid was working at the sandwich shop where I got lunch. He had a good look, so I took it. Brushed his hand when he gave me change and he went into my bank."

"Forever?" Jingshen asked.

"Nah. Once I change out of this form, I'll lose it unless I touch him again. Don't worry, I can't do you again unless I touch you, Rook." He held up a hand. "High five me?"

"Fuck you." Rook stepped back, clearly uncomfortable with the shapeshifter's ability.

"All right, boys. Quit playing with your dicks and let's get to work. *I* have a watch, and it says DuraGen should be here in twenty minutes." Bishop looked around the abandoned factory floor, rife with broken crates and tanks of some kind of sludge that Jingshen thought was probably toxic. "Looks like a great place for a party. Rook and I will get their attention once they show the asset. We'll keep DuraGen's goons occupied while the two of you retrieve the asset and stash it in the van." She grinned a predatory smile. "I would not recommend leaving without us."

* * *

"So how about the psycho twins, huh?" Nobody Special asked as he quietly tapped his fingers on the railing. He and Jingshen waited on a catwalk overlooking the main floor. Some enterprising crime lord with a technical bent had spliced into a utility trunk somewhere nearby, allowing a few of the building's interior lights to function. Most of them were down on the main floor, so Jingshen and Nobody Special were safely hidden in the shadows overhead. "Seems like the Source must really be scraping the bottom to dig up that trash."

"They hired you, did they not?" Jingshen wished Nobody Special would stop talking. Inane chatter prior to action was an indicator of someone unsure of himself. He'd seen it a thousand times in his life. Men who were all talk had an unfortunate tendency to get those around them killed. It was less of a concern for Jingshen than for most, but he preferred a more professional attitude.

Nobody Special didn't bite Jingshen's hook. "You fighting types always think with your fists first. You think you can only solve a problem by punching it until it curls up and dies. Well, there are other ways to win. It takes brains, dude. With a power like mine, you got to be quick on your feet. I've talked my way into more places I wasn't supposed to be than I can count."

Jingshen sighed. There would be no peace so long as Nobody Special was by his side. If they didn't have a contract to work together, he might have swept the other man's legs from under him and tossed him from the catwalk. That would have not only rendered his contract null and void, it would have earned him a black chip from the Source. It would have painted a target on his back. Assassins would find it difficult to collect upon that chip, but the Source had resources to rival the world's most powerful governments. If there was a parahuman somewhere in the world who could cash in Jingshen's chip, the Source would find them.

"What's your gig anyway, man? I saw you grow back your finger so you heal quick. Twins said you're hard to kill. What else can you do?"

"Be quiet when required," Jingshen said, hearing the sound of an approaching engine.

"What's that supposed to—oh shit!" Nobody Special said the last in a whisper as the loading ramp door opened, long-disused bearings squealing in protest. The rising door revealed a black step-van with no windows in the cargo area. A man hopped back into the driver's seat from the door controls and guided the van into the warehouse. He swung it around in a semicircle so it was pointing back at the open door. Jingshen noted how low the van rode on its suspension and suspected it was armored.

The engine shut down and the back doors opened to release four men in gray jumpsuits with SWAT-style tactical armor vests and headsets. They spread out into a standard cover pattern to maximize their fields of fire without needing to fire toward each other.

Jingshen took note of their Israeli-made submachine guns with their extra-long clips. The guards wouldn't be shy about spending ammunition if called upon to do so. Their vests would give them a false sense of security that could be exploited. Their smug expressions told him they were already confident in the success of their task.

Nobody Special leaned over, perhaps to whisper something to Jingshen, but with a simple economy of motion, Jingshen placed his finger against Nobody Special's lips. He wondered briefly if that meant Nobody Special would be able to mimic him at some point in the future, but then returned his attention to the tableau unfolding below them.

The van's driver didn't leave his seat, and although Jingshen couldn't see, he suspected there was someone in the passenger seat as well. That meant six opponents before the peripheral team arrived from DuraGen. If they had a similar security setup, the mercenaries would be solidly outnumbered by a factor of three.

Rook and Bishop should have plenty of playmates, Jingshen thought, and a wry smile crossed his lips. He knew the kind of music they preferred to dance to, and the building might very well not be standing by the time the song finished.

The guards stiffened to high alert as a late-model sedan rolled into the warehouse and stopped several yards away from the van. The driver shut it off and stepped clear. He wore an off-the-rack business suit and yellow-tinted glasses. He had a plastic ID badge clipped to his jacket and immediately went over to the nearest security guard. Three more men exited the sedan, one more in a nearly identical business suit and the other two wearing lab coats.

The security guard checked the driver's ID badge and apparently liked what he saw, for he pursed his lips into a cab-calling whistle. "It's all good," he called. "Let's get this show on the road."

"Open it up," called the driver.

One of the lab-coated men reached down under the sedan's steering wheel to pop the trunk release. The click of the latch was loud in the silent warehouse and the trunk lid raised on its own. The sedan faced toward where Jingshen and Nobody

Special watched, so neither could see what was in the trunk.

"Cute guns," said Rook as he stepped out from behind a shipping crate with his antitank gun lowered. "But size matters."

Chapter Three

September, 1993
Los Angeles, California

Despite their apparent overconfidence, the DuraGen security guards were good. Three out of the four immediately opened fire at Rook. The fourth didn't have a chance because Rook fired his antitank gun and the shell blew the guard into stew.

"Holy shit!" Nobody Special gasped.

Bullets ricocheted off Rook's armor and resistant skin. He laughed as the guards emptied their clips at him. "Kinda tickles!" he crowed.

A crackling wedge of energy punched through a guard's torso as Bishop appeared behind him. She raised him up on her naginata, then flung him away like a *jai alai* player hurling a ball with a cesta. His smoldering torso added the sweet stink of charred flesh to the reek of gun smoke.

"Go, go, go!" one of the two remaining guards shouted, and the suits and lab coats ran for the sedan.

Jingshen leaped off the catwalk. He rolled with the impact but a twenty-five foot drop was still a twenty-five foot drop, and both his legs shattered on the concrete floor. It wasn't the worst pain he'd felt, but it still hurt and he wound up on his back, staring up into the overhead lights. Rook fired his cannon again, taking down another security guard. Blood sprayed through the air, crimson mist floating like clouds in front of the sun.

"Ow! Son of a bitch!" Bishop's naginata went flying as a bullet struck the blade and she lost her grip on it. She pulled her pistol and put a bullet between the fourth guard's eyes.

Jingshen rolled onto his stomach, breathing hard with the effort, and started dragging himself toward the sedan as the engine roared. His leg bones were already knitting back together and with every inch he advanced he gained a little more mobility. He didn't worry about them healing crooked; his body knew its proper shape and would continue repairing itself until it was achieved.

"Stop them, Rook," Bishop shouted. "And don't damage the goddamn package!"

Rook put a shell into the sedan's engine compartment, sending shrapnel in all directions, cutting Jingshen's face. The suits and lab coat guys spilled out of the ruined car, pistols out and firing with more enthusiasm than aim.

The van driver floored the accelerator and made for the exit. Bishop sprang at the door, trying to grab hold, but her fingers slipped. "Shit!"

Jingshen pulled his legs up beneath him, feeling the last bones work themselves back to whole. He pulled the sticks from his back and took down one of the suits with precise blows delivered to kidney, collar bone, and temple. He spun into a leg sweep and knocked one of the lab coat men off his feet. His legs didn't hurt at all as he sprang into the air, one leg raised high. He dropped a solid axe kick onto the lab coat's rib cage, breaking everything from sternum to spine.

Rook pointed his cannon at the van and pulled the trigger but nothing happened. He looked stupidly down at his gun while Bishop screamed at him. A sound that began as a soft pop and ended with breaking glass made the van's steering wobble and it bumped against the edge of the exit door. The horn made a discordant drone and the engine stalled.

Almost as an afterthought, Bishop shot the last suit and lab coat guy while Rook was still trying to un-jam his gun.

Jingshen looked up toward the catwalks and saw a dark-skinned figure in the shadows, holstering his pistol. He nodded toward Nobody Special and wiped away the shrapnel his skin had pushed out of his face. The tiny pieces of metal tinkled against the concrete floor, almost inaudible over the persistent blare of the step-van's horn.

The horn stopped as suddenly as it had begun. A moment later, the door on the passenger side slid open and someone stepped down. Heels clacked against cement as whomever it was walked slowly and deliberately toward the back.

"What the shit is this?" Rook raised a pair of six shooters that looked like they might fire solid shotgun slugs and cocked the hammers.

Bishop slammed a clip into her own pistol and took aim. Still the footsteps came, paced like the beating of a heart.

She stepped around from the back of the van, a burgundy leather unitard zipped halfway up her chest and a heart-shaped tattoo exposed on her throat. She had stringy white-blonde hair with dark roots and heavy black makeup around her eyes. A braid with crimson ribbons mixed into it hung over one shoulder to end at her waist. Black leather straps crisscrossed her torso, supporting two scabbards across her back. Her lips were blood red and they curved into a smile.

Neither Rook nor Bishop fired their weapons. Both had grown pale, sweat pouring down their faces, eyes bulging in fear and surprise.

"Four of you," she said in a surprisingly sweet voice. "I thought they'd send more."

She raised a hand and made a twisting motion. Rook gasped and fell to the floor. One of his pistols discharged when it hit the cement and an overhead light shattered into splinters. Bishop pitched forward onto her face, moaning. With a rattling series of thuds, Nobody Special tumbled down a steel staircase and collapsed at its base.

Jingshen felt his heart grind to a halt, like an engine that ran itself out of oil. Then it started again. The woman frowned and twisted her hand again. Jingshen gasped as his heart stopped again. His vision grew blurry for a moment but then a flurry of contractions brought his circulation back up to speed. "Who . . . are you?" he asked through lips dull and lifeless.

"They call me Heartbreaker," she said sweetly. "Why aren't you having a massive heart attack right now? Don't you have a heart to break?"

Jingshen grimaced in pain but fought through it. "I have been called heartless before."

"Well, if that doesn't just beat all," Heartbreaker replied. "Maybe I'll just cut you open to check." She reached over her shoulders and slid two wicked katanas from their scabbards.

Jingshen raised his sticks to a ready position. "Better than you have tried."

The gibe created its intended response, and Heartbreaker charged him, swords whirling like silver lightning. Sticks met blades with a clacking chatter and the combatants fought back and forth across the warehouse floor.

It had been years, even decades since Jingshen faced an opponent in single combat he couldn't best in a few seconds. Heartbreaker wasn't any faster than a normal human, but she had exceptional training. She found adequate defenses for every attack Jingshen launched. When he changed from Chinese to Filipino to French to Israeli fighting styles, she matched him. Her razor-sharp blades sliced cuts in his simple black shirt and the skin beneath, which stung as his sweat rolled into them before they healed shut. He parried a blow that would have decapitated him and his hat went flying across the warehouse.

Heartbreaker suffered as many minor blows as she'd delivered. He knew he'd cracked one of the bones in her left forearm by the way she favored it. Blood trickled from a thin cut over her left ear where the very corner of his stick had caught her. If his blow had struck true, the end of his stick would have entered her eye socket and punched through the back of her skull.

Step, parry. Attack, defend. Jingshen back-flipped away from Heartbreaker's whirling spin kick and landed in disaster. He came down in the slimy remnants of one of Rook's cannon victims and his feet slipped from under him. He landed on his knees on the cement floor.

In that moment, Heartbreaker had him. He parried the blow that would have bisected his head at ear-height, but she twisted her arm with the broken bone further than he would have thought possible. Two feet of icy tempered steel slid between his fifth and sixth ribs, slicing through everything that kept a normal human alive. Heartbreaker held the sword in him, breathing heavily, her eyes sparkling as if she'd never felt so alive. Perhaps she hadn't.

"Aw," she said in her same sweet little-girl voice. Her gaze met his. "Guess you had a heart after all. If I can't break it one way . . ." She pulled the sword from his chest and blood gushed from the wound. "I'll find another."

Jingshen's vision grayed out and he fell forward without a sound, face down on the cement.

Heartbreaker hummed to herself and stepped away from him, her voice growing more quiet, as if she were traveling down a tunnel away from him.

No, he couldn't just let her walk away.

He clenched his teeth, and then he clenched a fist. He punched it onto the cement as if trying to battle gravity hand-to-hand. Blood splattered in all directions at the blow. The gush from his wound decreased to a defiant trickle. Complaining organs spliced themselves back together, fresh scars mapping across flesh. Muscle tissue knitted ragged edges like a zipper.

Jingshen rose like a specter from the grave, blood-soaked from head to toe. His senses returned like a projectionist adjusting the focus on a movie. His left leg dragged for a moment as he stepped forward. Nerve ends were still finding their way back together, each connection like broken glass dragged across raw skin.

"What the hell?" Heartbreaker's voice took on a cold edge.

"You missed," Jingshen said. "Try harder."

"I'm going to—"

Jingshen never got to hear what Heartbreaker was going to do, for Bishop's crackling naginata blade burst through her chest. Electricity arced all around her, blackening her eyes and igniting her hair. Her swords fell from nerveless fingers and she slumped to the ground, revealing Nobody Special standing behind her with the naginata haft clutched in his hands.

"Goddamn, Ghost. She fucked you up."

"I will recover."

"Yeah, okay, but still. Jesus, dude." Nobody Special nudged Heartbreaker's corpse with his toe as if to confirm she was dead. Seeing Jingshen arise after the grievous harm done to him could shake anybody's faith in the finality of death.

It was good to know how his teammates fought, Jingshen thought. He'd been alive long enough to learn much about people from the way they killed. Rook was a man of excess who secretly harbored terrible fears about his own inadequacy. He compensated with gigantic, loud, brash weaponry. Bishop was much more confident about herself, able to decide what weapons were most practical in any given situation. When her naginata proved ineffective, she would switch to guns. She trusted herself and knew her limitations. Nobody

Special was by far the most dangerous of them all, for he hid like a coward and took highly accurate shots of opportunity from the shadows. He'd killed as many DuraGen people as the others, and he was unharmed. Rook and Bishop were still recuperating from Heartbreaker's attacks, while Jingshen would have died several times over if his healing ability hadn't been active. Nobody Special had an assassin's eye, a marksman's skill, and ridiculous luck to boot.

He would bear watching more than the others.

"How did you recover from Heartbreaker's ability?" Jingshen asked.

Nobody Special shrugged. "Lucky for me when I fell down the stairs, I wound up right beside Bishop's toy here. I managed to activate it and defibrillated myself with the goddamn thing."

Jingshen snorted. It was so unlikely a solution that it was probably the truth. Pain and then the memory of pain remained as he walked across the warehouse floor, silent but for the quiet drips of draining blood onto cement.

"What's up?" Nobody Special asked.

"We still have a job to do," Jingshen said. "Check to see if Rook and Bishop are dead or alive."

"Alive," Rook coughed. "Jesus fuck, that hurts."

"You won't get rid of us that easily," Bishop added. "Keep your filthy hands off my naginata."

Nobody Special looked at his hands. "Like yours are any cleaner than mine."

Jingshen stepped around to the back of the sedan to see why Heartbreaker and the rest of the DuraGen security team had so dearly sold their lives.

Lying in the trunk, wrapped securely in a biohazard suit, was a young woman.

* * *

The girl stank, even through the coveralls she wore. That meant her suit wasn't airtight, so whatever contamination was at risk didn't involve biological threats. Jingshen had experienced most of the world's worst plagues and contagions over the course of his life. The most virulent diseases would reinfect him over and over again until he managed to get away from the carriers.

He wrinkled his nose at her unwashed reek, a melange of acrid sweat and filth that came from living on the streets. She was asleep or more likely drugged by the way her head lolled within the hood. She looked thin, with prominent cheekbones and a razor-sharp nose.

Nobody Special loped over to take a look. "What'd you—*oh shit!*" He gasped and staggered away, hand over his mouth as he caught a whiff of her. He managed to get three steps away before falling to his knees and vomiting.

"Major buzzkill, cruster," Rook said as he pushed himself to his feet, using his antitank gun as a crutch.

"Sorry." Nobody Special wiped his mouth with the back of his hand. "It's just . . . I've seen—I've *smelled* homeless people who weren't as stank ass as that chick."

"Oh, I don't know." Bishop stepped beside Jingshen to look down at the girl in the trunk. "I remember a crack house in Baltimore that smelled worse than this. Remember that one, Rook?"

Rook grinned. "The dude hanging by his intestines?"

"That's the one."

"Jesus, you guys," Nobody Special said. "Why you think she's wrapped up? She sick or something?"

"I don't know," Jingshen said. "But I don't think she's sick."

"Something's wrong with her," Bishop said. "But yeah, this isn't an airtight suit or we couldn't smell her ass. It's something else."

"It don't matter what it is," Rook said. "She's the package, and it's time to get paid." He raised a hand and his sister high-fived it.

Jingshen frowned. He'd traded in humans before. He'd *been* traded before. Neither was a pleasant experience. This was what he'd become, he thought, and he felt nothing except tired. He was tired of the mercenary game. He wasn't sure why he continued in the industry. It wasn't like he needed the money; one could earn staggering amounts of income if one had many lifetimes to live. He'd gained and lost more fortunes than he could count. At the moment, he was doing well financially, so that wasn't the driving factor behind his career. He certainly wasn't in it for the thrills. There was nothing pleasant about behind shot, stabbed, broken, and beaten over and over again. Healing or not, he felt every injury.

He could walk away right now. The others could try to stop him, but there was nothing any of them could do that hadn't already been done to him a hundred times. When they were done, and he was lying on the floor in pieces, he would heal. It would take a long time, but it would happen. He had no concerns about that. What was the worst that could happen? He might finally find the eternal sleep that had eluded him for centuries.

He was done, he decided. He would finish the current job, because he saw no reason to cut off the avenue of future employment with the Source should he feel the need later. Then he would inform them he was no longer available for contracts.

"Yes," Jingshen said to Rook. He turned and walked toward the depths of the warehouse.

"Where you going, Ghost?" Bishop's voice was full of suspicion.

"To get my hat."

"That fucking hat," Rook said with a laugh.

Jingshen spotted his missing chapeau and placed it back onto his head, setting it to his favorite angle. "Rook, bring the girl to the van." He started back toward the van himself, which was still stopped against a vertical warehouse support.

"You heard him, Rookie." Bishop chuckled as she lifted her naginata to rest on her shoulder. "Pick up the package and let's get going."

Rook called after them, "Hey, how come I gotta carry Miss Stank here?"

"You're the biggest?" Nobody Special suggested.

Jingshen pulled open the driver's side door. A dead man sat in the seat, leaning forward against the seat belt, the side of his face ruined by Nobody Special's shot through the windshield. He released the seat belt catch and dragged the corpse from the seat. The steering wheel was tacky with blood. He went to one of the dead lab coats and removed the man's coat, which was only slightly marred by the blood that had run down his neck.

"Jesus fuck, this chick is *ripe*," Rook grumbled.

"I wonder what's her deal," Nobody Special said. "I mean, we're getting paid bank for this."

"We're not getting paid to ask questions." Bishop opened the van's back doors. "Goddammit, there's no seats back here."

"Shotgun," Nobody Special said quickly.

"She's probably some kind of super-duper parahuman," Rook said as he set the young woman none-too-gently in the back of the van. "Like, toxic skin or something. She sure *smells* toxic."

"But it's not our business," Bishop said, elbowing her brother. "Now shut your cake hole and get in the van. Stop trying to figure shit out. Thinking isn't your strong suit." She climbed into the back of the van, laying her naginata against one of the sides and making herself as comfortable as she could on the bare floor.

"I'm not stupid," Rook said, climbing in after her. The van's springs sagged with the addition of his and his giant gun's weight.

"Perish the thought."

Jingshen ignored the sibling rivalry as he wiped the steering wheel and seat down with the lab coat.

"Hey," Nobody Special said, pointing at his watch. "How long will it take us to reach the hand-off?"

Jingshen looked at his own watch and did some calculation in his mind. "Too long. We'll have to turn the asset over at the second appointed time."

"Shit, you mean tomorrow?" Rook asked.

"Why, you got a date tonight?" Bishop retorted.

"Maybe."

"We need a safe place to hole up until tomorrow," Jingshen said. "Not here. This place is compromised."

Nobody Special nodded. "I know a place. It's out of the way but easy to get to. Unfinished neighborhood about an hour away."

"That will be fine." Jingshen slipped behind the wheel and started the van.

"Hey, roll the window down," Rook said. "It's like the ass end of a dumpster back here."

Jingshen tugged his hat down a bit lower so the draft wouldn't dislodge it. He cranked the window down into the door, then backed the van away from the vertical support and pointed it toward the exit doors.

"Why the hat?" Nobody Special asked as Jingshen pulled the van out of the warehouse. "Nobody wears hats like that. You look like Japanese Indiana Jones."

"He's Chinese, you complete toolbag," Bishop said.

"I like it," Jingshen said. "It suits me."

"It's . . . noticeable," Nobody Special said. "Kind of hard to lay low when you look like you just stepped out of a *Green Hornet* episode, Kato."

Jingshen didn't dignify the comment with a reply.

"Hey, pull over for a second," Rook said. "Gotta take care of something."

"You couldn't have gone before we left? I swear, it's like traveling with a toddler," Bishop said as Jingshen stopped the van.

"I don't need to take a leak." An ominous *kerchunk* sound came from the back of the van as Rook chambered a round into the under-barrel grenade launcher attached to his antitank gun. "But I ain't gonna let that mess stay untouched and leave behind a bunch of clues."

"What clues?" Nobody Special snorted.

"The ones they ain't gonna find after I do this." Rook opened the back of the van, stepped out, and fired four quick shots from the grenade launcher. Each one sounded like someone hitting a large plastic case with a bat. Windows shattered as the shells pierced them.

Fiery explosions tore through the warehouse as Rook's grenades detonated. From the brilliant flame and heat that washed over them, Jingshen thought he'd probably used thermite or some other kind of high explosive. The reflection of the flames licked across Rook's armor and he grinned back at the others. "Now that's what I'm talkin' about."

"So much for keeping a low profile," Nobody Special grimaced. "Cops can't overlook it now."

"Let 'em spend the next week combing through the wreckage," Rook said, shutting the van doors again. "By that time, we'll be on to the next job."

Jingshen drove the van away from the rising cloud of flame in the mirrors. Ahead, on the highway, he saw the flashing red and blue lights of approaching emergency vehicles. As they raced down the exit ramp, he steered up the on-ramp into the flickering crimson river of rush hour taillights.

"Shit, we should have taken side streets," Nobody Special complained. "I hate traffic."

"News flash, wankster. That's like sayin' the sky's blue." Stretched out on the floor behind Nobody Special, Rook busied himself reloading the antitank gun from the bandoleer of shells stretched across his torso.

"Not in Southern California it isn't." Bishop leaned over and smacked her brother. "Hey, hands off the merchandise."

Jingshen glanced back over his shoulder to see Rook guiltily withdrawing his hand from the girl in the biohazard suit. "The contract says she is to be undamaged."

"I wasn't damaging her. I was just—"

"You don't *just* anything, Rookie. Not when payday is at stake."

"Whatever. And don't call me that."

The siblings continued needling at each other, the rising and falling of their arguments matching the ebb and flow of traffic as Jingshen lost them amid the commuters.

Chapter Four

September, 1993
Los Angeles, California

As Nobody Special had promised, their destination was a dark, unfinished neighborhood an hour to the east. The developer, like so many others in the recession, had fallen on hard times and left several dozen houses in varying states of completion. Perhaps another developer would move in to complete the project, assuming demand picked up among suburbanites. Uniform cracker-box construction dominated the completed houses, lurking too close together and crouching around weed-ridden cul-de-sacs. Yards once carefully sculpted in preparation for lawn installation were choked with more weeds, spilling alluvial deltas of sediment across sidewalks and gutters.

Jingshen braked hard as the van's headlights illuminated a small herd of deer. They vanished into the darkness in a flash of white tails.

"It's just ahead," Nobody Special said. "Next street up, hang a left. First house on the right. I've had it prepped for awhile, just in case I needed a spot, you know?"

"You got running water?" Rook asked. "I gotta take a wicked shit."

"Nice," Bishop grumbled.

"Unless the city has shut down the entire neighborhood, there should still be water," Nobody

Special said. "No power, but I got battery-powered lanterns stashed in the basement."

"Medical supplies?" Jingshen asked.

Nobody Special snorted. "Why, you hurt after all?"

"Not for me." Jingshen turned the van as directed and parked it in the darkened house's driveway. He nodded his head toward the back. "For her."

"I'll see what I can scrounge up."

"How about food?" Rook asked. "I'm also gonna need to refill after I take that wicked shit."

"Dude, you are disgusting," Bishop said.

"There's no food in the house, but there's drive-throughs back by the highway. Twenty minute round trip."

"We are not going through a drive-through with a goddamn hostage in the back of the van," Bishop said.

"I agree," Jingshen said.

"I'll go," Nobody Special said. "No offense, but the rest of you stand out like a mohawk in a church choir."

"Let's get her inside first. Sooner we're out of sight, the better I'll feel," Bishop said.

"There's nobody out here," Nobody Special waved vaguely toward the neighborhood. "This place has been vacant for a year."

"No vagrants? No kids looking for windows to break or walls to graffiti? Can you be sure?" Bishop crossed her arms.

Nobody Special smiled back at her. "I can't be sure who I'll look like when I wake up in the morning, but I'm pretty sure there's nobody out here but us mercenaries."

Rook kicked open the back of the van. "Fuck it, I'm gonna go drop a deuce. The rest of you can piss in the van for all I care."

"Shit. I better go unlock the door. There's a . . ." Nobody Special grabbed at the door handle but the door slammed back shut as Rook's face appeared in the window.

"There's a what?" The huge man's face was fully hidden in shadow but Jingshen caught a predatory gleam in his eyes.

"A b-b-b . . ." Nobody Special stammered.

"A booby trap?" Jingshen asked softly.

Nobody Special nodded.

Rook burst out laughing and opened the door. "That's the first goddamn sensible thing I've heard come out of your mouth." He bowed. "Please, after you, wankster."

Bishop followed her brother out of the van, saying over her shoulder to Jingshen, "Bring the girl."

Nobody Special unlocked the house's front door and opened it just enough to reach his arm inside. "Anybody got a flashlight?"

The others all shrugged.

"All those goddamn pouches and not a single light," the shapeshifter grumbled.

Rook shrugged. "Where else am I gonna keep all my spare ammo?"

"Hang on, I know I got somebody taller in here . . ." Nobody Special's flesh and pseudo-clothing rippled in the darkness. His body and legs lengthened and narrowed. "Got it." Something clicked inside the door and he pushed it open the rest of the way. He stepped into the dark room and Jingshen heard another door open. He stiffened, anticipating an attack that never came, because situations like this always seemed to end up in ambushes.

Instead, a bluish fluorescent light flickered to life in the hand of a tall slender man with a bushy mustache and prominent cheekbones that made his face look skeletal. "Well don't just stand there like a bunch of cretins," he said. "Come inside."

The front room was bare but for a pair of wooden kitchen chairs with their legs duct-taped together to form a framework supporting a shotgun. A cord ran from the trigger to an eye bolt screwed into the opposite wall and back across the room to loop around the front door. Or at least, that was how Jingshen pictured the trap had been set before Nobody Special disarmed it.

"Charming," Bishop said. "Love what you've done with the place." She patted the shotgun barrel. "All the comforts of home." She shook her head at the three electric lanterns sitting on the nearby table.

"Dibs on the shitter," Rook said, grabbing a lantern and pushing past everyone in search of the bathroom.

Jingshen looked down at the girl he held and realized in the dim light that she was conscious. She looked up at him with wide eyes. "She is awake," he said.

"Shit, that complicates things," Bishop said. "Nobody, you got any drops or injectables or anything like that to knock her ass back out?"

"Sorry, no. I wasn't expecting the kind of company you need that for."

Bishop cracked her knuckles. "Then I guess we knock her out old school." She stepped forward, fist raised.

"Wait," Jingshen said. "She is not to be damaged. That is part of our contract."

Bishop snorted. "Knocking a bitch out isn't *damage*. That's incidental."

"I will not permit it. She may be our contract, but that doesn't mean we have to treat her like garbage."

"She certainly stinks like it." Bishop bent down to glare into the girl's face. "I've smelled week-old corpses better than you. You're nasty."

"Manners," Jingshen said. "Be professional."

"Eat my ass." Bishop gave him the finger.

Jingshen turned away from her and looked down at the girl in his arms. "Can you speak?"

The girl nodded and said something through chapped lips, but it didn't carry through her suit.

"Can you stand?"

She made a non-committal motion with her head. Jingshen set the girl upright on the floor, steadying her as she swayed. She found her balance as she clutched at him with her bound hands.

"Are you contagious?"

She shook her head.

"Are you in danger if we remove your suit?"

She shook her head again.

"Now, just a goddamn minute—" Bishop began.

Jingshen held up his hand and Bishop stopped her tirade as quickly as it had begun. "She appears dehydrated. She probably needs a toilet. Perhaps she could wash herself."

"Hey, there's no fucking toilet paper!" Rook called from down the hall. "Hope you ain't attached to these hand towels."

"Whatever," Nobody Special said.

"I don't know what you're playing at," Bishop said. "But whatever it is, it's on you. You take off her suit so you can play Barbie dress-up, anything that she does or happens to her is your responsibility. And if it means I don't get paid for the contract, I'm taking it out of your ass."

"That is fair." Jingshen removed the girl's hood. If she'd smelled bad before, the reek coming off her was ten times worse.

She took a deep shuddering breath, as if grateful to smell something besides herself. "Water," she rasped.

"Nobody, get her some water," Jingshen ordered.

"Why me?" the reedy man asked.

"Because the Ghost is watching the captive, and I'm watching the goddamn Ghost in case she turns him into a pillar of salt or some shit like that," Bishop retorted. "Now move your skinny ass before I find out if you can shapeshift when you're in two pieces." She thumped her naginata on the floor for emphasis.

Nobody Special left the front room, muttering under his breath. Jingshen studied the girl. Her thin face was framed by dark hair with lighter roots—clearly a bottle job. The unwashed, tangled hair looked like it was only days away from going into full-on dreadlocks. Her eyes were so shadowed she looked like she'd been punched in the face. Jingshen decided she was young, maybe still only a teen. She must have been exceptionally unusual to have garnered such a high price in mercenary contracts.

Parahuman? Undoubtedly. He couldn't fathom any other reason someone like her would be worth the huge investment from two rival corporations.

Nobody Special returned with a glass of water. He gave it to Jingshen then stepped away, wincing at the girl's stench. As her hands were still cuffed together, Jingshen raised the cup to her lips and carefully tipped it. She drank greedily, draining the glass in a few seconds, then coughed as the water got away from her.

"Are you all right?" Jingshen asked.

"I . . . I need to pee."

Jingshen glanced toward Bishop, who raised her hands. "Uh-uh. No. This isn't Girls' Night Out."

"Is there another bathroom in this house?" Jinshen asked Nobody Special. "I won't subject her to Rook."

Nobody Special shrugged. "Yeah, that's fair. Up the stairs, straight across the hall."

Jingshen slipped a handcuffs key from one of his pockets and unlocked the girl's wrists. "Don't run," he said. "You will not get very far."

She shrugged. "Where'm I gonna go, anyway? I'm just the *captive*." Her voice was bitter and Jingshen realized her youthful appearance was only skin-deep. The girl, whoever she was, had *seen some shit*. Any childhood innocence was long gone.

"That wing of the house is closed for business, know what I'm saying?" Rook said as he returned from the bathroom. He saw Jingshen leading the girl up the stairs, one of Nobody Special's electric lanterns in his hand. "Hey, where you going with my money?"

"To close another wing of the house."

* * *

Her name was Zoe, she said, but she was disinclined to share anything else about herself. "You gonna watch me pee?" she asked Jingshen as he stood in the bathroom door. "You get off on that shit?"

"There is a window. I am not going to let you leave by it."

Zoe looked up at the small window over the shower. "I'm no gymnast." She opened the toilet, shucked her filthy jeans and underwear to her ankles, and sat. The sound of a strong urine stream hitting the water followed.

Jingshen averted his gaze to give her as much privacy as he was willing to risk.

"Dude, I've been holding that for hours. If you only knew," Zoe said. "You got a cigarette, maybe?"

"I do not smoke."

"What's a straight edge like you doing with a couple of gigantic douches like Mr. and Mrs. NRA?"

"Right now, I'm trying to treat you like a human being instead of a piece of property."

Zoe stared at him. "Like I said, straight edge." She leaned forward, elbows resting on her knees, and chin on her hands. "You probably don't wanna let me go."

"I can't. I have a contract."

"So break it. People break deals all the time. All. The. Time." She said it with such vehemence Jingshen was sure she had suffered more than her fair share of dishonesty. After all, she was a high-value prisoner. One didn't become such a thing without some serious falsehoods laid down first.

"Why are you here?"

"You assholes brought me here."

"Yes, but why were we hired to retrieve you?"

Zoe sat back up, looking down at her hands. "I got the magic touch." She held a hand out to him. "See this? This is the money right here." She turned it over and raised her middle finger at him. "Also, fuck you and your contract. I'm going to take a shower. I've been wearing the same clothes for two weeks now." She stood, flushed the toilet, and stepped out of her crumpled jeans and underwear.

Jingshen looked away, embarrassed at her sudden willfulness as she pulled her t-shirt over her head. She spotted the half-full hand soap bottle on the vanity, grabbed it, and turned on the shower. There was no shower curtain and water splattered onto the floor.

"Shit, that's cold," she griped as she stepped under the spray. "You gonna watch me do this too, perv?"

"No," said Jingshen. "But I won't leave you alone either."

Zoe stuck her head under the spray, working the water through her matted hair. "Then make yourself useful. Wash out my clothes, since I don't see anywhere to get some new ones. You're Chinese. Isn't laundry, like, in your blood?"

Jingshen bristled at the girl's blatant racism, but then considered her position and decided maybe she was entitled to be a bit of an asshole. Besides, he'd spent several years working as a launderer in various mining towns along the mountains. It was better work than railroad labor, which he'd also done. "Very well. Give me the soap." He had cold running water, a sink, and whatever hand soap Zoe would leave after washing. He shrugged. It was better than smelling her. He wished he had some good old-fashioned soap chunks but he would make do. He plugged the drain and filled the sink with water, then poured in half of the remaining liquid soap, then set the bottle on the edge of the tub.

Zoe stared at him in frank astonishment. "Goddamn, you're really gonna do that."

"As you said, we have no new clothes for you, and the others will prefer you smell better."

Zoe stepped back from the spray and began soaping herself up, being frugal as possible so she wouldn't run out. "What's with the hat? You trying to be Chinese Indiana Jones?"

Jingshen didn't answer, but it amused him that she'd reached the same conclusion as Nobody Special, and at least she'd identified the correct ethnic background. He lost himself in the process of soaking Zoe's clothes in the soapy water, wringing them out, then repeating the steps. He removed the top of the toilet tank and pressed the clothes between it and the toilet lid, making an impromptu wringer. The clothes would still be damp, but it would be the only practical option.

Zoe rinsed herself off then shut down the water and stood in the tub, shivering. "You got a towel or blanket or anything I can wrap in? I'm freezing my skinny ass off here."

"Sorry, I don't."

Nobody Special appeared in the bathroom door, holding a rough gray blanket. "Oh, hey, I'm sorry to intrude." He looked anything but apologetic as he stared unabashedly at Zoe's nude body. "I found this in the van. Thought it might be useful. 'Scuse me." He pushed past Jingshen to hand the blanket to Zoe, who swiped it from his grasp.

"Give me that, you fucking creep."

"Ow! What the hell?" Nobody Special shook his hand and then looked at it. Jingshen thought the man's flesh seemed to waver for a moment before stabilizing. Perhaps he'd imagined it. "What, do you make static electricity or something?"

"Don't ever touch me!" Zoe snarled at him. "You could have died just then!"

Nobody Special raised his hands. "Hey, don't be so salty. You ain't all that." He turned to Jingshen. "I'm heading out for food." He lowered his voice. "Keep an eye on her. I don't trust Rook and Bishop."

Jingshen nodded. He didn't trust them either. Nor did he trust Nobody Special. "You said you will change your appearance when you return. How do we know it is you?"

"Give me a password. Something a random stranger isn't going to guess."

"*Laundry day*," Jingshen said.

Zoe snorted.

"Yeah, okay, I can remember that. *Laundry day*. You got a food preference?"

"Burger and fries," Zoe said immediately. "What? I'm hungry. Those assholes were into oatmeal and water. I probably got deficiencies on top of my deficiencies."

Jingshen nodded. "That will be fine. Get enough for all of us."

Nobody Special grimaced. "Man, I bet Rook can eat a whole side of beef by himself."

"You have money." Jingshen didn't make it a question, and Nobody Special didn't argue the point.

"I'll be back," Nobody Special said, aping Arnold Schwarzenegger's *Terminator* character. He paused as if waiting for someone to compliment his impression. When none was forthcoming, he left the bathroom.

"He's a joy," Zoe said as she stepped out of the tub. "You've got shitty friends, Indiana Jones."

"He is not my friend. We just work together."

"Yeah, maybe you need a change of jobs."

"I'm considering it."

"How about this? You start your career change by letting me go."

"Sorry, no. Your clothes are as clean as I can get them, but they will still be damp."

Zoe sniffled and suddenly her bravado disappeared. "Please. Please, Mister. I just want to go. I won't say anything. I don't want them to experiment on me any more."

Jingshen understood how she felt. He'd seen far too many people killed at the hands of those who professed to be medical doctors. He'd also seen far too many people tortured under the guise of experiments. If anyone like that discovered his ability to regrow lost appendages and to heal from the most grievous wounds, he would never again see the light of day. "I . . . I am sorry," he said at last, knowing it was a pathetic and underwhelming phrase.

"Hey, Ghost," Bishop called up the stairs. "You fucking her or something? Because that wasn't part of the arrangement."

Jingshen motioned to the bathroom door. "We should go back downstairs. Bishop is . . . less polite than I am."

"Yeah, you're a fucking Good Samaritan, Indiana Jones." Keeping the blanket wrapped around her as best she could, Zoe grabbed her damp clothing in her other hand and pushed past him.

He noticed how careful she was not to touch him with her bare skin and filed that away for future reference.

Jingshen followed Zoe to one of the empty adjacent bedrooms and watched her struggle to push her legs through her damp jeans. "Goddammit, Indiana Jones, can't you give me two seconds of privacy?"

He pulled the door partway shut and turned his back. "This is the best I can do."

Zoe didn't respond. He heard her step toward the window, but she stopped at the dusty glass and stared out at the dark abandoned neighborhood and the distant city lights beyond. "What a shithole," she murmured, quietly enough that Jingshen thought she probably hadn't intended him to hear.

"If you are finished dressing, come downstairs," Jingshen said. "Nobody will be back soon with food."

"What kind of name is *Nobody*?" Zoe's stomach rumbled loud enough for Jingshen to hear it across the room.

"It is the only name I know him by," Jingshen said. "As they only know me as *Ghost*."

"Ghost. It's like you're a superhero or something."

Jingshen snorted. Heroes didn't kidnap young women for profit.

"What's your real name? You got one, don't you?"

"Jingshen."

"I'm going to call you Chinese Indiana Jones."

"As long as I know it means me."

"Nothing gets to you, does it?"

Jingshen shrugged. "You might say I've seen it all."

Chapter Five

September, 1993
Los Angeles, California

Rook stood by the edge of the front window, alternately watching the street and turning to the others to complain that Nobody Special was taking too long getting their grub. "He better not have ditched us."

"Why would he do that?" Bishop said from where she sat against the wall with her legs folded and her naginata resting across her knees. While her brother kept an eye out for the van, she kept watch on Zoe, who sat glumly on a chair in the room's center. "He wants to get paid."

"I just don't trust him," Rook said.

Bishop snorted. "You? You're hardly a good judge of character."

Rook snorted in an almost perfect imitation of his sister. "Ghost, you've been around awhile. What's your take on Nobody Special? You trust him?"

"No," Jingshen said. "Nor do I trust you."

Bishop burst out laughing. "He's got you there, Rookie, dear."

"Goddammit, don't call me that!"

Rook's anger only made Bishop laugh harder.

Jingshen spotted the gleam of headlights off the windows from the house across the street. "The van is returning."

Bishop's laughter died and she stood, bits of energy crackling around her naginata. Rook kept his antitank gun slung across his back but drew one of his oversized pistols. "Fucker better have remembered the ketchup or I'm going to ventilate his ass."

The van parked in the driveway and the driver emerged. As promised, Nobody Special had changed his features again, now resembling a nondescript man in his early twenties with stringy hair and a soul patch beard on his pale skin. He clutched several bags from Taco Bell.

"Ah, hell. Now I'm gonna have the farts all night," Rook grumbled.

"H-hello?" Nobody Special said at the door. "It's, uh, laundry day. And my hands are full."

"What the fuck?" Bishop asked.

"Open the door," Jingshen said. "It's him."

Rook shrugged and pulled open the front door. Nobody Special came in, staggering under his load of cheap tacos. "I, uh, brought Taco Bell. It's the only thing open this late out by the highway."

Jingshen took one of the bags and handed it to Zoe, who tore into it with the intensity of someone who hadn't eaten in a few days.

"Anybody see you?" Bishop asked.

"No . . ." But even as he said so, Nobody Special looked over his shoulder and Jingshen saw more lights reflecting off the house across the street.

Flashing red and blue lights.

"Cops," he hissed.

"Cops? *Cops?*" Rook raised his pistol. "You dumb piece of shit brought the cops here?"

Nobody Special's eyes grew wide as he stared at the pistol. "No! No, I didn't do nothin'! He said—"

Rook fired once and Nobody Special's head evaporated into dark mist that splattered the far wall. Zoe screamed and Bishop whacked her on the side of the head with the butt of her naginata, hard enough to leave a welt but not knocking her unconscious.

"Shut your stupid ass up. Dammit, Rook, what the shit?"

"Cops! That sneaky little asshole led them right to us! I told you I didn't trust him!"

Police cruisers skidded to a halt on the street outside. Jingshen counted five, and the officers spilling out of them had tactical gear.

Rook swung his antitank gun from his back and slammed a fresh clip into it. Bishop drew her own pistol and pressed her back against the wall beside the front window. "Ghost, check the back door. It would be just like them to make all this noise out front and slip a sniper in the back."

Jingshen kicked Zoe's chair out from under her as he passed. "Keep your head down," he warned, and pulled his sticks from his back. He was no slouch with a firearm, but his preference was for weapons that were as swift and silent as a gust of wind.

The kitchen was dark, and Jingshen melted into the shadows in his black outfit and hat. He saw no movement through the kitchen window but anyone sneaking in would probably come in through the mudroom instead.

"Come out with your hands up," came an officious voice through a bullhorn outside. Such a phrase was normally followed with *we have you surrounded*, but Jingshen saw nobody lurking in or near the mudroom. He set one of his sticks on the kitchen counter and slipped a small cardboard box from a pocket of his cargo pants. Inside it was a handful of Fourth-of-July bang snaps. He spread them out in front of the mudroom door. The pops of anyone stepping on them would give just enough warning for everyone to act.

"You have until the count of three, and then we're coming in after you. We know you're in there. One . . ."

Jingshen returned to the front room. Rook immediately tossed a spare pistol at him. Jingshen snagged it out of the air, grimacing in distaste at what he considered to be an exceptionally uncouth weapon.

"Two . . ."

"Three!" Rook shouted, and fired his antitank gun through the window.

A police cruiser exploded in front of the house, the forceful eruption sending it skyward for a few feet before gravity brought it back down in a flaming wreck.

"Yeah, boy!" Rook shouted as the police opened fire upon the house. The bangs of shotguns mixed with the sharper reports of pistols. Bullets crashed through windows and smacked into drywall.

Bishop threw herself against the wall beside a ruined window, then spun around to fire several shots at the police before moving to the other side. Rook howled with glee and fired the cannon again, devastating another cruiser.

Jingshen fired out another window. An officer went down, holding his leg and screaming. A bullet thudded into Jingshen's bicep, making him drop the pistol. He didn't bother to retrieve it as Bishop and Rook were doing far more damage between them than he could have hoped to do himself.

Bullets ricocheted off Rook's giant gun and one lucky shot damaged his firing mechanism. When he pulled the trigger and nothing happened, he swore with the kind of vitriol reserved for the death of a loved one. He dropped the cannon and pulled two of his huge pistols. "You're gonna pay for that" he screamed over the din, and opened up with the pistols on full automatic.

"Jingshen, get the package out of here! Meet at the secondary drop tomorrow!" Bishop shouted from her knees as she reloaded her own weapon. "We'll hold them off." She popped up next to her brother and added the soprano chatter of her own pistol to the baritone chorus of Rook's arsenal.

Jingshen crawled across the floor to Nobody Special's body and dug the keys from the man's pocket.

Rook yelped as police bullets smacked into his breastplate. "Goddammit, that hurts!"

"Got you right in the man-gina?" Bishop shouted at her brother as she pulled an extra pistol from his hip holster. "Need a tampon, pussy?"

Rook dropped his pistols, their barrels glowing a dull red, and yanked two more from under his arms. "Take that! And that! And *that!*" he shouted as he emptied the clips at the police.

Despite their insulting banter toward each other, the siblings were a skilled, dangerous pair of fighters. One kept up a withering barrage of fire while the other reloaded. Jingshen crawled over to Zoe, who had her hands over her ears and her eyes scrunched up tight. "Come with me," he shouted over the gunfire. "I am getting you out of here. Stay low."

"No!" she screamed. "No, no, no no no . . ."

"I'll knock you out and carry you if I have to, but it will be faster if you run."

She gasped as the front doorknob shattered from a shotgun blast. "Okay."

They ran into the kitchen just as Jingshen heard the pops of his booby traps go off. A pair of officers had just entered through the mud room. With no room to use his sticks, Jingshen went after them with open hands. Bullets pounded into him like fists, splattering blood with every blow. He reached the first officer and disarmed him with a thousand-year-old technique. He drove the man's face into the washing machine, leaving a dark stain on the glass door from his shattered nose.

The second officer tried to back away, stumbled, and fell. Jingshen dropped a heavy axe kick on the man's shoulder, snapping bones and tearing ligaments. The officer screamed before Jingshen silenced him with a vicious kick to the temple.

Zoe screamed and kept screaming.

Jingshen straightened up, feeling his flesh push bullets out, a process which was nearly as painful as their initial entry. Sometimes they didn't leave by the same path they entered. "Shut up or you're going to get yourself killed," he said curtly, and Zoe stopped her screaming.

They left the mudroom and went along the back of the house toward the corner. He peeked around and saw the side was clear. He made sure Zoe was right behind him and trotted to the front corner to regard the scene of devastation wrought by Rook and Bishop.

Three police cars were ablaze, two flipped onto their roofs. The third had flames racing up the windshield and out from the fenders from an ignited engine. The police were firing toward the house to provide covering fire for those who were injured and trying to crawl to safety, or dragging those who couldn't. So much gunfire came from Bishop and Rook inside the house that the two of them had pinned down more than a dozen police.

Jingshen grabbed Zoe's hand and pulled her after him to the driver's side of the van. He opened the door and shoved her inside. "Stay there and keep your head down or you'll get shot," he said. He ripped aside the cover of the fuse box and pulled the fuses for the van's brake and tail lights.

Zoe wrapped her hand around the door handle as if getting ready to jump out, but a bullet spalled across the windshield frame and she screamed. Jingshen slipped into the seat and started the engine. The van's engine spun to life and he shifted into reverse. "Hold on."

The wheels spun as the van roared backward out of the driveway, crashing between two parked police cars. As he passed beyond their barricade, Jingshen saw the shocked expressions of the officers who'd been firing back toward the house. Keeping his foot jammed onto the accelerator, Jingshen cranked the steering wheel over and the van's front tires broke loose into a sloppy bootlegger's reverse. As the front end came around, he shifted back into drive as bullets punched holes in the van's rear doors. One struck the back of his seat and went most of the way through his shoulder. He cursed as his arm stopped working.

He wove the van through the neighborhood streets, waiting for his body to push the bullet free so he would have both his hands again. He knew the police would have backup on the way, including SWAT officers and air support. The sooner he got to new cover, the better.

Zoe huddled in her seat, whimpering and moaning. "Oh no, oh no."

Jingshen ignored her panic and found enough function in his injured arm to hold the steering wheel. With his other hand, he reached up to his shoulder and dug the bullet out from where it sat just below the skin. Zoe screamed at his casual self-mutilation. He ignored her and dropped the bullet onto the floor between the seats. Once it was gone, his healing would take care of the rest of the damage, but at a cost. He was famished. Dehydrated. Exhausted. Healing wasn't free, and he'd used a lot of energy recovering from injuries that would have slain a lesser man a dozen times over. He pulled the van onto the frontage road alongside the highway. Driving without lights on the highway would attract too much attention, but on the frontage road, he might not be noticed at all.

"Please, dude, can't you just let me go? Just pull over and let me out."

"No."

"I'll grab the wheel if you don't. I'll drive us right into an overpass," she said, showing some bravado at last.

"If you do, you'll die, and I'll walk away," Jingshen said. "You can't kill me that easily. People have been trying for a very long time."

Headlights flashed at them as a car came the other direction on the frontage road, reminding them that their own lights were off.

"So what happens now?" Zoe asked.

"Find a safe place to hole up for a few hours, then meet the others at the secondary drop."

"Meaning what, after all that you're just going to turn me over to Kokorotai?"

Jingshen frowned. "Yes. That hasn't changed."

* * *

Zoe actually fell asleep while Jingshen drove away from the carnage Rook and Bishop created. He couldn't blame her; he was exhausted as well. He needed a solid three or four hours of sleep and a few thousand calories. Before that, he needed a better disguise. Nothing could be done about the bullet holes decorating the body panels, but in Los Angeles that wasn't as uncommon as one might expect.

He spotted a commercial park a couple exits further to the north. If he stayed on the frontage road, he should run into it eventually. Before he reached it, he pulled off to the side of the road and replaced the fuses he'd removed from the fuse box. With lights functional once more, he turned into the park. The faceless glass and steel buildings had names on them that gave no indication of what business was transacted inside them.

Jingshen didn't care. He smiled when the headlights illuminated a few parked cars along the side of one building. He scanned the building for any cameras trained on the lot but didn't see any. Perfect.

He backed the van into a spot beside a minivan, shut off the engine, and stuck the keys in his pocket. He found the multitool he carried in one of his cargo pockets and opened the screwdriver attachment. A few hurried minutes and he'd switched the van's plates with the minivan's. It wasn't a perfect disguise but it would have to do.

When he returned to the driver's seat, he found Zoe awake and watching him.

"What are you doing?" she asked.

"Covering our tracks." He started the van and pulled away from the building. "Why didn't you run?"

She shrugged. "You'd have just caught me. You got me out of that firefight. I figure if nothing else, I'm safer with you than on my own."

"Even though I'm turning you over to Kokorotai?"

She shrugged again. "Dude, I'll cross that bridge when I come to it."

Jingshen frowned but said nothing. He kept his hands clenched on the steering wheel so they wouldn't shake with the exhaustion. The wound in his shoulder had closed, but it took longer than typical. He couldn't die—at least, nobody had managed to do him in despite making some impressive efforts, but his healing would grow slower and slower if he couldn't refuel and rest. Once it had taken him months to put himself back together after being beheaded in London for presumed offenses against the King.

The frontage road ended, forcing him to drive deeper into an industrial area. He cruised slowly, keeping an eye out for patrolling police or private security, until he found a factory with a couple isolated cars in its lot. He successfully hot-wired one and it not only started, but had almost a full tank of gas to boot. "Come on," he said to Zoe, leaving the van's keys in the ignition.

"Why'd you do that?" she asked, sitting beside him.

"Do what?"

"Leave the keys."

"We're stealing someone's car. Perhaps they can use the van if they need it."

"Why do you care, dude?"

"It's the things we do when we don't need to do them that matter most." Jingshen rubbed his jaw. He was so tired his eyes weren't focusing properly.

"That's really fucking deep."

They drove away from the bullet-ridden van and out onto the highway. Jingshen could barely focus enough to keep the car in the lane. He struggled past two exits and took the third, hoping to find an all-night drive-through and a motel. Fortunately, Los Angeles came through in the form of a 24-hour Taco Bell. "Not a word," he said to Zoe at the drive-through.

"Fine, whatever."

He ordered enough food for four people and inhaled a pair of flavorless burritos, chasing them with flat soda. It wasn't great, but he'd eaten worse in his life, and his body would process the calories regardless of what form they took.

"God, did you even taste those?" Zoe asked, eating her own burrito at a more leisurely pace.

Jingshen paused. "Why would you want to taste this? It's barely food."

"I guess."

Jingshen took their stolen car into the lot for a run-down motel called the Lamplighter, complete with a traditional-style box lantern lamp with cracked glass and peeling paint. *Rooms By the Day or By the Hour*, it advertised on a hand-painted piece of plywood screwed into the wall over the office window.

"Really? Hourly rates?" Zoe sneered. "You take me to the nicest places."

Jingshen reached out and casually snapped a set of handcuffs around one of Zoe's wrists and the other around the steering wheel.

"Hey, what the fuck, dude?" Zoe shouted.

Jingshen raised a fist. "Be quiet and it will only be handcuffs. Cause trouble, and it will still be handcuffs, but I will also knock you out."

Zoe glared at him. "Fuck you, dude. I thought we had something."

"We have nothing. We will spend a few hours here and rest. I recommend you take the opportunity to do so of your own accord. Otherwise . . ."

"Yeah, yeah. You'll knock me out. Asshole." Zoe sank in her seat, pouting. "You better not be expecting me to put out just because you bought me a burrito."

"I don't." Jingshen took the keys when he got out of the car and went to the window. A shadowy figure was watching a cable movie with topless women playing beach volleyball. Jingshen saw no bell, so he knocked politely upon the window. The figure stood and stepped into the harsh glow of the overhead light. He was an older man with a bald scalp and tufts of wild gray sticking out over his ears. He wore a stained wife-beater tank top and swimming trunks.

"Yeah?" the man asked, rubbing gray stubble around his jaw.

"How much for a room?"

"Hourly or all night?" The man looked at his cheap digital watch. "Checkout's at eleven, so all night ain't gonna get you your money's worth. Tell ya what. Twenty bucks and be gone by ten. Best I can do."

Jingshen handed him two twenty dollar bills. "I will be gone by four o'clock this afternoon."

The man made the money disappear and handed Jingshen a key. "Suit yourself, weirdo." He glanced at Jingshen's hat and snorted before returning to his movie.

Jingshen returned to the car. Zoe had her feet up on the dash and was going through the CDs in the glove compartment. "This is crap. Couldn't you have stolen a car with decent music?"

"We're not going to be in it long enough to listen to anything." Jingshen bent down to release the handcuffs. "Let's go."

The room was about what he had expected from a place that rented by the hour. The walls were marked with unrecognizable stains, at least one of which Jingshen thought was blood. The brown fjords of water stains crept across the ceiling and the carpet was so old that a rectangle of it was faded below the window. The management had bolted a window lock into the track so it couldn't be opened more than a couple of inches. A threadbare bedspread was smoothed over a mattress sunken in the middle. The shades on the bedside lamps were yellowed from old dust.

"Shit, there's no TV," Zoe said. Bare wires sprouted from the wall where a television might once have been plugged in.

"I suggest you sleep instead."

"Well I'm kind of going to have to now, dude." She crossed her arms and glared at him. "And don't get any ideas."

Jingshen shrugged. "That is fine."

Zoe stepped into the bathroom. "Oh *gawd* this place is the worst."

While she busied herself in the tiny bathroom, Jingshen took one of the two pillows off the bed and set it at the base of the room's door. He took his sticks from their back sheaths, removed his hat, and sat down on the pillow with his back to the door. He set the hat upon the floor beside him and placed the sticks across his folded legs.

Zoe emerged from the bathroom. "What the hell are you doing, dude?"

"You may sleep on the bed."

"You're just going to sleep sitting up right there?"

"Yes. Is that a problem for you?"

Zoe raised her hands. "Hey, I don't care what you do. Unless you're planning to let me go."

"No."

"You're a real asshole, you know that?"

"Yes."

Chapter Six

September, 1993
Los Angeles, California

Zoe was a restless sleeper, and every time the bed creaked, Jingshen cracked open an eye to check on her. He'd learned over the years to get the most out of his sleep when he needed to. He didn't need to get all his hours of rest in a row, so he passed the rest of the night and a portion of the morning in a half-awake state, drifting in and out of REM sleep.

When at last his eyes opened and didn't shut again a few seconds later, he knew it was time to awaken. He reached for his hat and slipped it onto his head, pulling the brim down low to shield his eyes. Sunlight streamed through the crack in the curtains, illuminating a narrow column of dust that shifted with his every motion. Beyond the door, the sounds of traffic on the highway competed with the occasional distant whoosh of jets on their approaches or departures.

Jingshen stepped softly across the carpet, toe to heel the way he'd been taught by a Japanese assassin. He stopped at the edge of the bed, sticks in hand, and looked down at Zoe. He wasn't sure what he'd expected to see, but when he saw the shadow of stubble on her cheek, he realized he wasn't surprised at all. He raised a stick and gave her a sharp, expertly aimed rap on the tip of her nose.

"Ow! Shit!" Zoe recoiled, still half asleep, fumbling at the blood streaming from her nose. "Dude, what—"

"No," Jingshen said, laying a stick across Zoe's wrist. When she tried to pull it back, he snapped the stick against the bump of bone jutting from her wrist. "Not *dude*. What do you call me?"

"Asshole!" Zoe shouted, then yelped when Jingshen cracked his stick against the point of her elbow. "Goddammit, stop!"

"At the safe house. What did you call me?"

"I don't know! Ghost, right? Jesus *fuck* that hurts."

"No."

Zoe paused, her sides heaving, blood running down either side of her mouth like a crimson mustache. "You want me to say it? Fine. It's me. Nobody Special."

"Take that face off. I don't want to see you wearing it anymore."

"Fine." Zoe's face filled out and grew a real mustache. Her feminine features disappeared beneath a fleshy middle-aged man's face framed by shaggy brown hair. Shoulders filled out with thatches of hair sprouting from them. His paunchy belly was barely contained inside a stained Lynyrd Skynyrd concert t-shirt with the sleeves torn off.

"What's your name? Your real name," Jingshen said.

"Corso."

"Who was the young man at the house? I assume it wasn't you who was shot."

"Just some delivery kid. I gave him a hundred bucks and told him it was a surprise party."

"You just let Rook kill him."

Corso snorted with laughter, blowing flecks of bloody snot across the bedspread. "I heard all about you, Ghost. There's more blood on your hands than most. You picked a hell of a time to go all noble and shit."

"Where's Zoe now?"

"Bishop and Rook have her. I swapped places with her when you went out to check the back door. I don't know where they took her."

"Tell me everything."

Corso shrugged. "It's the money, dude. It's always the money. You know that. DuraGen is paying a hell of a lot more money for your little hood rat than Kokorotai. I figured they might be real interested in making sure when all was said and done, they got to keep their cash cow."

"Rook and Bishop are in on it," Jingshen said.

"Of course they are. They're even more mercenary than I am. They don't care about the goddamn Source. Hell, for all I know, they're going to go work for DuraGen full-time. I mean, the cut we're all getting for this is fucking obscene."

"Why didn't you try to recruit me?"

"Are you serious? With your reputation? Shit, I don't expect to leave this room alive. Only reason I'm talking now is because maybe you'll decide letting me live is more noble. So how about it, huh? You want to just let me walk away? I'm not worth anything to you dead."

"You're not worth anything to me alive."

Corso raised his hands—slowly, so Jingshen wouldn't pop him one again. "That's not entirely true, Ghost. Right now you're on the outside looking in. Bishop and Rook turn Zoe back over to DuraGen, fulfilling the deal we made with them. DuraGen makes her disappear. Bishop and Rook blow away in the wind and me, well . . ." He smiled beneath his mustache. "I can be ten different people by this time tomorrow. Ain't nobody going to track me down. Kokorotai's not going to be happy that they got double-crossed, and you're going to be left holding the bag."

"I had nothing to do with this."

"Yeah, go ahead and tell them that and see how it plays out. You're burned, Ghost, unless you join forces with me. I'll talk to my DuraGen contact. Get you paid too. Enough for you to disappear."

Jingshen shook his head. "I don't renege on contracts."

"You're an idiot."

"Reputation is the only commodity worth anything in this business."

"Not when you see how many digits are on the DuraGen check. The Source can go fuck themselves."

Jingshen lowered his sticks.

"So you can make a smart decision," Corso said. "Good. I—"

"No," Jingshen said. "You will help me get Zoe back and fulfill the contract."

Corso laughed. "Are you high?"

"The price is your life. Help me, and I give it back to you freely. You may, as you say, walk away."

Corso glanced to one side, perhaps considering what he might use as a weapon. Jingshen rapped him across the knuckles with a stick. "Ow, goddammit. All right. Fuck. You and those damn sticks."

"Have Rook and Bishop already delivered Zoe back to DuraGen?"

"No, the meeting is set up for today. They wanted to make sure I got you far enough away and kept you off balance."

"Where?"

Corso rattled off an address that meant nothing to Jingshen. "Take me there."

"What, now?"

"I want to check the place out before anyone arrives."

Corso canted his head toward the cheap digital clock radio on the bedside table. "You're not going to have time, dude."

"Then I'll improvise. You're driving."

"How do you know I'll take you to the meeting place?"

"I don't. That's why you're driving. If I decide you're bullshitting me, I'll put one of these sticks through your head the hard way."

"There's an easy way?"

* * *

Corso kept up a litany of muttered complaints as he drove the stolen sedan through weekend highway traffic. "Why can't these assholes all stay home and watch the Raiders like regular people?"

"We're not watching football," Jingshen pointed out.

"We could be." Corso took an exit ramp into a commercial district. He rolled up to a stoplight and pinched the bridge of his nose. "I'm about done with this business anyway. Mercenary work is way too dangerous. I'm going to take my payout and go back to grifting. Never had anyone trying to take a shot at me doing that. Besides . . ." He turned to grin at Jingshen. "I got laid, like, all the time."

Jingshen turned to respond to Corso and froze. In the car in the next lane, staring at him from the passenger seat, was Rook. Their eyes locked. "Corso . . ." Jingshen began.

"What's up, playa?" Rook yelled gleefully as he raised one of his pistols.

"Drive!" Jingshen shouted, and Corso yelped in terror as Rook's pistol roared and a bullet blasted apart both men's headrests.

Corso hammered down the accelerator and the car roared across the intersection against the light. Horns blared at them and a small coupe skidded into the stoplight pole. The light broke free from the overhead bar and smashed to the pavement.

Jingshen spun around in his seat to see Rook and Bishop's car launch into pursuit. Bishop was behind the wheel and Rook pounded the outside of the door like he was whipping a racehorse. "I thought you were working with them!"

"I was!" Corso fishtailed around a slower car and switched lanes. "They must have decided to cut me out."

"That's the risk of a double cross," Jingshen said. "Do so once, and everyone knows you can do so again."

"Really goddamn helpful advice." Corso braked hard and took a sharp left. The car's engine redlined as he floored the pedal.

Behind them, Bishop's rear wheels slid out, spinning smoke against the pavement as she fought to follow. "Do you think Zoe is in there?"

"You want me to pull over so you can check?" They bounced over a railroad crossing, all four wheels leaving the road for a long second before crashing back down.

"Watch out," Jingshen said as Rook hung his pistol out the window.

Corso swerved right, cutting across the lanes as Rook fired. A bullet hole appeared in another car's rear window, matched by a crimson explosion against its windshield. The car drifted into oncoming traffic to collide with a box truck.

"We've got to get off this road. Rook doesn't care who he kills."

"I don't care who he kills either, as long as it's not me," Corso retorted. His driver's side mirror vanished with Rook's next shot.

"I'll stop them." Jingshen unhooked his seat belt.

"With what, your sticks?" The intersection ahead was clogged and Corso pulled onto the sidewalk, one hand jammed against the horn. Pedestrians screamed and dove out of the way as they roared past a café, smashing a table and chairs into splinters.

Corso swore as they cut in front of a minivan and it clipped the right rear quarter panel. The tires came loose and they spun a cloud of white smoke as Corso fought to regain his line. Behind them, Bishop swerved the wrong way around the minivan and flew past them.

"Go after them," Jingshen said.

"Are you fucking crazy?" Corso shouted back. He swerved as Rook leaned out from the window and fired back at them.

Jingshen pulled his hat down low over his forehead. It probably wouldn't stay in place, but he'd prefer not to replace it if he didn't have to. "Get me close to them, and then I don't care what you do." Before Corso could argue, he climbed out the window and crawled onto the roof where he wouldn't block Corso's view.

"Jesus Christ!" Corso said, but he acceded to Jingshen's order. Maybe he wanted to see how the action played out so he could claim his payday from the appropriate source.

Bishop plowed through another intersection, barely missing a taxicab and making Rook miss his next shot. "Faster, Corso," Jingshen shouted over the roar of the engine. Corso swerved around a truck, nearly dislodging Jingshen from the roof. Horns blared and tires squealed in their wake.

Rook fired again and the bullet caught Jingshen high on the scalp, gouging a furrow through his flesh and creasing his skull. His hat went flying away into the wind, much to his chagrin. His fingers stayed locked onto the car's roof as his healing ability sealed the wound. Rook glared at him and slipped back inside the car.

"Now, while he's reloading!" Jingshen shouted, and he slid down the windshield to perch on the hood. He glanced back at Corso, who had his teeth bared in an expression somewhere between a grimace of terror and a grin of anticipation.

Bishop cut into the oncoming lanes to swerve around a van stopped at the next light. Corso followed, only half a car length behind.

A dump truck entered the intersection from the right and broadsided Corso's car.

In the fraction of second Jingshen had as warning, he sprang from the car's hood. He felt the wash of heat as Corso's car burst into flame. Shrapnel from the collision peppered his back. He flew through the air, arms stretching as he strained to reach Bishop and Rook's car.

Time seemed to grind to a near halt as the pavement raced beneath him in a dusty blur. Bishop started to accelerate away—Jingshen heard the change in tone in the fleeing car's engine—and then he was falling, the car drifting tantalizingly just out of his reach.

The fingers of one hand closed around the steel bumper and time snapped back to its full blistering pace as he smashed to the ground. His wrist and shoulder dislocated simultaneously as his ribs and legs splintered at the impact.

Still, he held on doggedly. If the siblings got away from him now, he'd never find them before Zoe was back in DuraGen's possession and he was blacklisted by the Source for his unwitting participation in the double cross.

The broken ends of his ribs sliced into his lungs and blood poured from his mouth, leaving a dark trail along the pavement in his wake.

And still, he held on, knowing time was all he had left.

His world shrank to a few inches of bumper and the stink of exhaust blowing into his face. His body bounced over the rough road. And pain. So much pain.

Bones began knitting back together, righting themselves, fitting ends into sockets where they belonged. His broken organs and torn flesh sealed and made themselves whole once more, except for the constant damage that came from being dragged behind the fleeing car.

Horns blared around him as other drivers tried to alert the siblings to his presence. He wished he could have made them stop, but they were civilians, blissfully unaware of the life-or-death struggle inherent in the mercenary world.

He couldn't stay where he was; it wasn't accomplishing anything except wearing him down from the constant healing. He formed his free hand into a fist, steeled himself, and punched it into the tail light. The plastic cracked with his first blow and shattered with the second, sharp edges tearing through his skin. Inside the broken socket, he found he could reach all the way inside the trunk. His hand encountered something soft and warm, almost shocking him in the midst of the barrage of pain. *Zoe!*

"Holy shit, it's the Ghost!" Rook was leaning out of the window, bracing his hands on the door, looking back at Jingshen.

Bishop said something Jingshen couldn't hear, but he got the gist of it when Rook raised his pistol. Jingshen rolled himself back to the left, putting the body of the car between himself and Rook's pistol. Rook fired anyway, and the bullet banged through the trunk lid and out just above the bumper. More bullets followed and Jingshen flopped himself left and right. The bullets would hurt if they hit him, but he was more afraid of one blowing apart his hand and leaving him helpless and bleeding in the street.

Inside the trunk, his free hand happened upon a loose steel rod, and he realized he'd found the tire iron. He pulled it from the ruined tail light socket.

The car screeched to a halt and Jingshen bounced against it. "You get him?" Bishop asked over the sound of the motor.

"I'm sure I did. I must've put ten fucking bullets into the bastard."

"He heals, Rook. Make sure he's dead. We're gonna be late."

Jingshen heard the door open, followed by Rook's heavy footsteps on the pavement. He lay still to conserve every last erg of energy for his healing needs. From his prone position, he saw Rook's boots as the huge man approached. The boots were high quality but well-worn, ceramic plates over reinforced leather. They'd be heavy to wear, but the individual plates would give them enough flexibility to be comfortable. That flexibility gave them a weakness Rook might never have considered.

Jingshen would make sure he thought of it in the future, however brief that future would be.

"You tenacious son of a bitch," Rook said as he slapped a fresh clip into his pistol. "What the fuck does it take to kill you?"

Jingshen lashed out with the tire iron, aimed with long centuries of practice, and drove the wedge end in between two ceramic plates. Rook's damage resistance would have turned away a hard, fast blow, so Jingshen pushed it with just enough slow, inexorable force to pierce Rook's flesh. Steel met bone and bone was found wanting. The tire iron punched through Rook's ankle and severed his Achilles tendon. Rook screamed and collapsed, firing his pistol in reflex. Bullet shrapnel spattered into Jingshen's face as he yanked the iron free from Rook's flesh.

The big man had bracers protecting his wrists, but nothing to guard his hands, and Jingshen smashed Rook's knuckles, just hard enough to crack all the bones to splinters. The pistol clattered to the pavement. Tears of furious agony spilled down Rook's cheeks as he thrashed about. Jingshen rolled to his feet, reversed the tire iron, and shoved it through Rook's face like he was pinning a butterfly onto a card.

The big man's struggles ceased instantly.

Before Jingshen had even a moment to catch his breath, electricity crackled all around and through him. A long blade punched out of his chest, leaving his blood hissing like water on a stove burner. The stink of his burning flesh filled his head and he couldn't gasp because the shaft of the blade occluded his windpipe. The tire iron slipped from his suddenly clumsy fingers.

"Fuck you, you piece of shit!" Bishop screamed behind him. "You killed my brother!"

Spots danced in Jingshen's vision, but he'd been impaled before and knew what he had to do. He wrapped his hands around the naginata's shaft, feeling his skin blackening as electricity poured into him, and yanked the blade forward. Bishop hadn't expected the motion and the haft slipped from her grasp.

Jingshen pulled the rest of the shaft through the ragged hole in his torso, coughing reflexively as he tried and failed to draw a deep breath. The naginata was slick with his blood as he spun around. Bishop, startled at first losing her weapon and then having it turned against her, dodged far too late. The flat edge of the naginata crashed into the side of her head and she dropped as fast as Rook had.

Wind and breath whistled through the open wound in Jingshen's chest cavity. He let the naginata fall to the ground and slumped against the trunk. For the first time since the car came to a stop, he looked at his surroundings. They'd wound up on a narrow road between two large, mostly featureless warehouses with dusty windows high above and graffiti sprayed onto the bricks below.

Distant sirens meant he didn't have much time. Pain thudded through him with every step as he limped around the car, leaning on it for support and leaving bloodstains along the door panels. He yanked the trunk release lever and returned to the car's rear end. His internal organs shifted inside his body as the impalement hole closed. He gagged and spat up a thick glob of thickened blood shot through with pale streaks. Zoe lay inside the trunk, bound with duct tape and gagged with a tennis ball taped against her mouth. She blinked at the sunlight and her eyes widened in recognition as she saw Jingshen.

He bent to where Rook's body lay in the road. The man had a large fighting knife, practically a short sword, strapped to one of his boots. Jingshen pulled it from its sheath. It was poorly weighted and inexpertly sharpened—a peasant weapon, better suited for threatening than cutting.

Still, it was sharp enough to cut through the duct tape binding Zoe's ankles and wrists. "Hold still," he warned her as he raised the blade toward her head.

Zoe made frantic waving motions at him, pointing to her bare skin and shaking her head.

"I remember," Jingshen said. "I will be careful." He carefully sawed the knife blade through the duct tape behind her ear. He pulled it away and she sat up in the trunk, yanking the tennis ball from her mouth and tearing the tape from the back of her head. She winced at the pain of hair being pulled out of her scalp.

"Indiana Jones," she said. "Where's your hat?"

"I don't know. Come on."

She got out of the trunk and looked down at Rook and Bishop. "Jesus, you fucked them up pretty good. I didn't think you had it in you." She frowned at the bloodstained hole in his shirt and the ragged remains of his pants. "You don't look so good yourself."

"I will live. Now come on. You don't want to be here when either of these two awaken, or when the police arrive."

"The police?"

"Do you want to explain this to them?"

"No." Zoe paused beside Bishop and her face twisted into anger. Then she kicked Bishop in the side, hard enough to make Jingshen wince in sympathy. "Fuck you, bitch."

A pair of police cars screeched around the corner at the far end of the block, lights flashing, sirens howling.

"Last chance," Jingshen said as he slipped behind the wheel and shut the door.

Zoe jumped into the passenger seat. "I hate cops."

Jingshen hit the accelerator and the sedan leaped ahead, engine drowning out the pursuing police cars.

Zoe turned in her seat to look behind them. "They're cops. How are you going to outrun them? They've got, like radios and shit."

Jingshen crashed through a chain link fence and slid down a dirt embankment to the highway. "I don't have to drive faster than them. Just better."

He spotted a gap in the Jersey barriers separating the two directions of traffic. Sometimes police sat in the gaps on motorcycles, brandishing radar guns, but this one was empty. Jingshen cut across several lanes of traffic, making cars behind him honk and swerve. He yanked on the emergency brake and cranked the wheel hard. The sedan's rear end swung around as the car threaded through the gap. It wasn't a perfect maneuver; they lost their other tail light to a glancing blow at the end of the move. Jingshen dropped the hand brake and accelerated to match the flow of traffic.

The flashing lights of the police cars slowed as they followed through the gap in the barrier.

"Nice move, but it didn't work," Zoe said. "They're still back there. You got any other tricks, Indiana Jones?"

Jingshen frowned. At the moment, he didn't have any better ideas as he threaded his way through traffic. "Watch for helicopters," he said.

"Helicopters? You're shit at rescuing me, you know."

"I could have left you to Rook and Bishop."

A police SUV roared up an on-ramp to join the chase, much closer than the two cruisers following behind. Jingshen passed a semi truck on the left, pulled in front of it, and slammed on his brakes for a moment before he forgot he didn't have any functioning brake lights. The semi nearly rear-ended him but the driver reacted as he'd hoped and slammed on his own brakes. The trailer wheels locked and the trailer began to jackknife.

Jingshen swerved into the breakdown lane and accelerated again, trying to put space between him and the incipient calamity of the out-of-control semi. The police SUV pulled in behind them, siren blaring and lights bright in the rear view mirror. With his eyes on the pursuit, Jingshen almost missed the debris in the breakdown lane until Zoe screamed.

Debris was an inaccurate term for a full-sized dumpster on its side, burst trash bags spilling out of it. Jingshen swerved back into the lane at the last moment.

The police SUV did not move in time, and the truck vaulted sideways into the air from the collision. It smashed to the highway and other vehicles swerved and skidded to avoid the chain-reaction.

Between the jackknifing semi and the wrecked police truck, the highway behind them had become a catastrophe. Jingshen took the opportunity to swerve down an exit ramp into another industrial district.

"Hey, Jones . . ." Zoe had her face pressed against her window, looking into the sky. "You called it. There's a helicopter."

71

"Police or news?"

"How the hell do I know?"

"I guess it doesn't matter. Hold on."

"How are you—" Zoe's sentence ended in a squeak of terror as Jingshen swerved around a semi-trailer being towed by one of the odd-looking mule trucks used in freight yards. A truck freight terminal spread out before them, with dozens of loading docks at trailer height and a ramp for smaller vehicles. Jingshen slewed the car around a forklift and roared up the ramp into the freight terminal.

Almost immediately he found himself the odd man out in an orchestrated ballet of forklifts moving pallets and crates in and out of trailers. Dock workers dove out of their way as they raced down the terminal floor, weaving around stacks of staged freight. Forklifts beeped their horns and swung their massive loads out of the way with surprising nimbleness. Jingshen knew most of those lifts weighed as much as his car and colliding with one would end their bid for freedom in a fraction of a second.

The far end of the terminal was attached to a rail yard where cranes loaded containers on or off flatbed rail cars. Jingshen felt a flicker of hope. If they could get onto a train, they might lose their pursuers.

Flashing lights appeared in the rear view mirror as a pair of police motorcycles raced up the ramp and into the terminal. The bikes closed the distance with them at a disconcerting pace.

Jingshen misjudged the distance between two shipping containers and the car ground to a halt between them in a symphony of ruined metal and sparks. Zoe leaned back from where she'd hit the dashboard, rubbing her head. "Ow!"

The police would be on them in seconds, and opening the doors was impossible. Jingshen reached into the back seat where Rook had stashed his howitzer. It was heavy and awkward as Jingshen maneuvered it over the seats. He wasn't about to try to fire it and instead used it like a club to shatter the windshield and knock the safety glass out of the way.

"Come on," he said to Zoe. He crawled over the dash onto the hood. He could see daylight beyond the stacks of containers. They could lose themselves in the rail yard if they could just get there.

"Don't touch me," Zoe said as she crawled after him.

The police bikes braked to a halt at the rear of their wrecked car and the officers drew their sidearms. "Freeze!" one of them yelled. "Get down on the ground and put your hands behind your head!"

"Go," Jingshen said. "Run for the yard."

"What about you?"

"I'll be along." Jingshen grimaced. He was going to get shot again. Probably several times.

Chapter Seven

September, 1993
Los Angeles, California

As Zoe fled behind him, Jingshen snapped the antenna loose from the hood and sprang onto the car's roof.

"Freeze!" shouted the police officer again. "We will open fire!"

Jingshen leaped at them, twisting himself in midair in the hopes they would miss some of their shots.

And shoot they did. The reports from their service pistols thundered inside the freight terminal, echoing off the containers behind Jingshen. Two bullets thudded into his left shoulder and a third creased his ribs and then he was down between the two officers.

He whipped one's wrist with the antenna, flaying the skin open to the bone and making the man drop his pistol. With the follow-through, he slashed it across the man's forehead and opened a bloody gash.

More bullets slammed into his back as the other officer emptied his clip. Jingshen staggered from the wounds but still managed to whirl and bring the antenna across the man's knuckles. The antenna broke, but the officer still yelped and stepped back, fumbling for his *tonfa*-style baton.

The first officer threw himself upon Jingshen, driving the point of his own baton into the side of Jingshen's head. The blow made Jingshen's head spin and he dropped to the ground, using Brazilian *jiu jitsu* techniques to take the officer off his own feet. He wrestled and grappled with the officer, who was practically blinded with the blood flowing into his eyes. The other stood uncertainly over the two of them, his baton raised, afraid to bring it down and accidentally strike his partner.

Jingshen brought his legs around the police officer as if he were traveling along a horizontal rope. He delivered pressure to the man's armpit with one foot and twisted the man's arm back until he dislocated the shoulder, making the officer howl in pain.

The other officer grabbed hold of Zoe's wrist, screamed, and fell into the floor.

Literally, *into* the floor, like a pit had opened beneath his feet but instead he fell into solid concrete and vanished. Jingshen forgot to finish the officer he was grappling with, and that officer forgot to gasp in agony as his partner vanished. Behind where the officer had been, Zoe lowered her hand, her face a mask of terror.

Jingshen twisted himself around and locked his legs around the officer's throat. A moment later the man passed out from the lack of blood into his brain. He could have killed the man easily, but it wasn't the same as killing Rook. It would have been . . . disreputable.

"What did you do?" he asked Zoe as he stood, shaking bullet fragments from his shoulder.

"You got shot," she said, eyes wide. "I saw you get shot a bunch of times. Why aren't you dead?"

Jingshen shrugged, wincing at the stabbing pain from the bullet holes in his back. "Been asking myself that every day for a long time. Let's go." He wanted to ask Zoe about what she'd done to the other officer but they had no time for a long conversation. He tabled that for later.

They ran toward the far end of the terminal. Jingshen spotted a stairwell and directed Zoe up it. He followed behind and they found themselves upon a bridge gantry over the rail yard. Ahead of them, Jingshen saw a train pulling away with a variety of freight cars, both closed and open. "Faster," he urged Zoe.

"Why?" Zoe cursed and stumbled along, clearly unfit for such strenuous activity after however long she'd been a prisoner of DuraGen.

"We're getting on the train."

"What, *that* train?" Zoe sounded like she might have wanted to laugh if she'd had any breath to spare. "That's got to be, like, a fifty foot drop!"

"No more than twenty," Jingshen said. "Move your ass."

Zoe reached the spot on the gantry directly over the train. Behind them, Jingshen heard more sirens and knew the yard would be swarming with police in moments. They were out of time.

The rail cars passing beneath them were open, but loaded with scrap steel. Jingshen would survive falling into such material, but Zoe would be shredded as if falling into a meat grinder. Jingshen was about to suggest they continue their flight on foot, but then amid all the scrap metal, he saw it: a single car filled nearly to bursting with wood chips. It was their best bet for Zoe to survive.

Zoe's eyes were wide with panic as she stared down at the train, shaking her head. "Uh-uh. Nope. Not happening, Jones."

Jingshen shrugged and turned away as if to try something else. He'd already timed the motion in his mind and lashed out with his foot to strike Zoe in the center of her chest. She yelped at the sudden, unexpected blow. The force lifted her up and over the gantry safety railing. She flopped over the edge, screaming in terror. Jingshen dove after her only to plunge into a pile of wood chips a moment later.

Zoe's screaming continued, barely audible over the rattle of the cars as the train accelerated away from the yard. Jingshen heard her clearly enough and crawled through the chips toward her. The overwhelming smell of pine filled his head with a powerful citrus vanilla scent. He found her and clapped his hand over her mouth before she had a chance to react. Her eyes widened with a new panic and she struggled away from him, kicking chips in all directions. "What are you doing?" she shrieked. "Don't touch me!"

The brief contact had been painful, and Jingshen felt his body rebelling as if fighting off a rampaging virus. Nothing worse than that happened, and he didn't seem to be in any danger of sinking through the wood chips. "Dig yourself in," he said, taking his own advice and wriggling into the surface until he was mostly covered. "There is still a helicopter looking for us."

Jingshen closed his eyes and let himself drift. His body was beaten and worn, and he'd pushed himself further and harder than he had in decades, and exhaustion was taking its toll. Just because he'd never worked or fought himself to death in the past didn't mean it wasn't possible. The click-clack of the train wheels across the seams in the tracks made a soothing metronome beat. The gentle swaying of the hopper and its fragrant woody cargo sent him into a dreamless sleep.

* * *

"Jones! Or whatever your name is, wake up. Please, wake up." A tentative hand shook him and Jingshen's eyes flew open. Zoe knelt beside him in the wood chips, trying to wake him. She had bits of wood stuck in her hair.

"What is it?" Jingshen asked.

"I fell asleep." Zoe leaned back, keeping her hands well away from him. "And so did you. Aren't you supposed to be rescuing me or something? Because you're doing a shit job of it."

"You're not in DuraGen's hands." Jingshen dug himself out of the wood chips. Their heady scent reminded him of the forests of Tibet, half a world away and several lifetimes ago.

"No, but I'm on a goddamn train and I don't know what to do now. Don't you figure they're looking for us?"

"Of course they are looking for us. Money is at stake." Jingshen crawled across the top of the cargo to reach the side of the hopper. He peered over the top edge of the car to examine their surroundings. The train was heading east into the Tehachapi mountains. It would be cold there, but they were at best sparsely populated. Two fugitives could lose themselves pretty successfully there if at least one of them was skilled in survival. "Still, we should get off this train soon. It will be harder to disappear if we are at a scheduled stop."

"How the hell are we supposed to get off the train?"

"Same way we got on. Jump."

"Oh, hell no. You think for a second I'm going to—"

"Shut up."

Zoe's mouth snapped shut, and she was so surprised she almost started complaining again, but then apparently thought better of it and kept her own counsel.

"I'm sorry," Jingshen said after a moment. "That was rude of me. I'm not used to . . . this." He made a vague gesture to the hopper in which they sat. "Normally, I complete a job without complications."

"Is that all I am to you? A *complication*?" Zoe folded her arms.

Jingshen chose not to answer her, for he wasn't certain how to do so. He was thinking about walking away from the contract, something he'd never done since first signing up with The Source three decades previously. He'd been drifting around the world without direction or purpose, floating from petty dictator to minor warlord, picking all the wrong fights and killing all the wrong people.

The Source had offered a way out of that life. Their rules were simple. If you agreed to a contract, you were bound to complete it or your life was forfeit. With a clearinghouse providing the opportunities, it gave Jingshen the freedom not to have to choose his masters. He only had to choose his jobs. If he chose poorly, he only had to complete the contract and could move on to the next. If he chose well, it improved his reputation until jobs were offered to him first. He became sought-after; a man at the top of his field.

And now he was considering throwing that all away over a skinny young woman because he couldn't stand the idea of her being anybody's lab rat. He regarded her curiously. "What are you? A parahuman of some kind—that much is obvious. You made that man sink into the ground. That is your power?"

She shook her head. "Not always. I'm a . . . I don't know what to call it. I can trigger powers in other people."

"In anyone?"

"Anyone I touch."

Jingshen whistled. No wonder DuraGen and Kokorotai were willing to shell out the big bucks for her. Scientists had been trying to create parahuman powers for half a century since the Germans accidentally managed it in 1942. Any corporation or nation who could create parahuman abilities on demand would become the wealthiest in the world. But then, disappearing into the ground like the police officer had was something to reconsider. "You touched me. And Nobody Special touched you," Jingshen said at last.

"You heal, right? Maybe your powers kind of . . . block mine from changing you," Zoe said. "I don't know why it didn't work on him. Did he have powers too?"

Jingshen nodded. "He was a shapeshifter."

Zoe shrugged. "Maybe that power protected him."

"Why did the man you touched fall into the ground? What happened to him?"

Zoe looked away. "He probably died. A lot of people who touch me die."

"Why?"

The train rattled over a crossing and Zoe said nothing. Jingshen waited without pushing her. She would speak when she was ready. He'd been around long enough to have a firm understanding of human psychology.

"I can't control what powers people get," she said at last. "Sometimes they can't handle them. It's like being thrown out of an airplane and hoping you learn how to fly before you hit the ground."

"So his power made him . . . insubstantial?"

Zoe shrugged. "I don't know. Maybe? Whatever it was, if he couldn't figure out how to control it, he probably suffocated. Or solidified inside the ground. Or fell all the way to the Earth's core for all I know."

"How many people have you done this to?"

"I don't know. A lot. Too many. I hate it."

"And DuraGen?"

"They want to learn how to control it, so they can control what powers I give people. Or how those people can learn to control their powers when they get them. Or whatever the fuck, you know? They just want the power. Everyone wants the power." She flung a handful of wood chips across the hopper like a petulant child. "So now what? Are you going to turn me in for the reward money or whatever?"

"I haven't decided," Jingshen said. He was still considering his options, and for the moment, they were largely limited by their circumstances. "We need to get off this train."

Zoe sniffed. "You think I'm going to jump off this goddamn train just because you say so?"

"I can throw you off if you prefer." Jingshen crossed his arms but otherwise remained still.

"You know, I think you would," Zoe said. "Not everybody heals the way you do, Jones."

"Jingshen. I told you that before."

"And I told you I was going to call you Chinese Indiana Jones, so here we are."

"Yes, here we are."

The train continued along its solitary route into the mountains, with its two stowaways glaring at each other in the rising dusk.

* * *

The sinking sun gave the world a burnished orange shade as the train chugged north. The temperature dropped as they gained altitude. Jingshen knew the area well enough to know there were seasonal cabins where they might find a safe place to rest and plan their next move. He kept an eye on the surrounding terrain and occasionally leaned over the edge of the hopper to scan the track ahead.

The trees changed from the ubiquitous oaks common to the region to pines and firs, telling Jingshen they were on the downhill side heading toward the San Joaquin Valley. Up ahead, he saw the twin engines pulling the train disappear to the left.

"Let's go," he said.

"But it's almost dark!"

"It'll be harder for anyone to see us leave."

"It'll be harder for us to see what we're landing on. You're not very good at this. What is this, your first day as a mercenary?"

Jingshen snorted. He'd been determined not to let this young fugitive get a rise out of him, but she had a way of needling under his skin like a bamboo splinter. "No. Don't worry. The ground is soft enough."

"Says the guy who can heal. What if I get hurt when I land? You gonna nurse me back to health before turning me over to whoever's footing the bill?"

"Perhaps."

"So what do we do?" Zoe peeked over the edge of the hopper, uncertainty highlighting her prominent cheekbones in the low sunlight.

"Take my hand." Jingshen held his out to her.

She looked at it as if he were offering her a slimy tentacle. "Are you shitting me? What if I kill you?"

"Then I will die. However, I don't think you will. I've touched you before and I am unhurt."

Zoe hesitated. "Jones, I swear to God, if you burst into flame or dissolve or some shit like that and leave me all alone out here . . ." She lunged for him suddenly, like she was attacking or pushing him back, but instead clasped his hand with all the desperate strength of someone trying not to drown.

Sharp pain ran through Jingshen's hand and up his arm, and he felt his flesh threatening to change while his healing ability struggled to contain it. He made himself keep his face a stoic mask despite the discomfort. Pain was something familiar, and he could tolerate it for years. "See? Nothing to worry about."

Tears filled Zoe's eyes, and her lips quivered. Jingshen wondered how long it had been since she'd had any kind of human contact without an isolation suit in the way. Skin to skin contact could be magical when it was withheld for lengthy periods. He squeezed her fingers with his, gently so she knew it wasn't intended to hurt.

"O-okay," she said. "Now what?"

"We jump. Hurry, before the train straightens." Jingshen pulled her to the edge. "On three."

"You mean—"

"One. Two . . ."

"*Wait!*" Zoe screamed.

"What?"

"Thank you. For not killing me. For not—"

There would be time for conversation later. "Three."

Jingshen pulled Zoe over the edge with him. Her scream was drowned out by the distant horn of the train indicating a tunnel ahead. They spun through the darkness for a moment before striking the gravelly shoulder of the rail embankment. Jingshen let go of Zoe's hand at the impact so he wouldn't accidentally hurt her if she rolled in a different direction than he did. They slid down the side into a muddy ditch, chilly water squelching into their clothes. The heady scent of decaying vegetation filled Jingshen's nose, and a sharp pain filled his face as something struck his cheekbone hard enough to make him see stars.

They came to a stop only a few feet from each other. Zoe was gasping in pain, but she still managed to squeak out, "Bastard," at him.

Jingshen sat up and felt at his face. A piece of wood was sticking out of his cheek—he could feel the end of it emerging inside his mouth. He pulled it free and threw it away. He realized he'd lost a couple of teeth with the impact as well. No matter; they would grow back like they always did.

"Awe you huth?" he asked, discovering he couldn't pronounce Rs or Ts properly with the damage to his mouth.

"Yes, I'm hurt. I got thrown off a fucking train, Jones." She rolled up to a seated position and winced. "Ow."

The end of the train passed by at the top of the embankment and the clacking of wheels on rails receded.

Jingshen looked around, sniffing at the air and listening to the sounds of wind in treetops. He had a general idea of where they were, and knew if they continued in a northerly direction they would eventually run across some indication of civilization. Until that time, it would be hard going. He'd been living with electricity and gasoline for far too long. He'd gone soft. This would be good for him, like a return to his roots.

"Well, now what?" Zoe asked. She started to climb to her feet, but cried out and fell back, clutching her knee.

Jingshen knelt beside her. "Leth me see ith."

"Don't touch me! Don't move it!" Zoe cried, tears streaming down her cheeks.

Jingshen touched his fingers to her lips. Her power made his skin crawl but he suffered no worse effects. "Hush. I need tho see how badly you awe huth."

It was difficult to examine her while she was wearing jeans, but not impossible. After some gentle manipulation, he determined it was sprained but not broken. While he worked, the hole in his cheek closed. He spat out a piece of broken tooth, pushed free from the emerging nubs of new teeth.

"Well that's just great. Why don't you just break my neck and get it over with? I can't do anything like this." Zoe hung her head in defeat and sobbed.

"It is only a sprain," Jingshen said. "It will heal. I will splint it and then find us shelter."

"What, you're Doctor Quinn and Ranger Rick, on top of being Jackie Chan and Indiana Jones and Crackerjack too? What the hell are you?"

Jingshen folded his arms. "I am immortal." He spoke carefully as his mouth was returning to its usual shape.

"You're *what?*"

"As far as I know, I cannot die. I was born more than three hundred and fifty years ago, in . . . well, the specific village doesn't matter. It's been gone for a hundred years. Just say northern China and leave it at that. I'm not sure when I stopped aging, but I think it was before I turned thirty. You've seen how my body heals itself. It has been doing so for centuries." He drew a long breath, running his tongue along the newly healed flesh of his cheek. "You don't think I learned a thing or two in all that time?"

Zoe wiped her eyes. "Jesus, you really are all those people. Ranger Rick and . . . Indiana Jones . . . and all of them."

"Yes, now wait here while I make you a splint and crutch." He checked his pockets and was pleased to find he still had the multitool he carried. It would make Zoe's survival in the Tehachapis much easier.

"You . . . you're going to leave me here?" Zoe's voice took on a tinge of panic.

"Yes."

"But you're coming back, right? You're not going to just abandon me?"

"I will come back."

"Promise?" Zoe clutched at him, forgetting her own powers for a moment. Her touch burned his bare arm like fire. She pulled back immediately as if she'd burned herself, and wrapped her arms around herself to keep from touching him again. Her eyes shone with tears in the last rays of the setting sun.

Jingshen met her gaze. In the few hours he'd known her, she alternately exuded the confidence of a young adult and the helplessness of a child. Right now the child was driving her and she needed the comfort of someone else's maturity. "I promise. I will be back quickly."

His search in the dwindling light turned up some reasonably straight pieces of wood that could function as splints and crutches with a little work on his part. He picked some fibrous plants suitable for braiding into cord and made his way back to where he'd left Zoe.

She wasn't where he'd left her. With her injury, she couldn't have gotten far. Jingshen closed his eyes and listened to the sounds of the twilight. A few birds cried in the distance. Somewhere, a small creature squealed as an owl or other nighttime predator caught it. A chilly breeze whispered through the pines, carrying with it the hint of snow to come. A shaking breath and chattering teeth. He smiled. Indeed, she hadn't gotten far at all.

He stepped around a tree to find Zoe sitting with her back against it, knees drawn up to her chest. He couldn't see her face in the shadows, but her sniffle suggested she was crying and cold. "Were you trying to run away?" he asked.

"N-no." Her voice quavered. "I'm hiding in case there bears or dudes with guns or something. Where am I going to go? I don't know the goddamn mountains. I'm a city girl."

Jingshen nodded. "We will stay here tonight. Tomorrow we will find a cabin where we can be more comfortable."

Zoe's voice took on a hard note. "What do you mean, *stay here*? It's freezing!"

"I will make a fire."

"Yeah, I've heard about what happens with fires in the mountains. Hard pass."

"I am careful. But if I don't make a fire, you will freeze. I can hear it in the way you are breathing."

Zoe was quiet for a moment. "All right," she said at last. "Please hurry. I can't feel my feet, Jones."

Jingshen was well-versed in the science of building campfires, and in a few minutes he had a small blaze started within a ring of stones. He pushed more stones into place, close by the flames. They would retain the heat to keep him and Zoe warm.

Zoe watched as he worked, using his knife saw blade to cut apart longer branches. He stacked them nearby, ready to feed the flames. Although he was tired, he kept working, using the repetitive motions of his hands to distract him from unproductive thoughts about his future.

Eventually he decided he'd acquired enough firewood to last them the night, and turned his attention to Zoe's leg. Her knee had swollen inside her jeans and she whimpered when he touched it. "I am sorry," he said. "It will hurt while I am binding it."

"Your bedside manner sucks." Zoe winced as Jingshen slowly straightened her leg. He took the plants he'd picked earlier and braided them together to make short sections of fibrous rope. Using that rope and some sticks, he fashioned a splint around Zoe's knee to keep it from bending. He hoped the nighttime cold would help to slow the swelling, even with the fire nearby. He didn't think she required medical attention. Besides, her parahuman ability would make treatment from a regular doctor nearly impossible.

"Tell me about yourself," Jingshen said, less because he was interested and more to distract Zoe from her pain.

"Not much to tell, Jones," Zoe said through clenched teeth. "Spent my whole life in L.A.. Powers developed when I was sixteen. I found out about them when I turned my mom into a cloud of steam and never saw her again." Her jaw muscles worked like she was forcing out the words.

"It's all right," Jingshen said quickly. "You don't have to keep going."

"No, I want to," Zoe said. "You might as well know. Maybe you'll decide not to turn me in because mine is a sad, sad story." She wriggled a little closer to the fire. "That feels really good. Thank you."

"You're welcome," he said.

"I'm sorry I said you were doing a shit job of rescuing me." She looked up at him. Firelight reflected from her dark eyes, mirroring the stars appearing between the high clouds overhead. "You're doing all right."

"I am . . . glad you think so. Tomorrow we will find real shelter, food, water. But for now . . ." He pulled his last energy bar from his pocket and handed it to her. "Eat this."

Zoe tore into it and crammed half of it into her mouth in a single bite. She chewed with her eyes shut, devoting her entire person to the consumption of food. Jingshen suspected Bishop and Rook hadn't been particularly concerned about her welfare and she probably hadn't eaten since the suburban house. She checked inside the wrapper for any wayward crumbs and then sighed, crumpled it up, and tossed it away.

Jingshen retrieved it and put it into his pocket.

"Why'd you do that?" Zoe asked.

"The less evidence we leave here tomorrow, the better we will be able to disappear." He frowned. "Also, I do not like littering."

"Whatever you say, Smokey the Bear." She shivered. "Hey, you don't think it's going to snow tonight, do you? We don't have any blankets or a tent or anything."

"Frost, maybe," Jingshen said. "No snow tonight."

"That's your centuries of experience speaking?"

"Yes."

"Are you ever wrong?"

"Yes."

Chapter Eight

September, 1993
Tehachapi Mountains, California

As he'd said before they fell asleep beside the fire, Jingshen was occasionally wrong. He wondered if this was one of those times. He awoke to the ache of cold in his bones. He'd awakened a couple of times in the night, just enough to stoke up the fire and add more wood so it would keep burning. The temperature dropped enough for frost to form upon the tips of pine needles, giving the forest a magical appearance.

The cold necessitated the two fugitives huddling together for warmth. Zoe had resisted at first, not wanting to be touched. Eventually, her need not to freeze exceeded her need to avoid physical contact. After that, they slept wrapped around each other, like dogs in a bed. Jingshen tried to keep skin to skin contact to a minimum, as her power caused him discomfort as his skin constantly had to heal from her touch. Unfortunately, his clothes had suffered from being dragged along the highway, then jumping from the train. Calling them *tattered* would have been charitable. He suffered her physical touch in stoic silence, trusting to his healing ability to keep him alive and whole no matter what her wild card power did to him. By the time morning came around, Zoe was curled into a tight ball in Jingshen's arms. When he awakened to put the last couple sticks onto the fire, she awoke too and he found her staring into his eyes.

He backed away quickly to avoid any awkwardness. "How did you sleep?"

"I'm freezing, and my leg hurts like a son of a bitch," she said. "But I don't seem to be dead, so there's that." She yawned. "Thank you for saving my life. Again. What happens now, Jones?"

Jingshen stood and turned a slow circle, getting a sense of the surrounding terrain. "When it's light, I'll climb a tree. There should be any number of private cabins around here. Except for the odd hermit type, most of them shouldn't be occupied. We'll break into one and then at least we'll be out of the elements while we plan our next move."

"I hope the next move is something to eat. I was kind of getting used to food again." Zoe paused. "You can't starve, though, can you?"

"No." Jingshen sighed. "But it is appalling how hungry you can get when you can't die and there's no food."

Zoe shuddered. "I can't imagine."

"If you would rather me hunt first, I will do that before we seek shelter."

"I *am* hungry, but no. I would rather be out of the cold. Besides, a cabin might have food already in it."

"True. Can you walk?"

Jingshen helped Zoe to her feet. She tottered, unable to put more than a fraction of her weight on her knee. "Oh goddamn does that hurt."

He handed her the crutch he'd fashioned the night before. "This will help. You'll have to get along the best you can. Unfortunately I do not possess parahuman strength, so I can only help you instead of carrying you." That wasn't entirely true, he reflected. Zoe was skinny as a rail and he doubted she weighed much more than a hundred pounds. He could pick her up in a fireman's carry and his healing would help his stamina. In a pinch, he would do so, but he didn't want to. He still hadn't decided how he was going to proceed beyond their immediate needs.

A few minutes later, the sun had peeked over the eastern edge of the mountains and Jingshen found a tall, straight tree with branches conducive to a climb. He pulled himself up branch by branch, ignoring the occasional twig in the eye or splinter until he was high enough to see across the valley. A couple cabins on the far side had lights on and smoke curling from their chimneys. There would be others without inhabitants. He stared down, giving his eyes time to adjust until he picked out a roof from amid all the trees.

Getting down from the tree was easier than climbing. He could have just let himself fall, but if he hurt himself too much, it would take time to heal. Still, he came down faster and sloppier than a normal person would and finally dropped beside Zoe amid a shower of pine needles.

"Jesus!" she said as he drew himself upright. "Are you all right?"

"Yes. There's a cabin not far from here. Maybe an hour's hike."

"An hour for you or an hour for me?" Zoe asked. "I'm not getting anywhere quick with this leg."

Jingshen nodded. "Let's just head in the right direction and we'll get there when we get there."

"Very zen," Zoe said.

"What do you know about *zen*?" Jingshen asked in surprise.

"Nothing," Zoe admitted. "I just know the word. It's, like, meditation and stuff, right?"

"Yes."

"And martial arts too? Punchee-kickee?"

Jingshen laughed. "No. That's different."

"You're pretty good at that stuff."

"I've had a lot of time to practice."

Zoe grimaced as her crutch slipped and she tweaked her knee. Jingshen was at her side in a flash, arm around her to support her so she wouldn't fall. Her skin touched his, her power making twinges and tingles radiate from the contact point. "Thank you," she said, and pulled away from him. "I'm sorry. I know it probably hurts you to touch me. I don't have any control over it."

"Pain goes away," Jingshen said.

"Still. It's got to suck for you."

"It's not so bad. I've suffered far worse in my life."

"Three hundred fifty years is a long time."

"It is."

They crossed a small stream. Jingshen squatted to fill his hands with water and drink, then helped Zoe down so she could also slake her thirst. "I hope there isn't, like, bear piss in this water."

"I don't think there are bears around here."

Zoe shrugged. "It's outdoors. The wilderness. I figure there are bears everywhere, right? Just waiting to eat people foolish enough to be out in it."

"Bears don't eat people."

"Yeah? I bet they do."

"Most bears don't," Jingshen amended, recalling an incident in Canada seven or eight decades ago.

"What's the worst thing that ever happened to you?" Zoe asked as she used her crutch to lever herself to her feet. "Like, the worst injury you ever came back from?"

"I've come back from all of them," Jingshen pointed out. "It's why I'm here now."

"You know what I mean."

The pain of it, long buried in his mind, roared to the forefront of his memory and he shivered. "It was . . . bad."

"Yeah, but what was it?" Zoe asked. "Don't leave a girl hanging."

"I've *been* hanged. It's unpleasant."

"That's the worst thing that happened to you?"

"No." He sighed. "Around two hundred years ago, give or take, I was quartered in Peru by the Spanish colonial authorities."

Zoe gasped. "Quartered? You mean, like, tied to horses and pulled apart? That's fucking gruesome."

A wry smile crossed Jingshen's face. "An apt description." He still remembered the feel of his arms and one leg being torn from his body with the last horse left dragging his ruined torso by one leg. The Spaniards had convicted him of treasonous acts against them. Perhaps they'd been right. He'd refused to give up his accomplices, and paid what they thought was the ultimate price for it. After his violent dismemberment, his remains had been burned. Surely if anything was going to kill him, that had been it.

He'd awakened some time later, naked in the jungle, with vines growing over him, half buried in mud. It had been a dark time in his life, and he hadn't returned to South America since.

"Still, dude. It kind of puts this stupid knee into perspective." Zoe frowned down at her leg.

"My own struggles with pain and injury in no way diminish yours," Jingshen said.

"I . . . what? What does that mean?"

"Your pain is yours. It hurts you. Just because I have experienced far greater pain and suffering than you doesn't mean yours isn't real, or isn't legitimate."

"That's really . . . I guess *enlightened* is the word?"

Jingshen nodded. "It's as good as any other."

"Most guys would just laugh off a bum knee. They'd say to *buck up and shake it off*."

"Rub a little dirt on it." Jingshen smiled. "I knew a cavalry captain who said that for everything from a splinter to a bayonet wound."

"Sounds like he had it all figured out."

"He died from sepsis."

"Must have used the wrong sort of dirt." Zoe chuckled.

Almost as if by magic, they stepped around a small stand of trees and found a small log cabin. Its wooden walls made it the same color as the surrounding forest. "Wait here," Jingshen said. "Keep out of sight. I will check it out."

He gave the cabin a wide berth and circled around it, checking it from all angles. There was no car parked beside it. No recent tire tracks marred the dirt track leading up the hill toward a main road some distance away. He didn't see or smell any plumes of smoke from a fireplace or stove or generator. At last, he approached the building and peeked into the dirty windows, seeing nothing but spartan furnishings and dust. It had a deck with sliding glass doors facing south and a regular door to the north with a locked shed beside it.

"It's empty," he said as he returned to Zoe. "Let's get indoors and figure out our next move."

Zoe sighed long and loud while she waited for Jingshen to pick the lock with an implement from his multitool. "You can't just break a window?" she asked. "I mean, it's not like it'll leave a mark on you."

"Actually, I do get scars," Jingshen replied. "If you look close, I have them almost everywhere." The lattice of white scar tissue ran back and forth across his skin. Layers upon layers of scars had healed over until it seemed he was made of nothing *but* scars. "And yes, I could break a window and let us in, but it was cold last night. And it will be less cold without a broken window. Besides, this is not our place. We are only borrowing it for a day or two until you can get around on your leg again." With a click, the tumblers worked into place and Jingshen opened the cabin door.

It was a floor-and-a-half style of construction. They entered through a small kitchen with a half bath off to one side. The narrow kitchen smelled of liquid dishwasher soap and the linoleum glued onto the plywood was bulging where moisture had gotten beneath the wood. The kitchen opened into a main room, dominated by south-facing windows and the deck with firewood stacked upon it. A cast iron stove sat in the middle of the main room, with a couch facing it. A room off to the right had bookshelves packed with dusty paperbacks and boxes of board games. Upon a folding card table in the middle of the study was a half-completed puzzle of boats parked in an autumnal harbor, probably somewhere in New England, Jingshen thought.

An open wooden staircase went up to the half floor above, covering only the study room, bathroom and kitchen. There they found another sliding glass door facing west, a queen-sized bed, a six-drawer dresser, and a folding privacy screen. A railing across the edge stretched between the roof support posts, and would allow fireplace heat to rise to the loft.

"Well, this is cozy," Zoe said. She went back into the kitchen and opened the fridge. "Power's off and the fridge is empty."

Jingshen said nothing. The existence of a refrigerator meant power was available; he just had to get it turned on. As he came down from the stairs, he heard Zoe banging cupboards open and shut in the kitchen.

"There's a couple boxes of cereal. Old people kind. Nothing sugary. No milk, either. Coffee grounds. Tea bags. Sugar. Spices. I think this might be flour? Canned soup . . . chili . . . vegetables . . . Hey, mac and cheese and Cup O' Noodles." There was a pause. "Water's not working either. Goddammit. I need to pee."

"Go ahead and go," Jingshen said. "I will find out how to turn on the power. There's a faucet in the kitchen and fixtures in the bathroom. That means there's a water pump. It probably needs power to operate."

"Well, hurry up, Indiana Jones," Zoe said from behind the bathroom door. "Now that I know there's food here, I'm starving."

"You'll be fine." Jingshen spotted a key hanging from a piece of wood by the kitchen door that he hadn't seen upon entering. He took it back outside and was pleased to discover it unlocked the shed. Inside, he found a veritable treasure trove. There was a small gas generator and two ten-gallon cans of gasoline for it. Other tools were arranged on a tool bench. He saw a chainsaw he could use to cut wood quickly or an axe he could use quietly. Best of all, a two-person dual-sport motorcycle was leaning against the wall.

Jingshen smiled. Of all mankind's inventions in the three centuries of his life, motorcycles ranked consistently near the top of his favorites. Whistling at his good fortune, he dragged the generator out from the shed and found the panel where he could plug it in. He couldn't run it constantly, but it should get the water pump working. He figured there was probably a cistern that would fill from the well, which would give them running water. He fired up the generator and threw a switch on the panel, thoughtfully labeled *PUMP* in permanent black marker.

Pipes within and beneath the cabin clunked as water began to push its way upward. He stepped back inside, turned on the kitchen faucet, and then reached into the bathroom to turn on the shower head. Air burped from them and water spat and frothed for almost half a minute before transforming into uninterrupted streams. He shut them off and went into the front room.

Zoe was asleep on the couch, her cheek resting on its arm and her injured leg elevated on the coffee table. She looked vulnerable. Harmless. Not at all like the high-value target she was.

Jingshen frowned. He still wasn't sure what he was going to do about her. The job had been poison from the beginning. Between human trafficking, medical research on the unwilling, and the double-cross, Jingshen felt like maybe he'd gotten in over his head. The Source probably wouldn't see it that way.

A job was a job, and the Source didn't maintain its sterling reputation for one-hundred percent mission success without going to sometimes extreme lengths to ensure completion. Right now, Zoe represented a failure of the highest order for them. Jingshen knew even now they had to be making plans to track her down on their own. That wouldn't be financed by DuraGen, or by

Kokorotai. No, the Source had resources to clean up their own messes. Even though he couldn't be killed, the Source probably had someone on their payroll who could make his life a living hell for a very long time.

His only hope would be to reach out to them in the hope that he could salvage things. He might have to give up Zoe—at least temporarily—but that didn't mean he couldn't turn right around and free her again on his own.

Well, he couldn't do that on his own, either. He would need help. But who could he call? He'd have to think about it.

He found a blanket in one of the drawers in the dresser and took it downstairs to cover Zoe. He built a fire in the stove, filled a kettle with water, and set it to heating. At the moment, he reflected, he and Zoe were in a fairly good situation. They had shelter, food, available transportation, and he still had his retainer fee. He hadn't even bothered to count it, which went to show how jaded he'd become about the mercenary's life.

His trousers had seen better days after he'd been dragged behind a car, shot, stabbed, crashed, jumped onto and off of a train in them. Fortunately, he habitually bought the toughest clothes he could find. His pockets were all still in good condition and he hadn't lost anything from them. He sat at the card table and took the stack of bills from his pocket. Despite all his recent rough travels, the band still held the stack together. He flipped through the bills, counting in his mind.

Five thousand dollars. That wasn't an insignificant amount. It was enough to start a new life somewhere. Pay for rent, buy a cheap car, live on it while finding new work. It was, he considered, even enough for two people for a while. He had much more set aside in Credit Suisse, where the bulk of his income went. He'd been one of the bank's first customers almost a hundred and fifty years prior, and their discretion with their clients even extended to apparent immortals.

Money wasn't a factor for the decision he needed to make. Likewise, reputation wasn't really a consideration. Reputations came and went over the course of a lifetime. There were times when he could trade solely upon his reputation, as he had been during his employ with the Source. Other times, his anonymity was his most valuable asset. He suspected anonymity would be the next direction his life would take.

The kettle whistled and he poured himself a cup of tea and made a cup of instant noodles. He sighed, watching the steam curl from the paper cup. He still remembered the finest noodle soup he'd ever eaten, in a shop in Hiroshima at the turn of the century. The dry pasta in its sad, salty fake chicken broth was a disappointing substitute, had he not been so hungry. He blew on it, waiting for it to cool, and let his thoughts return to the dilemma at hand.

The question was his standing with the Source. If he was already blacklisted, there was nothing he could do except isolate himself so the innocent wouldn't get caught in the crossfire when the assassins came for him. If the Source considered him still in the grace period for completing the mission, he might have the chance to cut a deal. Nobody Special had gone around the Source and cut his own deal, and he'd brought Rook and Bishop along. The Source didn't take kindly to being made a fool of, and if Jingshen could prove it to them, he might just get away without a bounty placed upon his head.

If he did that, he would still be bound to complete the mission on his own, and that would mean turning Zoe over to Kokorotai. That felt like betrayal. He looked over at her. She was smiling just a little in her sleep, like she was having a pleasant dream.

Jingshen slurped his noodles, drank his tea, and thought and thought and thought.

Chapter Nine

September, 1993
Tehachapi Mountains, California

Movement beside him awakened Jingshen. He hadn't meant to drift to sleep, but the strain of the past couple of days had worn him out both physically and mentally. His ability to heal didn't come without cost, and lots of healing required lots of rest. He raised his head and saw the sun had set and the cabin was dark but for the ruddy glow of embers in the stove. At some point while he'd slept, Zoe had snuggled up next to him and curled in the crook of his arm like a cat. She'd pulled the blanket over both of them.

Where his skin contacted hers, it tingled, like he was touching a bare wire. It could have been an unpleasant sensation, but his healing ability was keeping up with Zoe's uncontrollable power. It occurred to him that she had probably been terribly isolated from physical contact ever since she'd discovered her terrible ability. Jingshen sometimes went months without physical contact with another human being. His isolation was by choice most of the time, and likewise, he could choose to interact with others. That choice had been taken away from Zoe. No wonder she seemed simultaneously vulnerable and cynical.

His arm was dead asleep and he wondered if he could shift his position enough to get circulation back into it. He moved a bit and Zoe's eyes opened, dark pools in her pale face. "Hi," she said softly.

"Hi, yourself." He pitched his voice at a near whisper even though there wasn't anyone else nearby whom they might accidentally awaken.

Zoe stretched her arms over her head and arched her back. "I was sleeping hard. Oh!" She realized she was nestled against Jingshen and backed away. "I'm sorry! That must have been really uncomfortable for you."

"I was asleep too. Healing's hard work."

"Especially when touching me means you have to heal all over again." She drew her knees up to her chest. "I'm sorry about that too."

"It's all right," Jingshen said. "For me, pain is a matter of perspective. Touching you isn't as bad as being shot."

Zoe snorted. "How about being stabbed? Is it worse than that?"

Jingshen shrugged. "Depends on where the blade goes in."

"How about being dragged behind a car?"

"It's different than being dragged behind a horse. A car drag tends to be smoother but faster. Horses kick you. I'd rather go behind a car."

"Is that worse than touching me?"

Jingshen found himself smiling. "Depends on the surface. Gravel roads are bad. I'd guess you fall somewhere between road base and beach."

"Dragged behind a car on the beach?"

"Beaches are worse than you think. You aspirate sand and there's a reason they use sand to scour cast iron pots."

"How many beaches have you really been dragged across, Jones?"

"By a car? One. And it was more of a dune buggy."

"Sounds like a real party."

"They were playing the Beach Boys on the buggy's eight track. I've hated *Wouldn't It Be Nice* ever since."

"What did you do? To get dragged, I mean."

Jingshen shrugged. "I'm pretty sure I killed someone important to them."

"You don't remember?"

"No, I don't remember. I've killed a lot of people over the course of three centuries. I can't possibly remember them all."

"Will you remember me?" Zoe canted her head to one side, as if doing so would make her understand better.

"I'm not going to kill you," Jingshen said.

"Thank you, but will you remember me? In a hundred years, when I'm long gone and you're talking to someone else—someone maybe like me—will you remember what I was like?"

Jingshen nodded. He'd met a few parahumans in his life, and he remembered all of them clearly. "I don't doubt it."

Zoe made a small noise, like a sigh that never really got going, then crawled back across the couch to straddle Jingshen's lap.

He should have stopped her, could have done so with a quick move—a strike to the throat, an uppercut to the sternum. Instead he froze in surprise as she smashed her face against his, kissing him like it was the only thing keeping her alive. He found himself responding to her touch. His lips and face burned like they were on fire, and he felt the flesh trying to rearrange itself in response to her power.

He put his arms around her waist and pulled her toward him. She buried her hands in his hair and his scalp felt electrified. Her power threatened to overwhelm his body's natural recuperative abilities, and it excited him. She yanked his shirt over his head and bit him where his neck joined his shoulder, sharp teeth digging in until she drew blood like a mythical vampire. The pain made his head buzz as she sat back and watched the wound she'd inflicted heal. She dragged her fingertips down his chest, leaving behind red marks that faded almost immediately.

Jingshen slid his hands beneath her shirt. Her breasts were tiny but her nipples bloomed beneath his fingers. She moaned, grinding against him, luxuriating in human contact. Then she was pressing against him tight, wrapping around him like a serpent until she wound up with her back against the couch and him twisted around to face her. She bumped her injured knee and hissed at the sudden twinge of pain. He covered her mouth with his, feeling his tongue flashing through transformation after transformation.

She dragged at his cargo pants, fingers latching into the belt loops. He reached down to help her, undoing his belt. Her hands traced fire across his back, actually leaving burning trails in their wake. He watched as his skin burned, cracked, and rehealed in a few seconds, appalled at the thought of what this would do to someone who couldn't heal the damage like he could.

Making love with Zoe was sensual and violent at the same time. She was so desperate for the contact that she clutched and grabbed at him like they were grappling. She bit, dragged her fingertips across his back, squeezed him between her thighs. It was like she was trying to experience years' worth of physical contact in their explosively passionate fucking. When she came the first time, she screamed raggedly right into Jingshen's ear, leaving it ringing. The second time, she burst into sobs and slapped him across the face, then kissed him tenderly.

Finally, too spent to do anything else, she collapsed into a puddle of sweat and tears on the threadbare carpet beside the couch. Her knee was swollen and purple from the sprain, and she had other bruises and bumps marring her pale flesh from their escape from the train.

Jingshen took the blanket and covered her naked body, then pulled on his pants so as not to parade around in the nude before her. He added some wood to the stove, went to the kitchen, and brought back a ceramic mug of water for Zoe. She accepted it gratefully and downed it in a few gulps.

"Thank you," she said.

"Are you all right?"

Zoe laughed bitterly. "It's been so long. Since my powers turned, a few guys tried to fuck me. Every one of them is dead now. Every one. I'm like a human chastity belt."

"I'm sorry."

"Don't be. It's not your fault. This is my life now."

Jingshen sat on the floor beside her, leaning back against the couch and letting the stove's heat wash over his scarred flesh. "It shouldn't be. Maybe you can get help. There's a medical facility in Paris specializing in treatment of parahumans."

"So instead of going to the place that hired you, I can go be a lab rat somewhere else? Fuck you for saying that."

Jingshen shook his head. "That's not what I meant."

"You think just because you got your dick wet means you can control me?"

"No." Suddenly Jingshen felt like he was treading on thin ice. Zoe was flipping through emotions like riffling the pages of a phone book. "I'm not trying to control you at all."

"*You're going to sell me!*" Zoe screamed at him. "Like I'm a fucking piece of meat!"

"No," Jingshen repeated. "I'm not going to do that." He surprised himself at the admission, and then realized he truly meant it. He wasn't going to turn her over to Kokorotai, or to DuraGen, and he was satisfied with that decision. "You're free to go anytime you want."

"Where am I going to go? I don't have anything. No money. No car. No fucking life skills. I've been living on the streets since I was sixteen, Indiana Jones. I can't even fuck men for money because they'll die and the word will get out."

"I have money. I can help you," Jingshen said. The weight of his decision lifted from him, and he felt better about picking his side of the fence instead of straddling it.

"So now you're going to be my sugar daddy, just because you think you can get some young ass with your healing powers." Zoe flung her coffee cup across the room. It smashed against the log wall. "Maybe the next time we touch, my power will get the better of yours, and you'll die."

"Or maybe I won't," Jingshen said. Over three centuries, he'd come back from everything that would have killed a normal person. Nothing suggested he wouldn't continue to do so. "There doesn't have to be a next time if you don't want it. It's your body."

"You're goddamn right it is, and I'm nobody's goddamn lab rat."

Jingshen had nothing to say to that.

* * *

Eventually they drifted to sleep on the couch again, bare feet pointed toward the stove and blankets wrapped over their torsos. In her sleep, Zoe once more moved to snuggle with Jingshen. He let her. Now that he'd decided not to fulfill his contract, he felt an even greater sense of responsibility toward the young woman. Whatever happened next between him and the Source, he would work to ensure she was safe from their reach.

As the glow from the stove died, Jingshen became aware of the blue-white light covering the world beyond the sliding glass door of the porch. Low clouds hung heavy, reflecting the lights of the distant city, and drifting speckles in the half-light began to coalesce into . . . snow.

Jingshen liked the snow. It brought a peace he didn't often get to experience. He watched it fall for a while. Snow reminded him of the Canadian Rockies, which he'd traveled extensively in the late 19th Century, working as a trapper and guide.

"What are you doing?" Zoe's sleepy voice interrupted his thoughts.

"Watching the snow."

"Snow?' She sat up, holding the blanket tight around her. She hadn't put her clothes back on and Jingshen was careful not to ogle her. If she wanted to show herself off, she would. "I've never seen snow in real life."

"What, never?"

"I spent my entire life in L. A. My mom used to call it the Land of No Weather."

Jingshen chuckled at that. "She isn't wrong."

"What's snow really like?"

"It's cold."

Zoe slipped off the couch, keeping the blanket around her shoulders. Her knee was still swollen and she hobbled across the room toward the sliding door. "How cold can it really be?"

"Pretty cold," Jingshen said. "Let me help you." He stepped over to her and offered his arm as a crutch. Zoe looked at it as if not understanding what to do. He pulled his own blanket down to make it a barrier between the two of them, and then she took hold of his arm through the fabric.

They slid the door open. There was maybe a quarter inch of snow on the patio outside. Although she had a blanket about her, Zoe shivered as the cold air hit her bare legs. "Oh, wow . . ." She stepped outside into the lazy flakes drifting down. She hissed at the freezing touch on the soles of her feet.

"Careful, it might be icy," Jingshen said softly.

"Hush." Zoe tilted her face upward, letting the snowflakes settle on her cheeks. She opened her mouth and waited until one drifted into her mouth and then smiled. "It doesn't taste like anything."

"It's only ice."

"I guess . . . I don't know, I thought it would be more magical or something."

"The world isn't a magical place. It's a hard place."

She sighed. "Don't I know it." Zoe turned to face him. "Thank you."

She didn't say what she was thanking him for, but that was all right with Jingshen. In the greater scheme of things, that didn't matter.

"So what happens now?" Zoe asked.

"Now we go back to sleep and see how things look in the morning. If it's safe, we'll take the motorcycle down into town and figure out our next move there."

"There's a town down there?"

"There's always a town."

* * *

Morning brought a cold breeze from the higher mountains, carrying the dusting of snow that had fallen overnight into swirling eddies that evaporated as they reached sunlight. Jingshen made a pot of hot tea and heated some canned enchiladas for breakfast.

"You sure know how to treat a girl right," Zoe said. "You stuck around to make breakfast and everything. Some guys, that gets your man card taken away."

"I never really thought about it. I don't have anything to prove." Jingshen handed her a plastic bowl with some steaming tamales in their salty, preservative-laden sauce that smelled vaguely of chili powder.

Zoe sniffed at it and grimaced. "You're not proving that you can cook."

"I can cook fine. There's nothing to make but canned stuff."

Zoe snickered. "I'm kidding, Indiana Jones." She swallowed a mouthful of processed masa and shredded meat. "You look weird without your hat."

"I liked that hat."

"Maybe you can find another one in town."

"Maybe." He sipped his tea, letting its bright flavor warm him. "How does your leg feel?"

"It hurts. I wish I had your healing powers."

"Do you think you can sit on a motorcycle?"

Zoe shrugged. "I don't know. I've never been on one before. Is it hard?"

"Not if you know what you're doing."

"I don't know what I'm doing."

"I'll teach you."

They finished their breakfast in silence. Jingshen went to the sink and washed the few dishes they'd used during their stay. Then he cleaned up the broken coffee mug Zoe had thrown the night before. "Why are you doing that?"

"Cleaning?"

"Yeah."

"We've imposed upon these cabin owners. The least we can do is to leave the place in clean condition."

"But you're going to take their motorcycle. You're not planning to bring it back, are you?"

"No . . . But I will leave some money."

"You've got a strange sense of honor, Indiana Jones," Zoe said. She grimaced as she pulled her jeans back on over her knee. "That's not so bad. You have any idea how far it is to town?"

"Not so much. We'll find it, though."

"And then what happens?"

That was the question Jingshen had been wrestling with most. What *was* he going to do? He needed to make a couple calls to get a sense of just how bad things were for him. That meant being out in public. He looked at himself and Zoe critically. Her clothing was stained and torn. His was ragged, practically indecent. If they were going to avoid standing out, they needed to look less like the threadbare homeless people they actually were.

He went back through the cabin, performing a thorough, top-to-bottom search. His explorations turned up precious few elements of clothing, but enough that he felt he could update his and Zoe's appearances sufficiently. Whomever owned the cabin was tall and had feet like gunboats. The western-style overcoat he found was cut for someone several inches taller than him, and the boots were like clown shoes on him. He didn't find any pants or shirts, but he did discover a small sewing kit he felt he could put to good use. For Zoe, there was only a child's parka, but she was slight enough to shrug her shoulders into it and zip it up. There was a balaclava she could wear as well, and that would have to suffice for their ride in the chilly mountain air.

Using skills he'd picked up a century and a half earlier, Jingshen made some alterations to the length of the overcoat's sleeves and hemmed the bottom so it wouldn't drag. Being a duster, it was designed for riding and had straps with snaps that could tighten it around his legs to allow freedom of movement. It could also snap snugly around his wrists. He cut fabric from the blanket they'd slept beneath the previous night and used it to repair his pants.

Zoe watched him work, thumbing idly through a paperback book. "You're good at sewing," she said. "I never learned anything useful like that."

"I've had a long time to pick up skills. I know how to do a lot of things that are pointless in today's world."

"Like what?"

"Trapping beaver. Laying narrow-gauge railroad track. Setting linotype."

"What's linotype?"

"It's a process for printing documents using hot metal typesetting."

"I don't know what you're even talking about, Indiana Jones."

"It's . . . old." Jingshen stood and checked the length of his repaired trousers. They were good enough for his needs. "I'm ready to leave if you are."

Zoe looked around the cabin. "It's kind of nice here. I wouldn't mind staying in a place like this. Away from people. Away from everything."

"Maybe we can find one after all this is over." Inwardly, Jingshen cursed himself for not being honest with Zoe that this might *never* truly be over. The Source would keep coming after him unless he could either convince them he was dead or somehow buy out his contract. The former was unlikely, given that the Source had records proving he couldn't be killed, and the latter was something he'd never heard of happening. In an industry that functioned entirely on the basis of reputation, the Source would never permit someone to walk free.

Jingshen cleaned up his mess of blanket bits and made a quick once-over of the cabin. At least he could minimize the work the owners would need to put in to return it to the condition in which he and Zoe found it.

"You and your weird sense of honor," Zoe said with a laugh.

"Details matter," Jingshen said. "Go on outside. I will be out in a minute."

Zoe limped out to wait by the shed.

Jingshen took a piece of charcoal from the stove and went upstairs. On the dresser, where it would be out of view of anyone looking in a first floor window, he set ten one-hundred dollar bills on the dresser. With the charcoal, he scratched *Apologies for the damage and theft. Thank you for the use of your cabin* on the dresser's top. He set the charcoal atop the stack of bills and went back down to the main floor.

He topped off the gas tank in the bike, rolled it out of the shed, and shifted it into second gear. There was enough of a slope that he easily push-started the bike after only a few yards. The engine roared to life, kicking out smoke and steam in the cold morning air. He put his foot down, turned the bike around, and climbed back up to stop beside Zoe.

"This looks really dangerous," she shouted over the bike's exhaust.

"It will be fine," Jingshen said. "Keep your arms around my waist and press yourself against me. Keep your feet up and move with me."

Zoe swung her bad leg up and over first, then situated herself behind him. "Like this?"

"Yes. Keep your balaclava pulled up over your face. It will get cold. If the wind is too much, keep your face against my neck."

"But what about—"

Zoe's last words were lost as Jingshen twisted the throttle and headed up the dirt road. Somewhere above would be either a paved or graded gravel road, and from there they could find their way back to civilization.

Chapter Ten

September, 1993
Tehachapi, California

They made their way up the dirt track, eventually finding their way to a graded road. It met up with Highway 58, which Jingshen recognized. He headed east, passing by downshifted freight trucks like they were standing still. Swirling wind whipped around them, rapidly growing warmer as they shed altitude. Ahead, Jingshen saw a small town with a huge wind farm beyond it, spreading out onto the plain of the Mojave.

The town was called Tehachapi, a wide spot in the road between Bakersfield and Barstow, at the gateway to the Mojave Desert. Jingshen knew of the town, though he'd never once stopped within it. He took the exit and rolled the bike into the small downtown. "Where are we going?" Zoe asked over his shoulder. She'd taken the ride like a champ, clinging to Jingshen and moving with him so fluidly he might have forgotten he had a passenger at all.

"First to a diner for some real coffee," Jingshen said. "And I need to make a couple phone calls. After that, we'll figure it out." He spotted a cafe called Henry's and pulled off the street.

The wind whipped through the town, making Jingshen glad his overcoat was designed for riding and strapped around his legs. It occurred to him he didn't know what day of the week it was, having lost track of time. If the stores in town were open, he'd take Zoe to buy some new clothes. It would probably be safe for them to spend one night in a motel in the town before they moved on. The motorcycle they'd taken from the cabin wouldn't be a pleasant way to cross the Mojave, so they'd need to acquire a more robust vehicle.

"Jesus, does the wind *always* blow like this here?" Zoe complained as her stringy locks flapped around her face.

"No," said an old man as he passed them with a small dog on a leash. "Sometimes it blows the other direction." He laughed at his own joke and Jingshen smiled. "Have a nice day," the man said and moved on down the street, pausing for his dog to pee on some scrub brush.

Jingshen opened the door into the diner and stepped inside, taking a few seconds for his eyes to adjust to the dim interior. A red and orange tile floor, wood-topped tables, and brown vinyl booths gave it a homey feel. Overhead fluorescent lighting presented food in an unappetizing, sanitized light. That said, the coffee smelled fresh and delicious odors emanated from the kitchen while a couple waitresses bustled back and forth with meals for the patrons. Jingshen looked across the patrons and from their general state of dress, decided it was Sunday and this was the after-church crowd.

A teenage hostess with hoop earrings sat them in a booth and brought them coffee and water. Jingshen drank his coffee quickly, not worrying about scalding his mouth. The momentary pain would heal almost immediately, and he needed the caffeine. A waitress with a name badge reading *Denise* took their orders. Before she headed back to the kitchen, Jingshen asked if she knew where they could buy some clothing. "We're traveling by motorcycle," he said when she asked why. "Someone stole our saddlebags last night. We don't have anything except what we're wearing."

"That sucks, man," Denise the waitress said. She told them where they could go and went to place their order with the kitchen.

Jingshen stood. "Wait here. I need to make a couple calls. I'll be back in a few minutes."

Zoe nodded in acknowledgment, sipped her water, and stared out the window.

After changing a twenty dollar bill at the front counter, Jingshen went outside to use the pay phone. The first number he called was his fixer at The Source, a man he only knew as AJ.

"Jesus H. Christ on a rubber crutch," AJ said as soon as Jingshen identified himself. "Ghost, you're in a world of trouble."

"I know. How bad is it?"

"It's bad. The Source is unhappy with you and your team. Didn't anybody ever tell you reputations matter in this business?"

"I'm aware."

"Well, now you're aware that there's a price on your head. And on Bishop, Rook and that asshole Nobody Special, for all the good it will do to find him when he can look like anyone."

"This is all his fault," Jingshen pointed out. "He made a backdoor deal with DuraGen, and Rook and Bishop played along to throw me under the bus."

"That doesn't matter," AJ said succinctly. "Kokorotai contracted you for the job through the Source, and paid a lot of money to make that happen. Now the Source is on the hook for your failure."

"They're trafficking in human beings, AJ. Lab experiments. Human guinea pigs."

"I don't care. A job is a job. You failed in yours, and now the Source has had to contract its own team to fulfill your job."

"Who is it?"

There was a long pause and Jingshen almost hung up before AJ answered. "Carnival, Bloodstone, and Stirge."

"Fuck me." Jingshen grimaced. He knew of all three mercenaries by reputation, and that was plenty. Stirge was basically a human syringe, able to generate a variety of compounds within his body and inject them into victims through bone needles in his fingers. Bloodstone could create slivers of razor-sharp obsidian and hurl them with lethal force and accuracy. And Carnival . . . Jingshen shivered. He'd never much liked clowns, and Carnival was everything terrifying about them. If the three of them were after Zoe, and caught up with her and Jingshen . . . Well, Jingshen didn't have high hopes he would be able to stop them. They couldn't kill him, but they'd leave him in pieces by the side of the road.

"Can I buy out the Kokorotai contract?" Jingshen had heard that in rare circumstances, the Source would allow a negotiated contract to be bought out by one of the interested parties. Unfortunately, such instances were invariably rare and extremely expensive.

"Not an option. Like I said, reputation is everything. Maybe you could have bought it out before it was reassigned, but not now. There's more, Ghost. I said the Source put a price on your head. Warhorse picked it up."

"Warhorse. Jesus." Warhorse was a veritable force of nature. He could have been one of the world's greatest superheroes if he'd chosen to walk the path of law and order. Instead, he kept himself busy through high-paying mercenary work and only took the jobs he felt were of sufficient personal interest. If one needed an army base razed to the ground, or a small country's government overthrown, Warhorse was the operative of choice; super-strong, super-tough, and with a team of weapon designers backing him. Having him on the warpath meant one's days were numbered. If anybody could figure out how to permanently kill Jingshen, Warhorse would manage it.

"I'm telling you this out of respect for our long-running business relationship," AJ said. "But that's it. I'm disconnecting this number. Nice knowing you, Ghost."

The line went dead.

Bloodstone, Stirge, and Carnival. And Warhorse. Jingshen shook his head. The Source had resources to track him and Zoe even when they'd taken care to cover their tracks. There was a psi named Medium, who could psychically trace interpersonal connections to find people, like drawing a path from person to person until she found the target. A projecting teleport named Gate could open portals through an alternate dimension, allowing instantaneous travel from point to point. Projecting teleports were rare, and he was exceptional in the ability to do so without being intimately familiar with his destination. Between the two of them, they could track down Jingshen and Zoe in a matter of hours and place the new Kokorotai team in position to reacquire Zoe. Warhorse could use them too, for that matter, and he had the resources to spend on hiring their services.

Jingshen needed some additional backup, and he only had one number left he could call. He started punching keys, entering the codes from his long-distance calling cards that he'd committed to memory, making a call all the way across the country. The phone rang, and then just when Jingshen had decided nobody was there, the call connected and a deep voice answered.

"Forsythe residence. This is James."

"Juice, it's the Ghost."

Juice's mind was as sharp as ever, and he didn't even have to pause while he figured out who was actually calling him. "Ghost. It's been a long time."

Before Just Cause, Juice had been an up-and-coming hero in the Boston area. He and Ghost had worked together briefly on a case involving a kidnapped heiress. It had been a simple, straightforward assault on a fortified Mafia compound, and the two of them had successfully rescued the victim. The mission had earned Juice his spot on Just Cause, and he'd cordially extended an invitation to Jingshen to join him as well.

"There's a spot for you on the greatest team in the world, if you want it," Juice had said.

Jingshen had politely declined. Heroism was a thing for others, not for him. He'd only been involved because he had a contract to remove some documents from the same compound. With their missions aligned, it had only been natural for the two men to work together.

"Almost ten years by my count," Jingshen said.

"A drop in the bucket for you, perhaps, but a long time for me."

Jingshen blinked. He hadn't told Juice about his lack of natural aging Had the man figured it out by himself? If so, Jingshen wasn't surprised. Juice was one of the smartest men Jingshen had met in his long life. "Yes, indeed."

"So tell me . . . what can I do for the Chinatown Ghost today?"

Jingshen grimaced at the confession he was about to make. "I'm in trouble, and I need your help."

Juice was silent for several long seconds, enough that Jingshen started to reach for the lever to disconnect the call, figuring AT&T had dropped the connection. "What's the problem?" Juice said at last.

"I accepted a job I shouldn't have, and now I've got two different parahuman strike teams after me and the civilian I'm protecting."

"Where are you?"

"California," Jingshen replied. "I can't be more specific than that. This isn't a secure line."

Juice's sigh was audible even over a couple thousand miles of phone line. "You could have picked a better time to reach out to me. How did you even know I'd be home today?"

Jingshen shrugged even though Juice couldn't see him. "I figured I was due for a win. Why is this a bad time?"

"I'm being promoted," Juice said. "Sunstorm is retiring. Effective tomorrow, I'm in charge of Just Cause."

"Congratulations." Jingshen's heart sank. He didn't always notice the changes that happened during the lives of normal people—a side effect of his own longevity. With Juice moving into a position of leadership, his orders would be subject to review. If it came out that he was helping a mercenary who had completed hundreds of criminal acts just in the past dozen years, it would undoubtedly mean his expulsion from the team. Reputation mattered among superheroes as much as it did among those who walked the opposite side of the line of law and order. Jingshen couldn't ask Juice to risk all that for him.

"That doesn't mean I'm not going to help you if I can," Juice said, as if he were following along Jingshen's thoughts. "But it may have to be . . . circumspect. What do you need?"

"Backup."

"Who's after you?"

"I don't know if any of these names will mean anything to you," Jingshen said. "One will for certain. Stirge, Carnival, Bloodstone . . . and Warhorse."

"Warhorse," Juice repeated. "What the hell did you do to earn his attention?"

"I broke a contract. He's the punishment."

"Never ask for anything small, Ghost," Juice said. "I'm not sure how much help I can be. How much time do you have?"

"Not much, I'm afraid."

"I've got an idea. Someone who may be able to help you. I trust her implicitly."

"If you trust her, then I trust her too."

"Tell me where you are and I'll see how fast she can get to you."

"Tehachapi." Jingshen felt like the entire world was listening when he said it. He wasn't verbalizing his death warrant—at least, he didn't think so. Perhaps Warhorse or one of the mercs on his tail might come up with a way to kill him at last. Whatever happened, and wherever it happened, the collateral damage might be extensive.

"Give me three hours to get her to you. Can you hold out that long?"

"I'll have to, won't I?"

"Ghost . . . if Warhorse is involved, you've got to get away from civilians."

"I'll do my best. I'll owe you after this."

"Damn right you will, and you can bet I'll come back and collect someday."

"Your friend . . . how will I know her?"

"Oh, you'll know."

* * *

Jingshen spotted a haberdasher two stores down from where he'd stood to make his phone call. Curious, he wandered over to do a little window-shopping and actually saw a reasonable copy of the hat he'd lost. It gave him a feeling of wistful hope. Maybe he had enough time to go in and buy it. It would be a stupid, pointless gesture that would accomplish nothing to help him survive the strike teams pursuing him and Zoe.

But it *would* make him feel better.

He checked his pocket out of habit before opening the door and froze.

His bankroll was gone.

There was no way he could have lost it. Money didn't just fall out of pockets without help. Zoe must have stolen it. He felt his ire rising as he turned and stalked back toward the diner, thoughts of hats forgotten.

He stepped inside and looked around, but Zoe was nowhere to be seen. He made himself take a deep, calming breath, and spotted the waitress who'd taken their orders earlier. Her gaze met his and her eyes narrowed. Jingshen knew she was about to lie to him as he walked up to her. "Excuse me, Denise. I had to step outside to make a phone call. Did you see where my friend went?"

"Your *friend* took off," Denise said, crossing her arms across her blue blouse. "Stiffed me with two plates of food. That ain't even a dine-and-dash. You got the money to pay for this order?"

"No. She took my money."

"Then you best get your Asian ass out of my restaurant before I call the cops on you."

Jingshen raised his hands slowly. "Easy. I'm gone. I apologize for my friend."

"I don't want your apology, asshole." Denise flounced away and Jingshen left Henry's.

The pervasive wind in the street seemed colder than it had been, even with the sun shining brightly overhead. Jingshen looked up and down the street, wondering where Zoe could have gone. She had about four thousand dollars in cash, which was enough to buy a car with no questions asked. On the other hand, she was from the street, which meant she might think more like someone for whom money wasn't normally readily available. It was tempting when one was suddenly flush to spend money profligately, buying luxuries. Maybe she was on a shopping binge. Or maybe she was looking to leave town on the down-low, which probably meant a bus ticket.

Jingshen raised a hand toward a man in a safety vest who was marking spots on the pavement with a wheeled sprayer. "Excuse me. Where is the nearest bus station?"

"*Lo siento, señor. No hablo inglés.*"

Jingshen smiled. He didn't need the man to speak English. He was fluent in nearly thirty languages. "*Todo está bien. Yo hablo español. ¿Donde esta la estación del bus?*"

The worker brightened at Jingshen's fluency and told him the bus station was two blocks to the north, near the railroad tracks. Jingshen thanked him and walked briskly up the street, his stolen coat billowing around him like a sail in the wind.

The bus station was contained in a wide, inviting building with a sloping roof and lots of windows. Jingshen kept his head down and hands in his pockets and crossed the street to the depot. He spotted Zoe right away, hunched down on a bench with her knees drawn to her chest. She saw him striding toward her and her face flushed red with embarrassment. To her credit, she didn't flee, or cry for help. Instead, she sat and waited until he stood before her.

"You stole my money," Jingshen said.

Zoe looked up at him with a streak of defiance in her face. "You weren't using it."

"That doesn't make it all right."

"What are you going to do, mug me right here in the bus station? Because I'll scream."

"No, I'm not going to mug you. You can keep the money. If you'd asked for it, I'd have given it to you. I have money. Not with me, but I can get to it. If you want, take it and get on your bus and I won't follow you. Maybe you'll get away."

Zoe blinked. "What do you mean, I'll *get away*?"

"You think just because I didn't turn you over to Kokorotai that they'd let you go? You think DuraGen won't try to get you back? You're a very popular young lady, Zoe, and I know a little bit about the next team that's coming after you."

"A . . . team?"

"Rook and Bishop were kittens compared to the trio who picked up your contract."

Zoe crossed her arms. "They're not going to hurt me. I'm too valuable."

Jingshen frowned. "You don't have to be conscious to use your power. I felt it when you slept next to me. I'm betting you don't have to be . . . whole, either."

"Wh-what do you mean, *whole*?"

"A double amputee can't run away. A quadruple amputee can't strike back at you."

"They wouldn't do that."

"Carnival, Bloodstone, and Stirge? They absolutely would. They're animals."

"Where are they? Do you know?"

"No, I don't know, but I know they will have access to resources that can get them close to you sooner rather than later. I can't promise you'll live if you come with me, but I'll do my best to keep you alive and get you off the target list."

"How are you going to do that?"

Jingshen shook his head. "I don't know yet. I'm still trying to figure that part out."

"So what should we do? I could buy you a ticket and we both get on that bus."

"No. We'll be too exposed on a bus, surrounded by people who the mercenaries will have no problem killing to get to you."

Zoe stood. "So let's get out of here another way. You're handy. You can steal a car."

"I think we should keep a low profile. Stealing a car isn't low profile. They'll be expecting us to run."

"So we're not going to run?"

Jingshen took Zoe's hand, feeling his skin threatening to come apart at her touch. He led her from the depot. "We are, but we're going to be smart about it. We're going to hide in plain sight for a couple hours until my help gets here and then we'll figure out our next move."

"Who's coming? More freaks like us?"

"I think so," Jingshen said. He had no idea who Juice could have sent to help. Maybe someone from Los Angeles who could fly could get to them within that three hour window he'd promised. Jingshen didn't know a lot of people in the parahuman community. He'd spent too much of his life on the fringes, avoiding getting close to anyone with abilities. Beyond Juice, he couldn't have recited the names of more than two or three other Just Cause heroes.

They went to the haberdasher after all. Shopping for clothes when parahuman strike teams were hunting them might have seemed foolish, but Jingshen had to consider the larger picture. Their clothes were ragged, ill-fitting, and coming apart. If they were going to disappear in plain sight, they would need to fit in with their surroundings. The saleswoman was suspicious from the moment they walked into the shop, until Jingshen gave her fifty dollars and asked her to help them outfit themselves.

A few minutes later, Zoe had new jeans, high-tops, a pullover sweatshirt, and a jean jacket. She'd pulled a Los Angeles Raiders knit cap over her stringy hair and she looked like someone who wouldn't stand out in a crowd—exactly what Jingshen was hoping. He purchased a new pair of heavy-duty cargo pants and a black turtleneck, but chose to keep the duster.

And, of course he bought the hat.

Chapter Eleven

September, 1993
Tehachapi, California

Jingshen and Zoe walked up the street, neither touching nor speaking, but staying close together. The persistent wind tried to catch Jingshen's fedora, but it was an excellent fit and stayed firmly in place. From beneath its brim, he watched cars and trucks as they passed. Some headed further into the small town in search of respite from the desolate vistas of the Mojave, others packed with travelers seemed only too glad to leave for more urban locales to the west.

Sooner or later, a vehicle would arrive bearing the parahumans hunting him and Zoe. The psychic Medium was probably already tracking him, or tracking Zoe—whichever she found had the most interpersonal connections in humanity's collective unconsciousness. Then Gate would open the portal and send them through.

Jingshen could almost feel the psychic crosshairs on his back as Medium traced back through people he'd met, people who'd seen him. As long as Jingshen had been alive, there were hundreds of thousands of potential threads to find him. All Medium had to do was follow threads until one led to him.

"Jones? Hey, snap out of it." Zoe squeezed his arm through his coat. "My leg hurts. How long are we going to just walk around here?"

"There." Jingshen canted his head toward a used-car dealership at the end of the block, an establishment that reeked of shady deals named *Jeff's Autos*.

"You don't want to steal a car? Don't you think that would be better?"

"No. Maybe in the short term, we'd get away, but there are only two directions someone can go from here in a stolen car. Into the desert, or back toward Bakersfield. Better to purchase a vehicle and not have anyone immediately looking for us."

"Maybe we wait until dark and steal one then?"

Jingshen shook his head. "I don't think we have that long."

"What about your friend? The one who's coming to help?"

"I don't know who is coming, and I don't know what they can do when they get here. My friend said they would find me. I believe him. We need to leave town, but we need to do so without raising suspicion. That means we buy a vehicle."

Zoe scrunched up her face as she looked at *Jeff's Autos*. "That looks like a pretty sketchy place."

"Then they won't mind being paid cash."

"Doesn't that raise suspicions?"

"Not at a sketchy place." Jingshen smiled.

"You're infuriating, Jones."

"I've had centuries of practice." Jingshen gave the row of dusty cars a quick once-over. He had a general idea of what he wanted and tried to estimate how much he might need to spend to get it quickly with no questions asked.

That one on the end, the Jeep Scrambler with the rusting quarter panels and dusty purple paint, he thought. It had only a bra-style soft top, barely enough to keep rain off the front seat passengers. The wheelbase was too long for the pastimes of rock-crawling but the bed was too short for any kind of real recreational or utilitarian purposes. It was ungainly, ugly, and clearly had spent far too much time too close to coastal environments from the salt corrosion along the edges of the body panels. Where some of the other cars had stickers on the windshields proclaiming *Low Mileage* or *Super Clean* or even *Economical*, the Scrambler's sole, peeling sticker read *Fun*.

Jingshen smiled.

He strolled onto the lot. Streamers with plastic flags flapped in the breeze. A dog lying in the shade beside a car raised its head to look at the newcomers before grunting and rolling back onto its side. At first, Jingshen thought the dealership was closed, but then he heard the sound of a television from inside the office building. He went to the door and looked inside.

A large bald man with a goatee sat in a decrepit office chair with an open beer in his hand and a TV remote in the other, grimacing at the spectacle on the screen as two football teams vied for supremacy. He looked up at Jingshen. "Goddamn Browns, man. You watch, they're gonna come back because Hostetler can't complete a fucking pass."

Jingshen smiled at the man and raised his hand. "Go Raiders." He didn't care about football—or sports in general—but when in Rome, one acted like a Roman.

"Goddamn right. Looking at that Scrambler?"

Jingshen blinked. "Yes, I was. How did you know?"

"I been selling goddamn cars for forty years. I can always tell."

"Tell me about the car."

"Been on the lot for three years. Before that it was from somewhere up near Mendocino. I can't get anyone to take a goddamn test drive in it because everyone wants a small offroader or a big truck. They see that rust and think it's a piece of shit."

"Is it?"

"A piece of shit? God, yes. AMC should have quit while they were ahead."

"You're not doing such a good job of selling it to me."

The man laughed. "It's Sunday. The Lord says I don't have to try to sell pieces of shit on Sundays." He stuck out his hand. "I'm Jeff. Want a beer?"

"No thank you."

Jeff's smile widened as he saw Zoe lurking behind Jingshen. "Nice hat, young lady."

"What?" Zoe's hands went to her knit cap. "Oh. Yeah. Go Raiders."

"The Scrambler. How does it run?" Jingshen asked.

Jeff shrugged. "Like it wants a better contract. It'll lose a little oil now and again, but if you keep a quart and a funnel handy, you shouldn't ever be in trouble with it." Jeff grunted and levered his bulk upright. He loped over to a cabinet of keys, picked one attached to a Warner Brothers Roadrunner keychain and tossed it over to Jingshen, who caught it out of midair. "Go start it up, see what you think."

Jingshen went back out to the lot and slipped into the Scrambler's driver's seat. It was a manual transmission and the clutch was uncomfortably stiff. Still, he'd driven Willys jeeps for the Allies in World War II and the Scrambler was nothing compared to that. The starter cranked strong, and the engine purred relatively smoothly. He shifted into neutral, put the emergency brake on, and waited to see if it would roll on him. When it didn't, he went around to open the hood and look at the engine while it ran. He didn't see any leaks or smoke that would spell problems later on. Although the engine could use a good steam cleaning and a new air filter, it wasn't spewing or spitting anything troublesome.

He checked underneath and saw the dark stains from a slow oil leak on the frame's steel crossmember. Jeff hadn't lied about the oil leak and didn't seem to have downplayed its severity. Jingshen approved of a salesman who didn't start off with a lie. Undoubtedly, the man would lie at some point—it was in the nature of salesmen to do so—but perhaps Jingshen had caught him on a good day. He shut off the engine. As long as it started, he would address any problems that came up with the car when they happened. He went back into the office just in time to see the Raiders quarterback swarmed by a sea of white jerseys and orange helmets.

"Goddammit, Hoss," Jeff said to the television, then looked up at Jingshen. "What'd you think of the Scrambler?"

"How much do you want for it?"

Jeff shrugged. "Hell, I'd take fifteen hundred for it and call it even."

Jingshen nodded. There was the lie. Jeff could be talked down maybe as low as a thousand if he was of a mind to negotiate, but time was a factor and money was not. He pulled out a stack of his cash. "I'll give you two thousand for it and you'll forget we were ever here." He peeled off twenty hundred dollar bills and passed them over to Jeff.

To his credit, Jeff merely nodded. He pulled out a temporary tag and handwrote a date on it in permanent marker. Then he slid it across his desk to Jingshen, along with an envelope that contained the vehicle's title. "Guess I finally gave up on that Scrambler and sent it to the crusher. Nice to get the space back for something that might sell. You sure you don't want a beer for the road?"

Thunder grumbled in the near distance. Jingshen glanced through the office window. It was still bright daylight and the only clouds were those carried by the wind, too fleeting to bother with anything so pedestrian as precipitation.

Jingshen passed another hundred to Jeff, who made it disappear. "No, thank you."

Jeff took a long pull from his beer, then turned back to the television. "Goddamn Browns," he said, making it sufficient as a fare-thee-well.

Jingshen took the hint and left the office. "That one," he said to Zoe. "Come on, we're leaving." That thunder had set his nerves to jumping. Thunder didn't happen from clear skies, but it did happen for, say, supersonic jets owned by powerful warlord mercenaries . . . or from the displacement of air due to teleportation. They were on borrowed time, and Jingshen knew they needed to leave.

"Where are we going?" Zoe asked as she climbed into the passenger seat. "Wherever it is, I hope it's not far. This car's a piece of shit."

"It is, but it is now our piece of shit," Jingshen agreed. "We're going east into the desert."

"What about your friend?"

"I don't think we have time to wait," Jingshen said. "Buckle your seat belt. I expect we'll have unpleasant company before long."

* * *

The Camaro was primer brown and had a homemade hood scoop that looked more like a half a keg sticking up than something mechanically sound. It passed by the Scrambler going the opposite direction. Jingshen might have thought nothing of it if he hadn't seen it perform a U-turn in the rear-view mirror.

He couldn't see the driver or passengers from the rear view mirror. Something about that hood scoop made him uncomfortable. It didn't *belong* on that car. It was too tall, too wide, too *wrong*. He took the Scrambler onto the highway, heading east. The Camaro followed, which might have been a coincidence, but Jingshen didn't believe in coincidences. Three centuries had proven that very little in the world happened independently, especially where money was involved.

He accelerated, taking the Scrambler past seventy, then past eighty, taking them deeper into the desert. The car didn't appreciate the hard work to which it was unaccustomed, and shook and vibrated with the velocity. "Jesus, Jones, could you maybe not try to wreck us?" Zoe shouted over the howl of wind whipping around them.

Jingshen glanced at the rear view mirror, which shook with erratic vibrations. In spite of that, he could plainly see the Camaro was closing the distance between them. The hood scoop was like a gaping, toothless mouth screaming its battle cry wordlessly at them.

In a matter of seconds, the Camaro was only a few hundred feet behind them and growing closer.

Jingshen floored the Scrambler's accelerator but it pulled ahead far too slowly for his liking. He switched lanes, passing a semi. Once he was past it, he changed back and slowed, letting the truck ride up on him while watching the approaching Camaro in his side mirror. The trucker laid on his horn, making Zoe nearly jump out of her seat. As the Camaro started to pass the trailer, Jingshen said, "Hold on," and drifted right onto the shoulder.

The Scrambler bounced and skittered across the sandy soil as Jingshen braked hard, letting the truck pass him on the left. As the rear wheels drew even with him, he accelerated again. The theory was he would be behind the Camaro when he pulled back onto the road, but the driver had clearly seen that trick before. As the Scrambler found pavement behind the trailer, the Camaro drifted back from the trailer's left and drew even with them.

A clown was standing up through the T-top with a bazooka pointing at them.

He had a thick mass of bright red curls—either a wig or a dye job—with an incongruously small blue top hat that steadfastly refused to blow away in the wind. His face was split into a horrific grin and his cackling laughter was audible even over the howl of the Camaro's motor. Bandoleers of ammunition and explosives crossed his shoulders the way suspenders would on a less threatening clown. Below it all, he wore a day-glo Hawaiian shirt. He fired just as Jingshen slammed on the brakes.

Like it happened in slow motion, the rocket skipped off the Scrambler's hood with a resounding *BANG* and crashed unexploded against a stunted desert tree beside the road.

Zoe screamed and Jingshen cranked the wheel over, sending the Scrambler crashing through a lightweight fence at an angle away from the road. The tires kicked up a spray of sand and dust in their wake.

"I thought they were trying to catch me, not kill me!" Zoe cried as the Scrambler bounced over the rough terrain. The rear view mirror broke off the windshield, leaving a long crack that spread from edge to edge.

"They're supposed to be," Jingshen retorted. "Carnival is crazy."

Carnival wasn't the only crazy one, for the driver of the Camaro locked the wheels and then skidded off the road to follow after the Scrambler. Jingshen tried to divide his attention between the terrain ahead and the pursuers behind, but the rough ground quickly became his priority. One bad choice could drop the Scrambler into an arroyo or smash it against an unyielding rock.

Something sharp slammed into the back of Jingshen's head, just below the brim of his hat. The impact made his vision blur. He risked taking one hand off the wheel and reached up to feel the wound. His hand came away bloody, holding a sliver of shiny black volcanic glass. "Shit," he said, and flung it away. "Get down."

Zoe hunkered down in her seat. "What now? Oh, you're bleeding!"

"Bloodstone. Trying to kill me."

"They're trying to kill us both!"

"I don't think so." The Scrambler bounded down a gentle slope. The steering wheel jerked sharply and broke one of Jingshen's fingers. He grimaced and kept his hands clenched on the shaking wheel. It would heal in seconds.

Behind them, the Camaro roared and fishtailed down the hill after them. The car's front clip had broken free already and the hood was bouncing loose. Carnival was still standing up through the T-top, howling with laughter, his face peppered with sand.

"If they'd actually wanted to kill us, Carnival would have used live ammo." The Scrambler flew across a narrow dry creek bed and the windshield shattered into a thousand pieces, bound by the safety glass. Jingshen took a hand off the wheel and punched at the glass in front of him, creating a fist-sized hole through which he could sort of see. "Kick it out," he said. "I'm too busy and we can't stop."

Zoe screamed in terror and didn't move.

"Zoe, if you don't clear that glass, you are going to die!" Jingshen shouted. They crashed through another fence and a forest of white metallic tree trunks spread out around them. They'd reached one of the wind farms spread across the western edge of the Mojave.

Zoe's teeth were bared in a frightened snarl as she leaned back and kicked at the broken windshield. It shivered but held. Jingshen swerved around a windmill base. "Hit it again. Harder."

Bracing herself against the seat, Zoe kicked the windshield again. It popped loose and dangled across the hood for a moment until Jingshen grabbed hold of it and flung it aside. Wind and dust blasted into their faces as they whipped past a forest of windmill pillars. Behind them, Carnival had thrown away his bazooka in favor of something a little less lethal in the form of an assault rifle. He was taking shot after shot at the Scrambler. Jingshen jerked the jeep left and right at random intervals. He didn't know whether the clown was shooting at him, at the tires, or something else. They had to know a bullet wouldn't do much more than inconvenience Jingshen for a few minutes unless it struck something important. Shooting at him introduced a risk of hitting Zoe, and she was still the reason they were there in the first place.

Despite the terrain, the Camaro was still closing with them, driven by someone with no concern about getting home in the same car. As she got the range, Bloodstone began firing off her shards of obsidian. She was accurate, and Jingshen's scalp became matted with his own blood as splinter after splinter of volcanic glass creased his flesh.

Suddenly the Scrambler hit the edge of a ridge and went airborne for long, terrifying seconds. The car's momentum made it twist in midair, plainly angling to land on its side.

Jingshen didn't have time to think. He reached down and released his and Zoe's seatbelts before she had a chance to scream, grabbed hold of her, and leaped clear of the tumbling car. He wrapped himself around her like a living crash suit. They hit the slope hard—but not as hard as if they'd still been in the Scrambler, which impacted ahead of them and barrel-rolled down the hill.

Jingshen squeezed Zoe tight, trying to keep her arms and legs from flailing. Loose limbs would break against the ground or other unyielding objects. His skin crackled and flaked where it touched hers as her power tore into him without mercy. They bounced off something hard and Jingshen felt a bone break in his forearm.

Zoe grunted and gasped as they skidded to a stop, showing the telltale signs of having the wind knocked out of her. Jingshen knew he only had seconds to work. He took a precious moment to push the splintered end of bone jutting from his forearm back beneath the ragged flesh so it would heal faster. Zoe clutched at him, panic spread across her face as she tried to inhale. He held up a hand and curled it into an *ippon ken* fist with one knuckle extended further than the others. With it, he delivered a series of four precise blows to points shown him by an acupuncturist. At the fourth strike, Zoe's diaphragm spasm halted and she drew a deep, quaking breath.

With a roar like a charging beast, the Camaro flew over the top of the ridge, flames shooting from the headers as the driver buried the accelerator.

Jingshen yanked Zoe to her feet. "Run!" he shouted. The only immediate cover was behind the wrecked Scrambler, and he pulled her behind it with him. The vehicle had given its all in their attempted escape. Where there had been a roll cage and windshield frame, the vehicle lay flat. If Jingshen and Zoe had remained in it when it crashed, Zoe would probably be dead, her head smashed against the unyielding ground.

Somehow, the driver kept the Camaro under control as it bore down the hill toward them, showing no signs of slowing or stopping. Jingshen saw Stirge behind the wheel, his teeth bared in a rictus of fierce joy while Carnival cackled and hooted above him. A cloud of obsidian splinters made Jingshen duck behind the Scrambler's carcass—not because he was afraid of them, but if they caught him in his eyes, he'd need hours before he could properly see again.

A moment later, Jingshen grabbed Zoe and dove away from the Scrambler, for Stirge aimed the Camaro right at the wrecked jeep and red-lined the engine.

The muscle car smashed into the wreck with the force of a missile. An explosion rocked the world and the shock wave sent Jingshen and Zoe flying. Hot shrapnel peppered Jingshen's back as the Camaro exploded into a fireball, probably with the aid of one or two of Carnival's thermite grenades.

Jingshen and Zoe smashed back to the ground, bleeding from their ears. Zoe hit hard and didn't move, either knocked unconscious or dead. Jingshen's ringing ears healed in a couple of seconds, just in time for him to hear the thudding footsteps across the rough ground. He rolled aside as an axe blade whistled down and buried itself in the dirt. Jingshen looked up to see a leering Carnival grinning his crooked smile, his face paint smeared and sloppy.

"It's playtime!" Carnival shrieked, and swung his axe again.

Jingshen rolled aside, timing the blow, and kicked hard at the clown's wrist. The wrist turned but didn't break. Carnival dropped his axe and yelled in surprise and pain.

Bloodstone appeared behind the clown, her black overcoat flowing in the breeze. Her polished obsidian buttons sparkled in the sun as she made a flicking motion with her hand. Jingshen raised his arm just in time to intercept a cloud of obsidian splinters that would have shredded his face. They embedded themselves into his flesh with a level of pain he hadn't experienced for many years.

With his uninjured arm, Jingshen picked up Carnival's axe and jumped to his feet. Before he could fling it at Bloodstone, a half dozen pinpricks pierced his neck and it was like his insides were aflame. He screamed and fell to his knees. The pain was so intense and acute, he couldn't move, couldn't even think. His world shrank to a crimson tinged fog of burning, and he knew Stirge had reached him, close enough to drive his fingertip needles into Jingshen's flesh.

He tried to draw a breath to scream, but his lungs couldn't move against the force of whatever Stirge had injected into him through his bone hypodermics.

Bloodstone stepped over to look at him. He could barely see her as his eyes kept unfocusing. "He doesn't look so tough. You sure this is the Ghost?"

"It's got to be. I've unloaded enough batrachotoxin into him to kill an elephant," Stirge said.

"He's lovely," Carnival shouted, clapping his hands. "I want his hat!"

Somehow, Jingshen found the strength to overcome the poison coursing through his veins to say, "Come and take it." He fought to cope with the damage to his nerves. Somewhere behind him, Zoe was on the ground, either unconscious or dead. He couldn't help her so long as Stirge still had his bone needles in Jingshen's neck.

Bloodstone began forming an obsidian splinter as long as her forearm. The black volcanic glass twisted in her hand like it was a living thing. "I heard this guy can't be killed," she said, licking her lips. Her razor-cut black hair fluttered like the wings of a crow. "That doesn't mean he can't be cut to pieces."

Carnival jumped up and down, clapping his hands. "Do it! Doooo it!" he shouted. "Not in the face, though. I want that hat."

Bloodstone raised her shard-spear. Stirge stepped back so he wouldn't get impaled. Jingshen's vision cleared just as Bloodstone flung her splinter.

A red and gold blur passed between Jingshen and Bloodstone and the obsidian spear shattered into a cloud of sharp but ultimately harmless splinters. While the three mercenaries goggled in disbelief at the newcomer, Jingshen took advantage of the distraction and moved.

Bracing his hands against the ground, he kicked back with both feet and caught Stirge in the side of his knee. The knee bent sideways with a sickening pop and Stirge went down screaming.

"What the fuck?" Bloodstone shouted, and launched a barrage of obsidian at the speedster like a machine gun on full automatic.

Carnival whooped with delight and pulled a pair of Uzis from holsters at his hips. He fired at Jingshen, who jumped over the howling Stirge. As bullets creased his flesh, he grabbed hold of Stirge beneath the man's arms and lifted.

Bullets slammed into Stirge, piercing his lightweight armored vest and making him jitter and jerk. Blood sprayed in all directions as the Uzis chattered themselves dry. "Two-way split!" Carnival shouted, and yanked a katana from a scabbard strapped to his back. The blade lit with flames, spitting and snapping in the wind.

Jingshen threw aside Stirge's lifeless body and dove for Carnival's discarded axe. The katana blade whistled over his head, sending his new hat flying away, its brim smoldering. His fingers wrapped around the axe's haft just as Carnival brought his sword down. Jingshen caught the flaming blade on the axe handle and turned it aside.

Carnival was a more dangerous melee fighter than Jingshen expected. From the man's reputation, he expected a lot of bullets and bluster and little skill beyond it. Instead, he found himself hard-pressed to battle against a man who fought like he had nothing to lose. The katana flashed in the sun and rang like a bell as it met the axe blade and sliced it in half like a piece of fruit.

There it was, the mistake Jingshen had hoped Carnival would make. He paused to gloat over his powerful strike. Jingshen lunged, wrapped both hands around the flaming sword blade, and twisted.

The blade slipped right out of Carnival's outstretched hand. The clown made a disappointed "Oh," sound before Jingshen spun around and drove the sword point backward under his arm, right beneath Carnival's sternum and into his heart. The clown fell backward without a sound, his gaily-colored baggy outfit igniting from the sword's flame.

Jingshen dropped to his knees, panting heavily as he struggled against the pain of his ruined hands. He knew they'd come back, but it would take time. Zoe would have to handle driving for the next leg of their journey. He turned his eyes toward her and saw she still lay where she'd fallen. A chill overcame the burns in his hands as it occurred to him she might be dead.

The speedster wielded something like . . . horseshoes? She used them to slap aside and shatter every obsidian missile fired by Bloodstone. She closed the distance to the mercenary in a couple seconds and delivered a forceful uppercut that lifted Bloodstone off her feet. The woman's head snapped back viciously and she crumpled to the ground to lie deathly still.

Jingshen nodded in appreciation for a well-delivered *coup de grâce*. The speedster turned to face him and he recognized her. Her tight-fitting bodysuit of gold formed a horse-head emblem across her chest, contrasted in crimson that covered her neck and face. "Pony Girl," Jingshen said. "I thought you retired."

Pony Girl hung a pair of shiny horseshoes from clips at her waist and raised her goggles. "I did. You're the Ghost?"

Jingshen nodded and knelt to check Zoe. Her pulse fluttered under his fingers, which took on a hard, bluish tint like steel before his body recovered. "Thank you for coming."

"Juice and I are old friends. When old friends call, you do what they ask. Even when it's running across two goddamn states just to get into a fight." She folded her arms. "This better not take long. My sitter charges like an attorney." She looked down at Zoe. "Is she with you?"

"She is. Don't touch her. Her skin is extremely dangerous. It's only safe for me to do so." Still, he needed to minimize the contact with Zoe's flesh, so he took Bloodstone's overcoat. Given the odd angle of her head, it was unlikely the mercenary would need it—or anything—ever again.

Pony Girl stretched her legs and bounced up and down a few times as she waited for Jingshen to wrap up Zoe in the coat. "Damn, I'm stiff. It's been awhile since I ran that far or that fast."

"You don't still train?"

Pony Girl's laugh was short and sharp. "I'm *retired*, Ghost. I'm forty years old. I did my time in the costume."

Jingshen hefted Zoe in his arms. It would have been more efficient to carry her over his shoulders, but that would have made it more likely for her skin to touch his, and there were appearances to maintain. "It still suits you."

Pony Girl blinked. "Are you . . . coming on to me?"

"No. Just making an observation."

"Your loss." She looked over at the burning wreckage of the Camaro and Scrambler, then down at the three corpses slowly drying out in the desert wind. "I've got an observation of my own. You made a hell of a mess here and I don't appreciate being called in to help you clean it up."

"I appreciate your timely intervention," Jingshen said. "They were trying to kidnap this young woman."

"Juice said as much. Why her?"

"She can bestow parahuman abilities on others."

"No shit?"

"No shit."

"Can she give you anything useful like being able to fly or run at superspeed?"

"No, it doesn't work like that. She can't control it. For most people, her touch is lethal. I heal from it."

Pony Girl sighed. "I'm guessing you need another car, then."

"It's a long walk."

"To where?"

Jingshen's lips curled into a slight smile. "To anywhere else."

Chapter Twelve

September, 1993
Mojave, California

Zoe stirred before Pony Girl returned. Jingshen had carried her to the shade of a windmill tower and made her as comfortable as possible. He didn't know if she had internal injuries and if so how severe they were. None of her limbs appeared to be broken and from what he could tell, her skull seemed intact. Maybe she'd been fortunate.

He hoped so, because getting medical care with her power would be difficult at best.

The pain from his own injuries subsided and his body had already knit itself back together. He wished he could transfer his power to help Zoe. He would have done so, he reflected, even if it were permanent. He'd been alive a very long time. Perhaps it was time he wasn't. He wasn't suicidal; he was just tired of life.

Zoe moaned and Jingshen knelt beside her. "How do you feel?"

She licked her lips. "Like I got thrown out of a moving car."

"That's fair."

"And I'm thirsty."

"There will be water soon," Jingshen said.

"So I guess we won, since you're still here and I'm not on my way to become a full-time lab animal."

Jingshen looked in the direction of the three corpses, still baking in the sun beyond Zoe's range of vision. "Yes, we won. For now."

"What happens now?" Zoe shifted position and groaned as the movement apparently introduced new pains to her.

"We're getting out of here, as soon as Pony Girl returns with a ride."

"Who's Pony Girl?"

"She used to be a superhero."

"Used to be?"

"She retired."

Zoe sniffed. "So she's old."

"Not like I am."

"Nobody's old like you are, Jones."

Jingshen said nothing and stood as he heard the sound of an approaching engine. He peeked around the edge of the windmill's base. A white International Scout rolled toward them with a tall antenna mount and an orange flag waving upon it in the breeze. He squinted into the sunlight and decided there was only one person behind the wheel. "Stay here," he said to Zoe.

"I hurt too much to run away," she retorted. "I'll leave it to you to beat the crap out of whoever's coming after us next."

Jingshen nodded, waiting. He could have gone after some of Carnival's weapons. The clown had been known to be a walking arsenal. If it wasn't Pony Girl behind the wheel, it was someone who'd come to investigate the dying fire of the wrecked cars. An innocent civilian didn't deserve Jingshen's wrath, especially with Zoe suffering unknown and potentially serious injuries.

The Scout rolled to a stop and Jingshen saw Pony Girl wave at him from the driver's seat. He trotted over to the window, which she rolled down. A blast of icy cold air conditioning greeted him.

"Found the truck parked by the office and the keys hanging on a peg inside," Pony Girl said.

"The office wasn't locked?" Jingshen asked.

"Desperate times call for desperate measures," Pony Girl retorted. "Don't tell Juice."

"I won't."

"How bad is your friend hurt?"

Jingshen shrugged. "She may have cracked ribs but I don't think any are broken. I'm worried about internal damage."

"And of course, you can't take her to a doctor to get her checked out."

"No."

"Well, get her in the back seat and we'll figure it out."

Jingshen returned to where Zoe lay. "We have a ride," he said. "Can you walk?"

Zoe grimaced. "Maybe? I don't know if I can get myself up."

Jingshen held out his hand to her. "Let me help you."

Working in tandem, slow and careful, Jingshen got Zoe to her feet. His skin blackened and sloughed off where he touched her. The droplets of blood that fell to the sand jumped and hissed like water droplets on a hot pan.

"That's messed up," Pony Girl declared. "Doesn't that hurt?"

"Yes, but it will get better." Jingshen raised his hand to show her the flesh was already knitting itself back into place.

He helped Zoe into the back seat. Pony Girl took one look at Jingshen and his blackened skin and said, "I'm driving."

"I was going to ask you to." Jingshen sank gratefully into the passenger seat.

"Where to?" Pony Girl put the Scout into gear and let off the clutch. The car jerked forward but didn't stall. "Goddamn manuals . . ." she muttered.

"East for now. Into the desert."

Pony Girl glanced down at the dashboard and tapped at a gauge with an impatient hand. "We have half a tank of gas. I'm sure this thing gets lousy mileage."

"We'll stop in the first town. I'll be healed by then and you be on your way."

Pony Girl snorted. "Juice would have some choice words for me if I abandoned you."

"What about your sitter?"

"She'll have some choice words for me too. So will my daughter."

"Then you should leave. You helped me when I needed it. I'll be all right." Jingshen found a smile somewhere in his psyche. "They haven't found a way to kill me yet."

"Not for lack of trying." Pony Girl slowed, checked, then turned onto the highway. "You're lucky I saw the explosion."

"I'm glad you did."

Pony Girl shifted into overdrive and the Scout's tires thumped with quick repetitions over the seams in the highway. "What are you going to do, Ghost?"

"Disappear. I've done it many times."

She glanced sidelong at him. "Ever spend any time in Chinatown?"

"I've spent time in several of them. They exist all over the world."

"New York, then."

"Yes."

Pony Girl stared straight ahead, focusing on the strip of gray road fading into the golden brown of the desert. "My father said he once worked with a man called the Chinatown Ghost. That was more than forty years ago. He said that man healed from injuries too. He said . . ." She looked at him again. "That man was a hero."

Jingshen remembered the time his path crossed that of the vigilante hero Dr. Danger. They'd only worked together the one time, but they'd done good, saving the lives of several Chinatown prostitutes and breaking up an opium den. "That man has been gone a long time," he said at last.

"I suppose he disappeared, like you're planning to. He was you, wasn't he?"

"What makes you think that?"

"Look, I may not have been the smartest egghead on the team. That was Javier. And now maybe it's Juice. But seeing the way you heal . . . Aging is just the body breaking down. Wearing out. I ought to know. God, I'm going to be feeling this run tomorrow. I may just rent a car and drive myself home. Me, a goddamn speedster, driving." She laughed bitterly.

"Go on," Jingshen said.

"So if you heal from injuries, you probably heal from aging too. How old are you, Ghost? Fifty? Eighty?"

"I'm . . . quite a bit older than that. More like three hundred and fifty. Give or take." He smiled. "After the second century, specific dates get a little fuzzy."

There was an audible clunk from behind them. Pony Girl glanced in the rear view mirror. "Oh, shit. Check on your friend."

Jingshen started guiltily, realizing he'd forgotten about Zoe. He turned to look and she was asleep or unconscious, her head against the rear window.

A trickle of blood leaked from her ear.

Pony Girl pulled the Scout off onto the dirt shoulder and turned the hazard lights on. Jingshen went around to the back seat to sit beside Zoe. "Go," he said.

"Are you sure?"

"There's nothing I can do to help her while we're sitting here that I couldn't do while you're driving."

"Fair enough. Which direction do you want to go?"

Jingshen thought for a moment. "East to Highway 14," he said at last. "Then south toward Lancaster. If she needs a real doctor, we'll find someone there. Maybe I can find one through my contacts."

"Ghost . . . I can take you as far as Lancaster, but you're on your own from there. I know it's a shitty thing to do, but I've got a parapowered seven-year-old at home who will absolutely run off on her own. I once had to chase her across the southwest because she decided she wanted to go to Disneyland. I need to be home."

"I understand. I appreciate what help you've given me." Jingshen reached down and brushed his fingers across Zoe's cheek, ignoring the sparks that danced across them. "Zoe, can you hear me?"

Zoe murmured something unintelligible but didn't open her eyes. The blood from her ear stopped as quickly as it had started, only dribbling a few drops onto her blouse. Jingshen felt an electric shock roll down his spine as he withdrew from her.

"She may have a cracked skull," Jingshen said. "And that may mean pressure against her brain. We're going to have to get her help. I can't do anything."

"Doctors can wear gloves and make sure they don't touch her," Pony Girl said, lowering the accelerator and pushing the Scout past seventy. "They can help her."

"I have to disclose her power to them. They may refuse to treat her because of it. Even if they do, the word will get back to . . ." He stopped, realizing what he was about to say.

"What? What is it?" Pony Girl asked.

"Pull over as soon as you see someplace that has a pay phone."

* * *

The sun beat down upon Jingshen's shoulders as he punched number after number on the roadside pay phone. He didn't have any change for it, but he did have prepaid phone card and that would suffice. The last digits he keyed were Kobura's number that he'd committed to memory—it felt like a lifetime ago.

Three rings. Four. Five.

"Anything?" Pony Girl called from the driver's seat of the Scout.

Jingshen shook his head. He raised the handset to hang it up when a voice answered at the other end.

"Yes?"

Jingshen cleared his throat. "Kobura, this is the Ghost."

Kobura was silent for several seconds. Jingshen suspected she was probably ordering a trace of the call. "What do you want, Ghost?"

"I want to make a deal."

Kobura's pause was much shorter and felt more like surprise to Jingshen. "I'm . . . listening."

"I want you to cancel the acquisition contract for Zoe."

"And why would I do something like that? We have a lot of money invested in her and are prepared to invest much more."

"She's injured. She needs medical attention."

"Then let us provide it. We already have a team on standby fully trained in protocols surrounding her abilities."

"I won't turn her over to you, but I am prepared to make a conciliatory offer."

Kobura said nothing. Jingshen imagined she was waving at whomever was tracing the call, telling them to hurry. "What can you offer?"

"Myself."

"What?" Pony Girl sat up straighter in surprise, clearly listening in even though she'd pretended not to be.

"Go on," Kobura said.

"You're familiar with my own abilities?"

"I know you have exceptional healing."

"I'm also unaging. I've been alive for over three hundred years. You cancel the contract on Zoe and you can have me. I'll turn myself over to your science team. They can examine me. Test me. For all I care, they can dissect me. Nobody's managed to kill me in three centuries. If they can recreate my powers, imagine the benefits to mankind and the financial reward for Kokorotai. I'll submit to all of it willingly in return for Zoe's freedom."

"I cannot approve this on my own," Kobura said. "Bring her in, and I will guarantee her safety and treatment. I have to go to my superiors."

"Bullshit," Jingshen said. "You're no middle manager. You have the authority to say yes or no. I know you're tracing this call. You give me an answer right now or we disappear and you don't get either of us."

"You're willing to risk her life? She's a stranger to you. A contract. Nothing more, Ghost."

"She's a human being, Kobura, and she deserves the chance to live her life on her own terms, not yours. Hell, I will give her your number. If she decides you can help her more than she can help herself, she can call you. Answer me now, yes or no."

"Yes," Kobura said immediately. "I accept your terms. It won't stop DuraGen from trying to get her back, and I cannot control what they do."

"You let me worry about that."

A note of amusement crept into Kobura's voice. "So heroic of you, Ghost. People are going to talk."

Jingshen ignored her needling. "I'm going to get her some help, and then I'll turn myself over to you."

"What assurances do I have? This could easily be a delaying tactic."

"Write these numbers down." Jingshen rattled off a lengthy series of digits. "That is a Swiss bank account and access code with a balance sufficient to cover the buyout of the contract hiring me and the others. If I don't meet with you in twenty-four hours, drain it."

"What's to stop me from draining it immediately and coming after Zoe anyway?"

Jingshen smiled even though Kobura couldn't see it. "I suppose I will just have to trust you."

"You must truly be as old as reports claim," Kobura said. "No modern man would be so naive as to expect trust when it comes to profit."

"You're Japanese. Are you familiar with the writings of Yamamoto Tsunetomo?"

"You are speaking of *Hagakure*?"

"Yes. I met Tsunetomo while spending some time in Hizen Province. We spent many afternoons drinking tea and discussing philosophy."

"Sounds fascinating," Kobura said, making it clear she thought the opposite.

"He considered *bushido* to be the way of dying instead of the way of living. A samurai should live each day as if he were already dead, prepared to die in an instant in the service of his lord."

"Are you telling me you're a samurai?" Kobura laughed. "More like a ronin, Ghost. A sellsword."

"I don't dispute that, but I can't live as if I were already a dead man. I can't be killed. I always come back. For all I know, I may never die."

"A true immortal."

"Perhaps. Since I can't be prepared to die in the service of my master, I must be prepared to give up other things in an instant. In modern times, that means material goods and wealth. I will leave behind a fortune without a second thought. I have done so many times, and am prepared to do so again. If I dishonor you by breaking our agreement, I lose another fortune and all I can do is start again from nothing. That is far more difficult today than it was fifty or a hundred years ago. It is all I can stake against my word."

Kobura said nothing for several seconds. "You are a peculiar dinosaur," she said at last. "But I find myself believing you. Meet me at this address at eight o'clock tomorrow evening." She gave him an address in Lancaster, obliquely telling Jingshen that she knew exactly where he was and where he was going. "Come with Zoe and nobody else. I will come alone. You will leave with me and Zoe will leave alone with a signed letter guaranteeing her safety from Kokorotai, a copy of which will be retained within corporate records."

"And how can I trust you?"

"You can't, and you shouldn't, because you'd a fool to do so otherwise."

"I've heard fortune favors fools."

"Don't quote Shakespeare at me, Ghost," Kobura chided, and disconnected.

"It's not—" Jingshen sighed as a dial tone emerged from the phone's handset. He turned back to the Scout to find Pony Girl standing before him, arms crossed, a frown creasing her face. "What?"

"You're an idiot, Ghost. You know that?"

"You're not the first person to tell me that. Not even the first one today." Jingshen walked around the car and got into the back seat beside Zoe to check on her.

Pony Girl bent down to glare in through the window at him. "I barely know what's going on in your life, but it sounds to me like you just sold yourself into slavery."

"Something like that," Jingshen admitted.

"And then what, you're expecting someone to rescue you?"

"No. I will accept whatever they choose to do to me."

"What if they kill you?"

"Then I will, at last, be able to rest." He sighed. "People talk about living forever. Books and poems and songs are full of the idea of immortality." He looked up at her. "It's not all it's cracked up to be."

"And you're just going to . . . give that away to this Kobura, whoever she is?"

"It will mean Zoe walks free. I can trade my freedom for hers." He smiled. "I am very patient."

Pony Girl stomped her foot in petulance. "Dammit, Ghost . . . why do you have to be so fucking honorable?"

He shrugged. "It feels right."

"Well, I can't let you just walk into a trap without backup. I'd never have a restful night's sleep again." She stalked over to the pay phone, pulled her wallet from a pouch, and started punching in numbers off a calling card of her own. "Hi, Mom? Can you go over and pick up Sally? I had to leave on an emergency." She listened to the voice on the other end. "Yes, it's superhero stuff . . . Yes, I know I retired . . . Yes, I'll be careful." She looked over at Jingshen. "Tell dad one of his old friends says hello. An old Ghost of a friend."

Chapter Thirteen

September, 1993
Lancaster, California

The sun had already dropped below the San Gabriel mountains when Pony Girl took the Scout off the highway to the first Lancaster exit. Stars poked through the dusty air with the patience and dedication borne of a million years. Jingshen wished he had more time to stand on the outskirts of town and stare into the heavens. Instead, he watched the passing buildings as the Scout rolled along, looking for the right mark.

He spotted his target. "There," he said, pointing to a run-down strip mall. A sports bar at one end was doing brisk evening business for whatever NFL game ESPN was showing. The lot was full of cheap imports and rusty pickups. The Scout wouldn't be particularly noticeable amid the other vehicles. "Park at the far end, away from the bar, and turn off the lights."

Pony Girl pulled into a parking spot and shut off the engine and lights. "Won't someone notice us, all the way over here?"

Jingshen shrugged. "They'll think we came over here to fuck."

Pony Girl cleared her throat. "Just so you know, that's not on the menu"

"How do you feel about breaking and entering?" Jingshen indicated the business in front of them.

Pony Girl looked up through the windshield. "Oh, I'm a huge fan of committing street-level crimes," Pony Girl said, an acidic tone in her voice. "Nothing better."

"I can't take Zoe to a regular hospital. Even if I assume Kobura holds to her word and cancels the contract on Zoe, there's a rival corporation still trying to get her back. They're surely monitoring hospitals and police, trying to catch any hint of where she might be. I won't put any more civilian lives at risk if I can avoid it." Jingshen inclined his head toward the closed dentist office. "That office should have an X-ray machine, painkillers, and surgical tools."

"And of course, you're an X-ray technician and can perform surgery?"

Jingshen shrugged. "You pick up a lot of odd skills over three hundred years. I'm no doctor, but I'm not bad when it comes to battlefield medicine."

"So you're just going to break in right here in plain view of everyone in the lot?"

Jingshen withdrew his multitool from his pocket. "Yes, and here's why. If anybody actually looks in my direction, they won't believe I'm actually breaking in right in full public view. People tend to draw the conclusions they want to. The bottom line is that unless the dentist or his employees happen to be hanging out in that sports bar on a Sunday night, nobody is going to care."

"Three hundred years and that's your best strategy? *Just do it?* You're going to piss off the Nike people."

Jingshen stepped out of the car. "Just keep an eye on Zoe and make sure nobody comes over to interrupt me."

"And what am I supposed to do if they do?"

"Improvise."

"Fuck you, Ghost. I'm retired."

Jingshen walked around to the front of the Scout, unfolding his multitool. He glanced in the direction of the tandem at the end of the strip mall, but as he'd predicted, nobody so much as glanced in his direction. He looked around the edge of the dentist office door, checking for any of the telltale indications of security systems. This was a backwater dentist in a backwater town, and he didn't find anything besides the basic lock.

He popped it open quickly with his tool. He wasn't an exceptional locksmith, but he knew the basics of the trade. After a couple of attempts, the tumblers clicked into place and the deadbolt slid back. He pulled open the door and stepped into the darkened office.

No cameras, not even a motion detector in a top corner of the lobby. For a place that certainly kept narcotic painkillers on hand, the dentist didn't take security seriously in the least. Jingshen clucked his tongue in judgment.

He went back to the door and waved at Pony Girl to come in. She did so in a quick blur of crimson and gold. "Now what? I'm not an experienced criminal."

"Wait here. I'll bring in Zoe, and then we'll X-ray her skull to make sure it's not fractured." He frowned. "If it is, we've got no choice but to turn her in to a hospital. That might save her life, but it will almost certainly get her recaptured. Imprisoned as a medical experiment is no easy to spend the rest of one's life."

"Isn't that what you just offered for yourself?" Pony Girl had a sharp note on her voice.

"Yes," Jingshen admitted. "But it's different for me. I will outlive anything they do to me. Unless I don't." He smiled suddenly. "And actually, I'm all right with that too. I've already lived far more lifetimes than any one person should."

Pony Girl put her hand on his arm. "You've lived a long life, but it's what you do with the extra time you're given that matters. My father said you were a hero. Juice wouldn't have called me to help if you weren't worthy of it. You're a good man, Ghost. Centuries won't change that. Maybe when all this is done, you can join Just Cause."

He shook his head. "I'm not that kind of hero." He turned his back to Pony Girl so he wouldn't have to continue the conversation and went back out to the Scout.

The single dribble of blood from Zoe's ear had not repeated itself. He lifted her in his arms, careful to maintain the appearance of keeping her more or less upright for the benefit of anyone looking in his direction. Nobody seemed to be watching so he moved with quick purpose to get her into the dentist office.

Once they were inside, Pony Girl locked the door and they took Zoe into an examination room to set her in a chair.

"What should I do?" Pony Girl asked. "I can't touch her, and I don't know what to do with anything here."

"Find where they store the drugs. Look for lidocaine and halcion if they have any."

"I know what lidocaine does. What's halcion?"

"Downers. Sleeping pills. If we have to knock her out to do anything more . . . invasive."

"You better not mean surgery, Ghost. There's no way I'm doing that."

"I hope it won't come to that. I'm not qualified to do anything more than quick and dirty battlefield medicine." Jingshen turned on the overhead light and lowered it so he could examine Zoe's head. Despite the discomfort in his fingers, he felt around her head, focusing on the area around the ear that had bled. He found a large swelling behind her ear, hidden by her hair until exposed by the bright dental light. The skin was reddish purple with bruising and shiny from the pressure beneath it. He grimaced. He'd seen injuries like that before. At the very least, the pressure would have to be relieved. He went to rummage through the drawers along one wall, searching for appropriate tools.

Pony Girl returned bearing a couple of syringes and some ampoules of medication. "Novocaine and halcion. How is she?"

"She's got swelling behind her ear. We need to X-ray it to make sure there's no swelling beneath the skull."

"What happens if—no, don't answer that. You'll probably say we have to drill a hole in her head."

Jingshen looked down to see he was holding a dentist's drill.

Pony Girl's face went pale. "Oh God, I'm gonna throw up."

Jingshen set the drill on the counter top. "Let's just do the X-ray for right now." He opened a tall cabinet and withdrew the X-ray camera on its articulated armature. He covered Zoe's torso with the lead-lined smock, turned her head to expose the swelling behind her ear, and pointed the camera at it. Pony Girl paced back and forth at nervous super-speed while Jingshen took pictures.

After taking the third picture, he looked over at Pony Girl. "Do you know how to develop film?"

She shook her head.

"Then you'll have to keep waiting."

Her sigh was loud.

Jingshen took the photo plates into the dentist's darkroom and went through the painstaking process of developing each one. Developer fluid, fixer, rinse. He hung them to dry, then slipped past the curtain and out of the darkroom to check on Zoe.

The swelling behind her ear was darkening into a bruise. She was still unconscious, which worried him.

"What do you think?" Pony Girl asked. "You still sure we shouldn't take her to a hospital instead?"

"No, I'm not sure," he said. "If we do, we're putting dozens of innocent bystanders at risk. You saw the trio sent to recover her. I promise you DuraGen will send others They will want their cash cow back. The first group found her so quickly that I'm sure she won't stay hidden for long from the next team. They're certainly searching for her already."

"You think they're going to come here?"

Jingshen nodded. "The faster we can resolve this, the better it will be for everyone."

"How are you going to stop DuraGen? You made a deal with the other company but you can't very well give yourself to them too."

He frowned. That was the part of his plan he hadn't yet figured out. "I'm not sure," he admitted. "We have to make her disappear in such a way that they won't come after her."

"That means you need to fake her death,"

"Yes. Do you have any ideas how to do that?"

"No. This is outside my area of expertise. I run fast and hit things."

The thought of Warhorse came to him unbidden. The Source had hired the powerful mercenary to come after Jingshen. If his mission could somehow be redirected, that might be the best bet. It would take a large financial incentive and involve buying off the Source contract. Kokorotai would have to put up more capital. Kobura wasn't going to be happy. Jingshen hoped the woman wouldn't go back on her word. "I'll figure something out."

Jingshen went back to retrieve the x-rays and examined them under the light in the office.

Pony Girl crowded in behind him, peering past his shoulder at the images. "What are we looking at here?"

He pointed to the images. "This white part is her skull. That's brain tissue. This gray mass here is fluid buildup. It looks like she might have a crack in her skull."

"Are we going to have to drill a hole?"

"I don't think so. We'll drain the fluid to reduce pressure and reduce the risk of it getting beneath the skull and that will have to do."

"Tell me that's an easy process."

"It is. I just need a clean, empty syringe."

"I can do that." Pony Girl flashed from the room to retrieve the requested item. In a moment, she returned bearing a syringe wrapped in plastic. Jingshen removed it from its packaging and placed it into the dentist's autoclave. He went to wash his hands and put on gloves and a surgical mask while the autoclave sterilized the syringe. The package had a label that it was pre-sterilized, but Jingshen didn't trust it.

Once the autoclave was finished, he took the syringe and carefully inserted it into the swelling. A centimeter of cloudy, pinkish fluid withdrew into the chamber. Zoe moaned a little. "Hold still," he said softly. "I apologize for the pain. I'll take care of it shortly." He changed the syringe's angle and managed to pull out an additional couple of milliliters of fluid before removing the syringe completely.

"Did you get it?" Pony Girl asked

"Yes, I think so." He dropped the syringe into the container the dentist's office had for used needles and took up the novocaine syringe.

"Didn't you just drain all that fluid and now you're putting some back?"

"Yes, but to help with the pain."

"Do you really know what you're doing?"

Jingshen looked up at Pony Girl, whose arms were crossed and face was plain with suspicion.

"Sometimes."

* * *

Jingshen had long ago trained himself to awaken at a scheduled time. When alarm clocks had finally been invented, he felt grateful not to need them. The jangling bells inevitably launched him into full battle readiness when it wasn't required. It was an unpleasant way to begin one's day and ruined the benefits of rest. Many inventions over the course of his life he'd found beneficial; alarm clocks were not one of them.

His eyes opened at the time he'd picked, just before sunrise. The dentist office was quiet. Zoe slept in the chair beside him. She'd awakened briefly after he'd dosed her with the novocaine and said she was thirsty. He gave her water and a halcion tablet to help her rest and she was unconscious again. Pony Girl had curled up like a cat in one of the lobby chairs and was still asleep when Jingshen walked in from the back. "Pony Girl," he said softly, repeating it a little louder each time until she stirred.

"Oh, hey," she said, and grimaced. "It tastes like a cat shit in my mouth. What time is it?"

"Early. We need to leave."

"At least I can brush my teeth here," she said, and stretched. "How's Zoe?"

"Resting. Her swelling is lower today. I think she will be all right."

"Good." Pony Girl disappeared into the bathroom while Jingshen looked into the lot in the pre-dawn light. Their Scout was undisturbed where they'd parked it.

"Do you want to leave?" Jingshen asked as Pony Girl returned. "You don't have to stay with me. I've got this from here. Go home to your daughter."

"Believe me, I'd love to," Pony Girl said, "but a promise is a promise. What's your name, Ghost? Your real name?"

"Jingshen."

"I'm Faith. Nice to meet you behind the mask at last. Or maybe that should be under the hat. What's the story with the hat?"

Jingshen shrugged. "I like the style."

Pony Girl nodded. "Not all costumes have to be armorplast and spandex. It works for you."

"I'll bring out Zoe. We need to drive back to L.A."

"On a Monday morning. I hope you don't have any other plans today."

"No. Go on out to the car. I need a moment and then I'll bring out Zoe."

Pony Girl checked the lot for anyone who might be watching before leaving the dentist's office and stepping back into the Scout.

Jingshen went into the dentist's main office, identifiable as such by the diplomas and licenses hanging framed in the walls. He handwrote a brief note on a plain piece of paper: *I apologize for the damage and use of your supplies.* He slipped the note along with five hundred dollars into an envelope, wrote the dentist's name in it, and set it on the center of the desk.

He'd spent his bankroll profligately over the past few days. He had barely a thousand dollars remaining. It was fortunate he wouldn't need it after turning himself in to Kokorotai.

Zoe was still asleep. With time to prepare himself and materials at hand, Jingshen pulled on a pair of surgical gloves and lifted Zoe without her skin contacting his. He carried her out to the Scout and set her in the back seat. "Let's go," he said to Pony Girl.

Pony Girl shifted gears and took the Scout back onto the streets of Lancaster.

Chapter Fourteen

September, 1993
Lancaster, California

Pony Girl took them north of town to the undeveloped highlands. With Jingshen's help, she locked the Scout's wheel hubs and put it into four-wheel drive. They went deep into the hills and parked in a windblown arroyo nobody would find unless they were flying directly overhead and looking down.

"You going to have anyone flying after you?" Pony Girl asked as if she were reading Jingshen's mind.

Jingshen shrugged. "I don't know who we'll see next."

"You're sure it will be someone, though?"

"I don't doubt it. Zoe is worth a lot of money to DuraGen, and there's a contract on my head as well. We're both pretty popular right now, unfortunately."

Pony Girl shook her head. "You ever think maybe you're in the wrong line of work? Life's too short to have so many enemies."

"Not for me."

Pony Girl laughed. "I guess that's true. It's going to get hot and dry here, and we're going to be hungry if we're waiting all day until your meeting tonight. Think I'll jog back into town for some supplies." She slipped out of the driver's seat.

"Dressed like that? You're going to announce our presence to the world."

"I didn't exactly pack a change of clothes," she said. "Give me your coat. It's not ideal, but it's probably the best we can manage under the circumstances."

Jingshen shrugged out of his black coat and passed it over to Pony Girl. She slipped her arms into it and fastened it tightly around her waist and legs. "Running in this thing is going to be like wearing a sail."

"Like you said, it's the best we can manage . . . under the circumstances."

Pony Girl laughed. "I did say that. You know, Ghost, you almost make me miss this life. Almost." She turned to leave, then paused. "You got cash? If I use my credit card, it can be tracked."

Jingshen handed her a twenty dollar bill.

She tucked it deep into a pocket. "That'll work. Any preferences in particular?"

Jingshen smiled. "Something that travels well."

Pony Girl disappeared in a flash, leaving a swirling cloud of dust in her wake.

Jingshen waited until the dust settled before opening the back door of the Scout and sitting beside Zoe. Her breathing was slow and regular. Her face was serene, the kind of innocence reserved for young children and ingenues. He shut his eyes, not quite falling asleep, but maximizing his rest while retaining a sufficient level of awareness.

The wind blew across the arroyo, carrying occasional streams of dust skittering across the Scout's hood. Beside Jingshen, Zoe coughed suddenly and groaned. Jingshen opened his eyes and turned to see her eyes were open and she was looking at him.

"Hey, Jones," she said in a voice thick with sleep and dehydration. "What's up?"

"We're waiting."

"For what?"

"Pony Girl. She went to get us food and water. She'll be back soon."

"Oh, she's still around?" Zoe yawned. "Good. I'm thirsty."

"How do you feel?"

"I've been a lot better. What's the plan? Where are we going?" Zoe felt at the abused lump behind her ear and winced.

"Lancaster. I've . . . made a deal."

Zoe narrowed her eyes. "What kind of deal, Jones? Are you turning me in?"

"No. The opposite, actually. I'm making an arrangement for Kokorotai to leave you alone after today." Jingshen was being intentionally vague and he hated himself for it. Zoe deserved better than that.

"What about the other company? The one that already had me? What about DuraGen, Jones?"

Jingshen shook his head. "I'm still figuring that part out. I need to convince them it's a lost cause to come after you."

"How are you going to do that?"

He shrugged. "Faking your death seems like the best option."

Zoe blinked. "How are you going to do that?"

"Creatively."

A rapid patter of approaching footsteps preceded a blast of air as Pony Girl returned. "What are you going to do creatively? Or should I be sorry I asked?" She handed Jingshen and Zoe each a bottle of water.

"Fake my death," Zoe said as she opened her water.

"Yep, sorry I asked." Pony Girl pulled some plastic-wrapped gas station sandwiches from the inside pocket of her borrowed coat and some bags of chips from the hip pockets.

"It's the only way to ensure DuraGen doesn't come after Zoe. We have to convince them she's dead."

"How do you plan to do that without a body?" Pony Girl popped her bag of chips open.

"A body?" Zoe asked.

"I wouldn't believe anyone was dead without a body," Pony Girl replied, crunching a potato chip. "Especially if I had a sizable investment in them."

"It would require an incident which wouldn't leave a body behind," Jingshen said thoughtfully. "Like an explosion."

"Any explosion powerful enough to vaporize a human body is one I'm not going to let you set off without some kind of assurances," Pony Girl said.

"I thought you were retired," Jingshen said.

"Yet here I am."

"I don't have any explosives handy," Jingshen pointed out, neglecting to mention he knew enough about bombs and demolitions to work without them.

"You seem like a resourceful type, Ghost. I'll thank you not to blow shit up."

"I'll do my best."

"Can't they, like, identify bodies by their dental records? I saw that on TV," Zoe said.

"When's the last time you went to the dentist?" Jingshen asked.

Zoe shrugged. "I don't know. Maybe I was a kid?"

"Then they're not going to identify you by dental records. Besides, if we do it right, they'll have no reason to think you're anything but dead."

Pony Girl balled up the plastic wrap that had covered her sandwich and stuck it into her empty chip bag. "You don't have any convenient illusion powers or anything, do you? Either of you?"

"No." Jingshen drank his water. "Do you?"

"I'm a speedster, Ghost."

"You never know if you don't ask."

"Well, I don't have any powers like that," Zoe said.

"Can you give them to someone? Don't you give people powers?"

"I don't have any control over it. If I did, I'd be a millionaire. Most of the people I give powers to die before they can figure out how to use them, if they even can."

"That's not very helpful," Pony Girl said.

"Oh, my bad," Zoe sneered.

"You're too young to be so cynical."

"And you're too much of a celebrity to know what it's really like for poor assholes like me."

Jingshen cleared his throat, trying to broker peace before the two women came to blows over their differences. "We'll work it out," Jingshen said. "Perhaps Kobura will have resources that can assist us."

"You're trusting a corporate stooge?" Pony Girl laughed. "Three hundred years old and you're still that naive?"

"No, I don't trust her. That's why we have to make Zoe disappear."

"Fair enough, but no blowing shit up," Pony Girl said.

"I promise nothing."

* * *

The address Kobura had given him was yet another abandoned industrial facility. Instead of a warehouse, this one was a refinery. It was on the southern edge of town, just off the frontage road for Highway 14. The conglomeration of tanks and towering stacks was strangely quiet but for the wind whistling around the pipes. Jingshen examined it through some binoculars they'd found in the Scout.

"This is bad," the superhero said. "You're going to walk in that area and they're going to kill you and take Zoe anyway."

"I'm trusting you to make sure the latter doesn't happen," Jingshen said without lowering the binoculars. "They'll find me hard to kill. That's the entire point of me turning myself over to them."

"Well it's a stupid idea. I think you'll be better off on the run."

"You're a speedster. Of course you'd think that. No, they'll find us. Nobody can hide forever, especially nowadays. There are parahumans out there who could track me down in minutes. All they need is a large enough paycheck."

"Then what's your plan?" The color in Pony Girl's cheeks suggested Jingshen's speedster comment hadn't gone unnoticed.

"I'm going to appeal to Kobura's better side to . . ." Jingshen paused as he saw the vehicle pull up to the refinery's front office. Kobura emerged. She apparently had a key to the office door for she opened it easily and stepped inside, leaving behind the growing dusk.

He lowered the binoculars and must have had a peculiar expression on his face, for Pony Girl asked him what was wrong.

"I'm not sure," he said, truthfully. "But I believe you are correct that this is a trap. Kobura is much earlier than I would have expected."

"So now you're going to bail out, right? Shit, Ghost, go to New York. Appeal to Juice and the rest of Just Cause. Get help against these bastards and get Zoe the help she needs. I bet Doc Devereaux in Paris could fix her right up."

Pony Girl was speaking of the Institute of Parahuman Medicine in Paris. Jingshen had intentionally stayed away for the same reason he was now planning to turn himself over to Kokorotai. His own ability would make him a prime candidate for medical research.

"No, I need to resolve this now. I'm not sure Zoe would survive a cross-country trip with the kind of people coming after her that DuraGen has sent."

"They're not going to kill me," Zoe said. "I'm worth too much."

"You have no control over your powers," Jingshen said softly. "Therefore you may not need to be conscious for their research purposes. Or mobile."

"Jesus, Ghost," Pony Girl said. "That's pretty grim."

"These are the kind of people we're dealing with."

"So what are you going to do, then? Kobura's here and it looked like she came alone, like you wanted. Maybe you can get this resolved right now."

"Maybe," Jingshen admitted. "Still, I would feel better if you and Zoe moved to a different location after I leave so I truly don't know where you are. There are almost certainly telepaths on the hunt for her and I'd rather not make it any easier for them."

"I can do that," Pony Girl said "What if we're right and this turns out to be a trap? You'll be captured and they'll probably still be hunting for Zoe."

"I will abide. I always do. You should take Zoe and run. Find the deepest, darkest hole you can and disappear into it."

"You know, I'm pretty annoyed with you for getting me into this," Pony Girl said. "I'm retired."

Jingshen gave her a tight smile. "You're bad at it."

Chapter Fifteen

September, 1993
Lancaster, California

The lights burned in the refinery office as Jingshen cautiously approached the facility from across the road. The breeze made his long coat blow around his legs as he moved from shadow to shadow, keeping as well hidden as he could. The office was a two-story building adjacent to a large warehouse that must have been for equipment storage when the refinery was still functioning.

Jingshen hadn't seen anyone else come to the refinery, either by vehicle or on foot, since he'd begun his own approach. Perhaps Kobura had truly followed through and come alone, but somehow he doubted anything would be so simple and upfront with devious corporate types.

The doors into the offices were top-to-bottom smoked glass. Anyone within the building watching the entrance would see him there. All his sneaking up to this point no longer mattered as he would be exposed the moment he stepped from cover to open the door.

He stood as tall as he could, adjusted his hat to his favorite jaunty angle, and marched straight to the doors from his hiding spot. He kept his hands outside his pockets, visibly empty to all watchers. The doors were unlocked and he pulled one open to step into the building. It faced a reception lobby, well-lit but abandoned. There were faded spots on the walls where pictures might have once hung, and the receptionist desk had a dingy patina of dust marring its polished granite finish. Behind the desk, a camera regarded him with its single dark lens. A baleful red light indicated it was active.

"Ghost?" Kobura's voice crackled from the speaker on the desktop phone.

"Yes," he said.

"Come into the warehouse. Straight back through the hall. I'll meet you there."

Jingshen passed through the offices along the central hall. Most of the office doors were shut with blank nameplates giving no indication to whom they might have belonged. A couple doors were open and within them, Jingshen saw offices stripped of furnishings and decorations, just bare rooms with vinyl floors and cheap stucco ceilings.

Another camera perched over the door leading into the warehouse, watching his progress along the hall. He kept his brim pulled down and his head down. Kobura could see he was alone. He was about to enslave himself to her. She didn't need to stare down at him as well. The door to the warehouse was steel with only a vertical window over the handle, crisscrossed with a lattice of wires suspended within the glass. Jingshen turned the knob and pushed it open.

The warehouse was dark and dusty, with only a few pools of light from overhead sodium arc lamps. The warehouse floor was empty of equipment and crates, an unbroken expanse of stained and dusty concrete. Catwalks overhead reminded Jingshen of the warehouse where he had first met Zoe. It seemed like a lifetime ago, even though it had barely been a week.

Kobura stood in one of the pools of light. She wore a charcoal and dove gray business suit offset by a golden silk scarf knotted loosely about her neck. Both her hands were clasped atop the head of her cane as Jingshen approached. A modern mobile telephone sat on a chair beside her, its antenna extended, ready for use.

"Welcome, Ghost," she said.

"Kobura," Jingshen said. He didn't trust her, and was content to let her guide things until he knew for sure what was going on.

"So, here we are," she said in her husky voice, clearly expecting him to make the first move.

He wouldn't be baited. "Yes. As we agreed." He spread his hands wide to show he was unarmed. "Your move."

"Where's the girl?" Kobura asked.

"I do not know," Jingshen said, assuming Pony Girl had indeed relocated with Zoe since he departed. "That wasn't the arrangement."

"I'm altering the arrangement. Turn her over and you're free to go."

"I saw that movie, Kobura. You're no Darth Vader."

Kobura blinked and her cheeks darkened. "Enough games, Ghost. Give me the girl. Now."

"No." Jingshen felt his nerves sparking, sensing the trap was about to be sprung. "The deal was she goes free."

Kobura's face twisted into a smile. Her hand blurred in a remarkably swift speed-draw, whipping a pistol from within the folds of her coat, and pumping four bullets into him.

All four bullets struck the same spot, punching through his throat and severing his spinal cord. Jingshen felt no pain as he fell to the floor, gasping to draw breath through a ruined windpipe. Blood filled his mouth and flooded his lungs. He choked and gagged, unable to feel anything except the panic of suffocation.

Kobura appeared in his field of vision, standing over him with a look of smug satisfaction across her face. She held her cane lightly upon one shoulder. "That is the damnedest thing to see," she said as she regarded Jingshen's body trying to heal itself from the massive damage she'd wrought upon it. "I bet that hurts like a son of a bitch."

Jingshen couldn't move his lips to curse her out. He could barely even focus his eyes upon her. Once again, he'd suffered wounds that should have killed him, but his body refused to let him pass into the peaceful beyond. The severed nerves in the ruin of his spine ensured he felt nothing but the disquiet and panic as his lungs filled with his own blood. If Kobura did nothing worse to him, it would be perhaps hours before he was able to return to action as required.

She bent to take his hat. Then she brushed the spatters of his blood into the felt until they were unrecognizable as such, and set it upon her own head at a rakish angle. "Suits me, don't you think?" She put a hand up to her ear. "What's that? Speak up, dude." She chuckled at her own joke.

Jingshen made small gurgling sound but couldn't manage anything else.

Kobura tucked her cane into the top of his shirt where it slowly became coated with his blood. She reached down to take his limp hands and started dragging him across the floor. "You know, Ghost, I'm truly sorry this is the way things worked out. We could have been a hell of a team, you and I. There's a lot of money to be made out there doing this shit. You would know that better than most." She grunted as she tugged him back behind a hulking abandoned machine of unidentifiable purpose. "I know this isn't going to kill you, and I'm kind of glad about that. It'd be like destroying a piece of art." Her face and body rearranged into a mirror image of Jingshen's own, skin reshaping to match his clothing. "Although, to be fair, I'll do a lot of awful shit if the price is right."

Still unable to move, Jingshen could do nothing but blink his eyes furiously, over and over again. Somehow, Nobody Special had survived the horrific car crash a few days earlier and appeared no worse for the wear.

The impostor smiled at Jingshen, apparently divining the question in his gaze. "You're probably wondering how I'm not dead. Funny thing about what happens when I load a new body. It reduces any injuries I've suffered. Each time I change, I get better. It's not as fancy as your power, but it keeps me upright and breathing." He chuckled. "Let me tell you, I had to blow through almost everyone I had stored to come back from that one. Lucky I didn't die." He paused. "Well . . . not so lucky for you."

Keep talking, Jingshen thought. He could feel his nerves knitting back together by the way flickers of pain raced through his body that had been numb moments ago.

"I know we're not supposed to shit where we eat, but this was just too good a chance to pass up," Nobody Special said. "I tapped a mole in Kokorotai when I first got wind of this job. He's been feeding me information for weeks. That's how I knew you'd be here. I figure Kobura's going to show with a big payday for you and you're turning the kid over to her." He grinned. It was unnerving for Jingshen to see his own smile reflected at him on someone else's form. "I'll get paid twice. First as you, then I take Kobura out, then DuraGen pays me to return the kid to them. Then I think I'll take a long vacation. Somewhere tropical with underage girls who'll do anything for a twenty dollar bill, you know what I mean? 'Course you do."

Keep talking, Jingshen repeated to himself like a mantra. He knew he would heal and it was only a matter of time before he could move sufficiently to kill Nobody Special. Until then, he would suffer in silence.

Whistling, Nobody Special disappeared from Jingshen's view. Jingshen closed his eyes, trying to speed his body's natural healing process—as if such a thing were possible despite all his years of experience to the contrary.

Nobody Special returned to Jingshen's side. He held a hammer and tent spikes up to show Jingshen. "Sorry. I know you're going to heal eventually no matter what I do to you, and I can't have you fucking up my plan. At first, I was thinking, why not burn you to a crisp? I figure you've had that done to you before. But you didn't tell me where the girl is, and I don't have however long it takes you to come back from that kind of massive trauma. Same reason I'm not decapitating you."

Keep talking.

Nobody Special stretched out one of Jingshen's arms and drove the spike through it. Jingshen felt the pain faintly, as if he'd been numbed by an anesthetic. The second spike went through his opposite wrist and two more went through his ankles, leaving him spread-eagled on the floor. Nobody Special stepped back to admire his handiwork. "Damn, that's got to be uncomfortable as shit." He pulled a digital camera from a pocket. "You mind? I kind of like to keep a scrapbook. You know, something to show my grandkids someday." He raised the camera and it clicked a couple times.

He put the camera away and checked his watch. "Well, looks like I've got just enough time to clean up my mess before my first payday shows up." He winked at Jingshen. "Don't go anywhere."

* * *

While Nobody Special worked elsewhere on the warehouse floor, Jingshen lay where he'd been staked. He knew the exact moment his spinal nerves reconnected. One moment he was in mild discomfort and the next was filled with excruciating pain. He still gasped and choked as his lungs and stomach struggled to eject the blood he'd swallowed and inhaled due to the throat wound. His larynx was still a shredded ruin and he couldn't have cried out in agony even if he'd wanted to. His wrists and ankles were on fire from the spikes holding him down. Nobody Special had staked him with professional skill, leaving him stretched out in such a way that he couldn't lever himself free.

He kept his coughs as quiet as he could to avoid attracting Nobody Special's attention. Every cough sent spasms of wracking pain from head to toe, fingertip to fingertip. When he discovered he could turn his head, he did so and spat out mouthful after mouthful of thick, chunky blood. He saw he'd been nailed down onto a large pallet of some kind and that gave him hope that he might be able to free himself.

All it would take was more grievous injury.

At last, his lungs and stomach stopped clenching and he found he could breathe without gagging on his own blood. Every breath pulled at the stakes holding his wrists. The pain alternated between the burning hot of trauma and the icy sting of metal upon nerves.

Footsteps approached and Jingshen turned his head back to face straight up, as if he hadn't moved it at all. Nobody Special appeared, still wearing Jingshen's hat and a crooked grin. "So how are we doing?" He knelt beside Jingshen and tweaked the stakes holding down his limbs. Fresh waves of pain made tears spill from Jingshen's eyes. "Dude, I bet that's painful as shit. I'd probably cry too. I'm sure glad it isn't me." His face took on a hard cast. "This is what you get for smacking me with those fucking sticks. Asshole." He bent and placed a strip of duct tape across Jingshen's mouth. "Just in case you get any ideas about trying to warn Kobura." He checked his watch again. "Speaking of which, I should get into position. It's too bad you and me can't work together on this. This is a beautiful con, and I'm going to be laughing all the way to the bank."

Keep talking.

Nobody Special disappeared again, his whistle fading into the distance.

Jingshen swallowed his pain, grateful that he could, and waited for several minutes until he was sure Nobody Special wasn't coming right back. While he waited, his body continued repairing itself. His throat wound closed and stopped leaking blood, which was good, but his wrists and ankles also healed around the spikes through them, which wasn't good at all. He was going to damage himself to get free. It was nothing he hadn't done countless times in the past, but it took a special kind of fatalism to repeatedly injure oneself.

Fortunately, the spikes through his extremities didn't have large heads, which would have meant he'd need to cause far worse trauma. He steeled himself against the approaching agony and began to flex his right tricep, trying to push his hand further away from his body. His muscles and skin slowly ripped as he forced the spike further up his arm. A tendon let go with an audible pop and blood sprayed from the fresh wound he opened. Another tendon tore and his fingers flopped bonelessly, leaving him unable to move his hand at all. He clenched his teeth against the pain, wishing he had a leather strap to bite upon, for the next part would be even harder.

His shoulder protested at the resistance the spike offered as he struggled to raise his arm off the pallet. Ever so slowly, muscles aching with fatigue and toxins, Jingshen's arm came up fraction of inch by fraction of inch. When he'd raised it as far as he could, the head of the spike resting against the flesh of his forearm, he dropped it back down. He had maybe three inches of play. Before his flesh had a chance to knit back together, he raised his arm again, as fast and hard as he could. Flesh tore and blood fountained as the head of the spike ripped through his forearm, passing between his radius and ulna, and out the bottom.

A tiny moan escaped his lips despite his best efforts to keep silent. His body felt more abused than it had been in many years—since he'd been a soldier in World War I. Forcing himself to inflict even more self-harm was damaging on every level from emotional to psychological to physical.

Blood soaked through his sleeve as he held his arm against his chest, willing it to stop hurting. He knew it wouldn't, but if he could convince himself it would, he might make it through the process of freeing himself from the remaining three spikes.

His freed hand didn't want to work right while the tendons reconnected and his flesh regenerated. He was terribly thirsty, and his stomach clenched from the amount of blood he'd swallowed. His ears rang, an artifact from the bullets that had torn through his throat. The buzzing would disappear—eventually—until then, it was distracting to a fault.

At last, using his free hand to brace himself, he ripped his other hand free. The pain made his vision gray out and he lost track of himself. He'd lost blood faster than his healing could reproduce it, and he was literally running on empty. It would take time—more time than he knew he had—to get himself fully healed. Kobura was walking into a trap. As smart as she seemed to be, Nobody Special was one devious son of a bitch and the shapeshifter might just pull one over on the corporate shark.

Eyes rolling in his head, Jingshen struggled to make his hands work well enough to try to free his legs. He couldn't tear them free as the spikes were too close to his ankles. He wiggled one of the spikes loose from the pallet wood. It was slick from his blood, but he used it as a pry bar to release first one leg and then the other. He'd have loved nothing more than to close his eyes and sleep. The exhaustion and pain and blood loss had taken a tremendous toll. It would have killed someone without his healing ability. At times like this, it was far more a curse than a boon.

He waited until the wounds in his arms and legs stopped dribbling blood—less because they'd healed and more because he had virtually no blood left. Once they'd healed enough,   started resolutely crawling toward the shadows where he hoped he could disappear before Nobody Special found him.

Chapter Sixteen

September, 1993
Lancaster, California

Jingshen managed to heave his broken, battered body up a staircase. He dragged himself along a gantry until he was lying in the overhead shadows, watching the warehouse floor below. It gave him a sense of déjà vu, for the entire incident had began similarly. Below, Nobody Special walked around the abandoned machine behind which he'd sequestered Jingshen, whistling softly. He froze when he saw the blood-soaked pallet with no sign of his captive. His pistol came out immediately and he twisted his face into a wry smile Jingshen had never made with his own face.

"Huh," Nobody Special said, as if it explained everything. He looked at his watch. "Still got time." He raised his voice and called, "Come out, come out, wherever you are."

Jingshen was no fool; he said nothing. The best thing he could do was to remain silent and still, allowing his body to use every bit of energy to heal him.

"Where you at, Ghost?" Nobody Special called. "You couldn't have got far. I made sure of that. What'd you do, chew your arms and legs off?" He chuckled. "That's what wild animals do, Ghost."

From overhead, Jingshen watched as Nobody Special made a cursory search of the immediate area around where he'd been spiked down. The shapeshifter paid special attention to the drying blood trails Jingshen left when he'd crawled away.

"Yoo-hoo!" Nobody Special called in a tremulous falsetto. "Where'd you go, chop-socky?"

He stopped at the staircase Jingshen had ascended and looked toward the top, pistol unwavering.

"You didn't actually go up there, did you? That's the best you could come up with?" Nobody Special ascended the first step and Jingshen tensed, waiting for the inevitable discovery. With Nobody Special looking in his direction, the shadows wouldn't hide him if he moved.

A clear beeping came from Nobody Special. He took another step but the insistent beeping continued. "Shit," the shapeshifter said at last and pushed a button on his watch. He glanced up into the shadows. "Don't fuck with me, Ghost. I bet if I can't kill you outright, I'll find someone who can."

Keep talking.

Nobody Special moved to the center of the warehouse floor, standing in a pool of dingy light from the dust-caked overhead halogens. He clasped his hands behind his back and stood with his head tilted forward, hat hiding his face in shadow.

The glow of headlights appeared through the frosted warehouse windows facing the street. They shut off and the door from the front lot opened a moment later to reveal a shadowy figure in a long coat with a cane. If it wasn't Kobura, Jingshen thought, it was a convincing fake.

She walked slowly across the floor to halt at the edge of the next pool of light. She wore a dark business suit with a gray overcoat, very similar to the outfit she'd sported the first time Jingshen saw her. The scarf knotted around her throat was lemon yellow. "That's far enough, Kobura," Nobody Special called. "Send away your security men."

"I came alone, Ghost," Kobura replied. "I have no need of security men."

Jingshen heard the half-smile in Nobody Special's voice. "You're not afraid I'll try something?"

"I'm not afraid of you." Kobura matched Nobody Special with a half-smile of her own.

"Did you bring it? The letter?"

Kobura nodded. She reached into her coat and Nobody Special whipped his pistol out from behind his back. "Easy, there."

Kobura didn't move, keeping her hand inside her coat. "You're afraid I'll shoot you?"

"I don't know what you're planning. Take it out, whatever it is, nice and slow."

She withdrew a white envelope and held it up for his review. "It's the letter you asked me to bring."

"And what about the money?"

Kobura's brow wrinkled. "What money?"

"The—" A tremendous bang echoed through the warehouse and a crater appeared in the warehouse floor, cement dust exploding upward in a gray mushroom cloud. The explosion knocked Kobura off her feet. Nobody Special remained strangely upright, swaying slightly with an expression of surprise frozen on his stolen face.

A basketball-sized hole had appeared in his torso.

* * *

For the eternity of a second, everything was silent and frozen but for the ringing echo of the projectile's impact upon the floor and the pattering of pebbles and blood droplets. Then a scream rent the air as Nobody Special collapsed into a bloody heap. "No-o-o!"

Zoe ran across the floor toward Nobody Special. Kobura stepped backward toward the shadows but Pony Girl appeared beside her, holding Nobody Special's pistol against the executive's head.

"Don't move," the speedster ordered.

Kobura raised her hands without seeming particularly upset about it.

"He'll heal, right?" Zoe cried. "He heals. That's his thing, right?" She knelt beside Nobody Special, her hands fluttering around him as if she wanted to touch him but knew she shouldn't. "Why isn't he healing?"

"Call him off, Kobura," Pony Girl ordered.

"Call who off?" Kobura asked.

"Your shooter," Pony Girl hissed.

"He's not mine," Kobura said. "I suggest you deal with him, superhero."

The ground shook with a heavy impact, but it wasn't another gunshot. A large figure Jingshen hadn't seen previously dropped from an overhead support beam. A chill ran down his healing spine. Tens of thousands of people had tried to kill him over the past three centuries. If anyone was going to succeed, it would be the man called Warhorse.

Warhorse was a huge man, of a size that would have made even Rook appear petite were they side by side. Jingshen had never seen him in person, and knew he would never forget Warhorse if he lived another thousand years or more. The man must have been over seven feet tall, with gargantuan boots that only added more inches to his height. His ruddy skin and straight black ponytail spoke of his Apache ancestry. He was super-strong, super-tough, and if rumors were to be believed, one of the wealthiest men in the world. He could have lived in seclusion on a privately-owned island, enjoying the fruits of his wealth were he so inclined, but he would have found that a boring existence.

He eschewed body armor, wearing only a black t-shirt stretched tightly across his massive chest and combat fatigues. A bandoleer of shells the size of soup cans was slung over one shoulder. As he landed, he was loading one into some kind of hybrid weapon like the bastardized offspring of a sawed-off shotgun and a man-portable rocket launcher. He snapped the weapon shut and held it with the barrel facing skyward. His eyes were covered by aviator mirror shades and he rolled a toothpick around his mouth. He might have glanced in Pony Girl's direction but his attention seemed primarily focused on the bloody ruin that had been Nobody Special.

Zoe screamed and scrambled backward as Warhorse stepped closer. The cement behind him was cracked where he'd landed.

"I'm retired, goddammit," Pony Girl said to nobody in particular.

"Don't move, either of you." Warhorse produced a second pistol from a thigh holster and pointed it behind him toward Pony Girl and Kobura. Jingshen knew it was impossible to aim accurately at two targets so far apart— the man wasn't even *looking* in Pony Girl's direction!—but somehow, Warhorse gave the impression that not only *could* he do it, he was deadly accurate with it. "You, skinny," he motioned with the business end of the weapon he pointed toward Nobody Special and Zoe. "Get on your knees and put your hands behind your head."

Zoe complied, tears streaming down her face.

"He's not healing," Warhorse said, observing the spreading puddle of blood beneath Nobody Special's body and the complete lack of movement. "*Goddammit, I said don't move!*" The pistol he had aimed behind him roared and a section of warehouse wall exploded outward.

"Jesus fucking Christ!" Pony Girl shouted as shrapnel and debris rained down.

Warhorse turned so his pistol pointed toward Zoe and Nobody Special was now behind him so he could look directly at Pony Girl and Kobura. "The next one goes through your head, Pony Girl. I know how fast you are and you can't beat a shell at this range. Not even if you were twenty years younger."

"He's got some kind of tech or power," Kobura said softly. "He can see in all directions."

"All right, all right," Pony Girl said. "Fine, you made your point. Look, you came for the Ghost, right? Well, you bagged him. Cut off your trophy or take your picture or whatever kind of fucked-up thing you do to prove you got him and walk away. I'll let you."

Warhorse snorted. "*Let*? You don't *let* me do anything. You can't stop me."

"You might be surprised," Pony Girl growled.

"H-he's still not healing," Zoe said, her voice quavering. "I've seen how he heals. He should be."

"That's because it's not the Ghost," Warhorse said without looking at her. "Where is he?"

"What do you mean it's not the Ghost?" Pony Girl asked, aghast. "Who's this, then?"

"That son of a bitch . . ." Kobura murmured. "Nobody Special."

"Who?"

"I hired him—originally—to retrieve the asset." She tipped her head toward Zoe. "He decided to double cross me and my company."

"Looks like he got what was coming to him," Warhorse said. "That doesn't help me right now. So where is the Ghost?"

"I have no idea," Kobura said.

"Me neither," Pony Girl said. "But if he's smart, he's long gone with you on his trail."

Warhorse snorted in amusement. "I'm not accusing him of being smart. He's surely watching us right now."

"Wh-what?" Zoe asked.

Warhorse raised his voice. "Come out, Ghost, or I'll kill everyone else in here."

Kobura laughed. "He's a mercenary, just like you, Warhorse. He doesn't care about us."

"Then you should prepare to meet your god," Warhorse said. "Count of three, Ghost. One . . . two . . ."

"Don't shoot," Jingshen called. "I'm coming down."

Warhorse chuckled. "Like I said, not smart." He turned his attention away from Pony Girl and Kobura, keeping one pistol trained upon them, and raised the other toward Jingshen.

Jingshen limped down the stairs. He'd expended a tremendous amount of energy healing first the bullet wound trauma and then the piercings of his wrists and ankles. He hurt. A lot. The longer it took to get sustenance, the slower his healing would go. Experience had taught him even then it wouldn't stop, but the time frame would be measured in days or weeks instead of minutes or hours. He kept his bloodstained hands in plain view as he descended, only occasionally dropping them to support himself on the railings.

"Damn, Ghost, you look like someone already did a hell of a number on you." Warhorse cocked his head toward Nobody Special. "That guy, I presume?"

"Yes."

"What happens if I shoot you with this?" Warhorse twitched the barrel of his pistol.

"I'll heal from it, eventually."

"That's what I hear, which puts me into a quandary. I said don't move!" Warhorse didn't turn to look at Pony Girl.

"Oh, for fuck's sake, Warhorse. Neither of us have anything to do with this!" Pony Girl yelled.

"Fine. You can both come around to the front here so we can all have a conversation and figure this out." Warhorse kept one pistol trained on Pony Girl and Kobura as they walked around to stand beside Jingshen, who waited beside Zoe. "Now . . ." said the huge mercenary. "What am I going to do with the lot of you?"

"Let the others go," Jingshen said. "I'm who you want."

"No, we had a deal," Kobura said immediately.

"Let him go," Zoe said. "I'm the one this is all about."

"I'm fucking retired," Pony Girl said. "I'd like to leave now, thanks."

Warhorse lowered one of his guns but kept the other trained on the quartet. "Quiet. Let me think."

Zoe's sigh was audible. Pony Girl's foot tapped in impatience, sounding like a muted snare drum roll. Jingshen waited, conserving his energy.

Kobura interrupted the stony silence. "I have a proposal for you, Warhorse."

Warhorse's remaining pistol didn't waver. "Make it a good one. I'm on a tight schedule."

"How do you prove to your employers that you have fulfilled a contract?"

Warhorse canted his head a little to one side in a gesture reminiscent of a dog. "When my word isn't sufficient for their needs, a picture is generally acceptable."

Kobura bowed her head a precise millimeter toward the leaking corpse on the floor before her. "You have a body here that appears to be your target for all intents and purposes. Take your picture and you've completed your mission, as far as your employers are concerned."

"The Source knows I heal," Jingshen said.

"If I tell them I killed you, they will believe me." Warhorse's voice was full of unflappable confidence. He returned his attention to Kobura. "Go on. You haven't told me anything I don't already know."

"I want to hire you."

"I already have a job." Warhorse nodded toward Jingshen. "He's it."

"If you sell the Source on Nobody Special here, your job is done."

"Problem is, the real Ghost is still around. All he has to do is pop up his head once and then I look like a chump."

"What is she doing?" Pony Girl whispered to Jingshen.

He shrugged. "Making a deal."

"I can guarantee he won't appear publicly again," Kobura said. "He and I have negotiated a deal that will preclude that from happening."

"So what do you want from me, then?"

"As much as I'd like to hope Nobody Special was running a scam all by himself, he was being financed by my competitors at a company called DuraGen. I expect their reinforcements to arrive any minute and try to take by force what he couldn't take by deception."

"And what is that?" Warhorse asked.

"Me," Zoe said in a small voice.

"Who are you?"

"She's the touchstone," Kobura said. "Her parahuman ability allows her to give others parahuman powers, even if they are not genetically predisposed toward them."

"Shit, no wonder they're after her. And you're not?"

Kobura smiled and let her gaze turn toward Jingshen. "Not right now. I've made . . . other arrangements."

Warhorse's face rearranged itself into a wry grin. "I suppose I don't need to know those details. Lay out your offer for me."

"Get me and the Ghost out of here, alive and in one piece." She produced an envelope from within the folds of her coat with such swift precision that Warhorse didn't even have time to get angry about her doing so. Jingshen realized if she'd had a gun, she'd have had time to fire it. He couldn't have drawn nearly as fast. There was more to the Japanese woman than met the eye. "This envelope contains ten thousand dollars. Consider it your retainer. The remainder of your fee will be paid upon our safe delivery to my company."

Warhorse laughed. "Ten thousand? I don't even get out of bed for that. My retainer starts at one hundred thousand dollars. The job you're asking me to do . . ." He paused, lips moving as he did some figuring in his head. "Call it two million dollars."

"Done," Jingshen said before Kobura could answer. "But make it three million, and Zoe gets to safety too."

"You're awfully free with my money, Ghost," Kobura snarled.

"No, I'm paying it. From my Credit Suisse account,," Jingshen said.

"Can you guys haggle about this later? If there's a bunch of armed mercenaries on their way here, I'd kind of like to be somewhere else. Like home," Pony Girl said. "Not all of us are bulletproof or heal instantly."

"It's not instant," Jingshen murmured.

Warhorse sighed. "Fine." He twitched his gun toward Kobura. "Her ten grand buys me as far as my truck. I've got an uplink in there that you can use to pay me the rest. When that's done, you get my full services for the duration. Deal?"

"Deal," Ghost said.

Kobura tossed the envelope to Warhorse. He caught it in his empty hand, opened it with a dexterous twist of his fingers, and flipped through the contents. He smiled and lowered his gun. "Congratulations. You've hired the Warhorse."

Chapter Seventeen

September, 1993
Lancaster, California

The group was severely under-armed for the trouble Jingshen expected they were about to encounter.

Pony Girl had only a pair of iron horseshoes that she used like brass knuckles. Driven by a super-speed punch, they could deliver a powerful blow, but she would be at risk for bullets and parahuman abilities. At least she had extensive experience after spending two decades in Just Cause.

Zoe had nothing but her toxic touch.

Kobura carried a pair of custom weapons superficially resembling Japanese sais. Unlike the blunt-tipped traditional weapons, Kobura's were sharpened to points and smeared with a gummy substance that was almost certainly some kind of poison. They'd been strapped to her back, hiding beneath her long coat. Anybody who carried weapons like that were either highly skilled or far more interested in projecting a certain image. Kobura didn't strike Jingshen as a pretender, so he assumed she knew what she was doing with the poisoned blades.

With no free hand to carry her cane, Kobura had apparently been content to leave it lying on the floor. Jingshen asked if he might wield it, since he had both a free hand and the skill to use it as a weapon if required. She agreed, and he carried it. He had retrieved Nobody

Special's pistol and when nobody else offered to use it, he slipped it into a pocket along with the erstwhile mercenary's spare clip. He had twenty bullets to help fend off what might be an army. He wished he had sticks to use; he disliked guns . . . but that didn't mean he was incompetent with them.

Warhorse, on the other hand, was well-prepared to perform as his namesake. He had his two huge pistols and a bandoleer of ammunition for them, interspersed with a dozen thumb size devices he called high-efficiency grenades. He also had a knife as big as Jingshen's forearm strapped across the small of his back. Coupled with his super-strength and resistance to damage, Jingshen figured Warhorse would come out all right no matter what happened to the others.

The huge mercenary led the others toward the door facing the street. "Stay close," he said. "I think there's already company out there."

"Where is your truck parked?" Kobura asked.

"Opposite side of the refinery. I trekked in on foot. Truck's too loud for when stealth is required."

"Shouldn't we be heading for it?" Jingshen asked.

"We will. I want to see what we're up against. Keep away from the door opening," Warhorse said, raising a pistol in one hand and grasping the door's handle with the other. "Unless you're bulletproof, and I don't think any of you are."

They moved to take cover.

Warhorse pushed the door open. It swung wide before the hinge arm started to pull it shut again. Before it did, he poked his head out to get a look at what was awaiting them. A single gunshot cracked and Warhorse staggered clear before falling upon his back on the warehouse floor. His sunglasses fell away from his face to reveal a welt above the bridge of his nose. His eyes stared straight upward and for a moment, Jingshen thought perhaps the man wasn't quite as bulletproof as he was rumored to be. Then his eyes focused and he grimaced. "They have a sniper," he announced as he sat up. "A good one."

"Are you all right?" Pony Girl asked.

He rubbed the welt on his forehead. "I don't always feel shots. I felt that one." He looked down at his shattered sunglasses. "Dammit. Those were custom fit." He looked at Kobura. "You sure attracted a lot of attention. I counted three SUVs out there, probably full of armed men. There's at least one flier, all done up in black PVC. Didn't recognize him, but I was a little distracted by the bullet hitting my face."

Jingshen recreated the surrounding terrain in his mind's eye. "There's a factory across the street," he said. "The sniper is probably on that rooftop."

"Leave him to me," Pony Girl said.

"Thought you were retired," Warhorse said.

Pony Girl clinked her horseshoes together. "I'm not *that* retired." She sped off to find another exit.

Windows broke as gas grenades were fired through them. The cylinders clattered across the cement floor, spewing noxious white smoke. "Fall back!" Warhorse ordered.

The motley group moved through the warehouse. Warhorse covered their retreat while Jingshen watched for any surprises as they approached the exit leading deeper into the refinery complex.

Red targeting lasers pierced the fog as DuraGen troops entered the warehouse. Warhorse's pistol roared. An explosive round dispersed smoke with its shockwave and sent several troopers flying. They wore tactical gear with helmets and gas masks and carried short bullpup-style assault carbines. These were no corporate security types; DuraGen had invested in a top-notch paramilitary unit.

The rear warehouse door exploded inward, ringing not from a detonation but from a powerful blow from the masked woman in the reinforced leather suit. She was old school in her costume, with a distinctive logo reminiscent of an upside-down anchor with the arms stretching down her own arms. Above her, a man flew into the warehouse in a striped gold and black outfit. He fired golden energy slivers from his fists that spat and smoked where they struck the floor.

Jingshen didn't bother warning Warhorse; the man seemed to have the ability to see in all directions. The huge mercenary would be better-suited to fighting parahumans. "Climb the stairs," Jingshen said to Kobura and Zoe. "I'll follow when it's safe."

"Are you kidding?" Zoe cried, but Jingshen was already moving toward the armed troopers.

Whether the troops used tear gas or simple smoke didn't matter to him. Tear gas was uncomfortable but the minimal amount of harm it did meant he healed with every breath. Their targeting lasers were like arrows pointing to each man, and he dove into their midst so they couldn't easily shoot at him without hitting each other. Behind him, Warhorse's pistol fired again, followed by the man's shout of anger and surprise.

Then Jingshen was in the thick of battle, and had no time for anything except fighting.

A trooper loomed out of the smoke before him, carbine raised. Jingshen drove the cane into the man's throat, just beneath the straps of his gas mask. He dropped his gun and fell, clawing at his face. Jingshen kicked the carbine away, preferring the precision of single bullets and targeted stick blows over masses of poorly-aimed bullets. A laser light flickered toward him in the smoke and he threw himself to one side as another carbine opened up on full auto. Someone behind him cursed as they were struck. A line of fire creased his forearm as a bullet left a raw trail across his skin.

He dropped low and swept his leg across the ankles of another trooper. The man fell and Jingshen brought the cane down upon his gas mask, shattering the lenses, then kicked the man's knee sideways, dislocating it. The man howled, then gagged as he inhaled the tear gas.

Jingshen was already up and moving. He sprang high as a spray of bullets flew beneath him. He wrapped his arms around the trooper in a vicious embrace, swung himself around the man's body, and used his momentum to fling the man into a warehouse support beam.

A sharp, burning impact struck him from above, spinning him around and nearly getting him skewered by a trooper wielding a combat knife. He swung the cane at the man's wrist, intending to break it, but the man neatly parried the blow. Jingshen raised his pistol and put a bullet through one of the gas mask eye holes.

Golden energy rained down around and into him as the flying mercenary unleashed shot after shot at him. The energy bolts didn't do much physical damage, but they were intensely painful and Jingshen gasped as it felt like every nerve in his body was aflame. He fell, his body trying to clench itself against the pain. He forced himself to move through the agony and fired the pistol toward his attacker above. He didn't hit the man, but the man stopped firing for a second, giving Jingshen the chance to move.

He shoulder-rolled onto his feet and ran, dodging as the flying man rose higher, taking shot after shot. He ran out of the tear gas and ducked behind a support post as the man raced in toward him. He leaned out and snapped off a pair of bullets at the flyer. One struck the man's armored breastplate and the other whistled off into the darkness of the warehouse's upper reaches. "Damn," Jingshen muttered and ducked back behind cover.

Warhorse was engaged in a rousing fistfight with the woman with the anchor logo. Despite his resistance to damage, he had a seeping cut on one cheek and looked like he was enjoying himself tremendously. As Jingshen watched, he parried a blow from his smaller opponent but left himself open to a follow-up punch to his solar plexus. Anchor was so strong that her upward punch lifted Warhorse off his feet and sent him crashing right through the wall he'd weakened earlier with his hand cannon. It was such an impressive feat that for a moment bullets and golden energy bolts quit ricocheting off the beam behind which Jingshen crouched. He spun around, preparing to send a bullet through the energy blaster's face when a massive wall of foam struck him like a wave crashing ashore. It swept him beneath its inexorable tide.

Over his three centuries of existence, Jingshen had never been on the wrong end of an avalanche. Even though he knew deep down he couldn't die, panic tore through him as the foam compressed and hardened around him. He couldn't move or breathe. His body was crushed on all sides by the expanding compound. He couldn't tell which way was up, even if he could have started digging his way to freedom.

He forced himself to remain calm, even as he kept suffocating. He'd been buried alive before Could he move anything at all, even a finger or a toe? He began patiently moving his toes up and down inside his boots. His leg muscles screamed in agony as the drying foam crushed against them. He felt his boots begin to give, millimeter by millimeter. The foam was still made from material surrounding air pockets, and that lattice could be broken given enough time.

His lungs ached. He kept blacking out from the suffocation, only to awaken a moment later as his healing ability rejuvenated his blood. It was a perpetuity of choking darkness. He kept wiggling his toes. The foam muffled exterior sounds, but it did carry the vibration of several massive thuds to his ears and across his body. He wondered if Warhorse was winning or losing the battle. The sounds of combat receded, leaving him to suffocate in silence but for the scritch-scratch of his boots working back and forth in the tiny pocket he'd managed to excavate within the foam.

Something sharp grazed his face, then was withdrawn and a shaft of light and fresh air penetrated into the darkness. A faint burning in his cheek told him it had been one of Kobura's poisoned sais that had found him.

"Ghost? You are still alive?" came her faint voice.

"Yes," Jingshen managed, and then coughed as foam dust fell into his mouth.

"I thought you would be."

"Where is Zoe?"

"Safe. For now."

Jingshen didn't believe Zoe was safe anywhere in the vicinity. That said, Kobura was certainly into self-preservation, and she wouldn't be risking herself to rescue him if the DuraGen team was still in the warehouse. "Can you get me out of here?"

"I can try."

Despite the doubt in her voice, Kobura worked quickly and efficiently with her sais. They cut through the dried foam in great swaths, and she peeled away layers, excavating Jingshen's upper body. When he could move his arms, he did what he could to help. Between the two of them they got enough of the material moved that he was able to pull himself free. His skin itched from the particles of foam that still clung to it, but compared to suffocating, it was a most tolerable discomfort.

As he emerged from the foam, he saw Kobura holding his hat out to him. "I thought you might like to have this back. It suits you."

"Thank you," Jingshen said as he straightened the hat upon his head. A crash sounded outside the warehouse. "Warhorse is still fighting?"

"It sounds that way."

"He said his truck was at the opposite side of the refinery. We should head for it. Where's Zoe?"

Kobura indicated the upper catwalks of the warehouse with a slight nod of her head. "Seemed to be the safest place."

"Let's go. Stay alert. Warhorse may be the noisy distraction we need, but that doesn't mean everyone is battling him alone."

The stairs were twisted from a glancing impact, and creaked when Jingshen stepped upon them. He grimaced at the sound, for if he could hear it clearly over the sounds of the exterior battle, so could anyone else in the warehouse.

The stairs led up to the maintenance catwalks for the bridge crane that stretched the length of the warehouse. Several of the lights were out at the far end of the catwalk. Zoe had to be hiding in those shadows. He turned to Kobura. "Wait here. Watch my back."

The corporate woman nodded. "Hurry."

Jingshen trotted up the steps, his footsteps echoing off the walls as the muted sounds of mayhem filtered in through broken windows. He advanced down the catwalk toward the shadows. He wished he still had the gun, or Kobura's cane, but he'd lost both of them when the foam had overwhelmed him. Where had that foam come from, anyway? Someone had made it . . . someone he hadn't yet met. "Zoe?" he whispered. "Are you up here?"

A figure stepped from the shadows, hesitant in her movements. "Jingshen? Is that really you?" Apprehension filled Zoe's face.

"Yes. Come on, we're getting out of here."

She narrowed her eyes. "What do I call you?"

"Chinese Indiana Jones," he said immediately.

She practically jumped at him, throwing her arms around him. "Oh my God, I thought you died. And then I thought you died *again*, you son of a bitch."

Jingshen suffered her embrace in silence. His skin crawled where it contacted hers.

A moment later, she stepped away in shame. "Oh God, I'm so sorry. I know that hurts you. I just . . ."

"Just what?" asked a new voice.

Jingshen whirled to see a woman crouched in a fighting stance on the catwalk between him and the steps back to the ground floor.

Chapter Eighteen

September, 1993
Lancaster, California

The woman wore a high-necked dark blue leather leotard that would allow her great freedom of movement. Her arms and legs were bare but for bracers around her wrists and ankles. Her feet were encased in simple soft shoes. A form-fitting fabric navy sleeve covered the lower half of her face with a matching headband over her forehead. Her black hair was pulled into two long, slender braids, reinforced with silvery wire and holding bare knife blades at the ends. The only concession to decoration was a blood red sash around her waist and a thin golden circlet over her forehead.

Her name was Killer Queen, and she'd beaten Jingshen twice in the past two years.

He couldn't see her face beneath the mask, but the smile was evident in her voice. "Ghost. When they said ye were involved, I didn't dare tae hope." She had a gentle brogue that spoke of her Irish heritage.

Jingshen said nothing. Queen liked to hear herself talk, but engaging her in dialogue or—heaven forbid, *interrupting her*—only led to increasingly vicious attacks. Experience had taught him that much.

"Looks like I get tae go for the hat trick here." She flipped her head, making the knife blades in her braids jingle together. "Speaking of hats, maybe I'll take yours this time." Her giggle was almost musical.

"Stay behind me," Jingshen said to Zoe without looking back. "You can't do anything to this one."

"Why not?" Zoe asked.

"She's not real."

"Now that's rude," Queen said. "I'm right here."

"She's a construct, like a character in a video game, but tangible." Jingshen took a fighting stance of his own.

"Still right here, ye bastard," Queen said. "Why don't ye save us all the time and trouble and take a header?"

"Even if I beat her, she can come back. At least, that's what I've heard."

Queen laughed. "Shows what ye know. Nobody's beat me yet. Maybe I'm just better than everyone else." He eyes narrowed. "I already know I'm better than you." She leaped forward, her knife-braids swinging around like tentacles.

Jingshen met her attack with a counterstrike of his own, driving his fingers upward into where her solar plexus would be if she were a living being. Her knife-braids looped around, slicing at his shoulders. Zoe screamed and backed away out of reach.

Queen pivoted on her toes, driving a hard kick toward Jingshen's midsection as her braids swung around to open his throat. He threw himself to the deck of the catwalk, letting both foot and braids pass inches over him. Queen followed up her roundhouse with an axe kick that Jingshen deflected into the railing with one of his feet.

He slipped through the bottom of the railing as if he were rolling right off the catwalk to plunge to the warehouse floor thirty feet below. Zoe screamed as he went over the edge. He used his momentum to swing himself completely underneath the catwalk. He came back up on the other side feet first, driving into Queen's side. She staggered from the blow. Her braid blades lashed down and he narrowly missed having all his fingers severed, which would have sent him falling.

As Queen regrouped, Jingshen rolled back onto the catwalk and up to his feet. He pressed his attack, punching high then low, straight and from unexpected angles. Queen parried and dodged his blows, counterattacking with strikes of her own and those whirling blades that kept nicking and slicing like a straight razor in a hurricane.

One whirring blade opened a slit right across Jingshen's forehead, cutting him to the bone just beneath the brim of his hat. Blood poured down his face, blinding him for a moment. Queen took full advantage and drove his face into the catwalk railing, shattering his nose. Mouth full of blood, eyes full of stars, Jingshen kicked blindly and caught his opponent a glancing blow. She grunted in surprise and he dove at her, hoping the unexpected flying tackle would catch her off-guard.

They both went down to the catwalk, flailing at each other. He dropped an elbow hard into her shoulder, hoping to immobilize that arm. In her other hand, Queen wielded one of her braid knives like a dagger and slit across Jingshen's wrist. Then she used a ground-fighting technique to fling him up and over her. He bounced painfully off a catwalk support but came up right away, realizing that now Queen was between him and Zoe, and Zoe had nowhere to go.

"Get back!" Jingshen called to Zoe, who seemed like maybe she wanted to try to help.

She screamed as one of Queen's blades narrowly missed opening her throat and scrabbled backward against the wall.

Behind him, the bridge crane thrummed to life and began its inexorable crossing of the warehouse ceiling toward them.

Queen's face was a mask of joy as she charged at him. "I'm going to keep yer hat," she taunted. "It'll be the new addition to my trophy room." She punched at him. He deflected the blow and one of her blades buried itself in his shoulder. She yanked it free before he could grab hold of her braid and drove a knee into his crotch. "Actually, it'll be the first addition."

Jingshen swept her legs out from under her as she gloated. She rolled as she fell, sliding forward to straddle him. She pounded hard fist after hard fist across his jaw, pinning his arms against his side with her knees. She snapped her head forward and both braid blades sliced across his cheeks.

With a scream borne of terror, Zoe crashed into Queen from behind, knocking her forward, over Jingshen's head. He kicked his feet up, pushed off his shoulders in a kip-up, and immediately kicked backward, pushing her further away. "Get back," he said to Zoe. Zoe's feet tangled in one another and she fell backward onto the catwalk. Jingshen lunged at her, grabbing hold of an ankle to keep her from rebounding awkwardly and perhaps going over the side.

His hand ignited in blue flames.

Whatever Zoe had done to him wasn't harming him, so his healing didn't kick in as the flames flickered around his hand like a burning glove. It must have been one of the rare incidences where she granted someone a power that wasn't immediately fatal or uncontrollable. Still, she'd given him a weapon he hadn't possessed previously and he would use anything he could against Killer Queen.

He whirled just as she closed in on him and struck out with his flaming fist. She recoiled from the unexpected flame and her braids coiled around her neck as their momentum continued unabated. He reached for her but she danced back out of his range. She whipped her head around to sling her braid blades at him once more, but disaster struck. Queen hadn't been mindful of the approaching bridge crane and both her braids snagged in the crane's trolley. The sudden cessation of motion made her lose her balance. In the space of a scant few seconds, she was dragged headfirst into the trolley. Jingshen turned away at the sudden explosion of blood before the crane ground to a halt, warning buzzers announcing too late that it was obstructed. Only Killer Queen's hips and legs were still visible, and a good portion of the crane and surrounding gantry had been splattered crimson.

"Ghost!" called a voice from the floor below.

He looked down to see Kobura standing beside the warehouse building, her hand on what must have been the crane controls. "We're coming down."

The flame on Jingshen's hand went out as quickly as it had started and he couldn't reignite it. Perhaps his healing power finally realized something was wrong and fixed it. Or perhaps the ability Zoe had granted him only lasted a few seconds. He turned to her. Her face was so pale it practically shone like moonlight in the shadows of the catwalk.

"Are you going to be all right?" he asked her.

She swallowed hard and nodded, keeping her eyes averted from the carnage that remained of Killer Queen.

"She will be back, someday," Jingshen said. "As I said, she is a construct. She has flesh and . . . blood—" Zoe gave a short burst of laughter, verging on hysterics at that. "But she is not real like you or I. The term I like best to describe her is *golem*."

"I don't know w-what that is," Zoe said.

"It doesn't matter," Jingshen admitted. "Let's go. It's time to leave while we still can."

He and Zoe descended to the warehouse floor where Kobura waited for them. Off to one side, blood droplets splattered the cement from above. "I trust you are both uninjured," Kobura said.

Zoe wouldn't meet anyone's gaze, keeping her eyes firmly fixed on her own feet.

"We're fine," Jingshen said. "Thank you for your help. Killer Queen is a difficult opponent and I probably wouldn't have beaten her under different circumstances."

"Cranes are dangerous places to fight," Kobura said. "I should know. Now, let's get out of here before more reinforcements show up. I haven't heard any crashing outside for two minutes. I don't know if that means Warhorse is alive or dead."

"We should be so lucky," Jingshen mumbled.

"For which, alive or dead?"

"Either."

* * *

The area immediately outside the warehouse looked like several bombs had gone off, with the kind of carnage that could only come from parahuman-scale combat. The SUVs in which the tactical team had arrived were twisted into unrecognizable hulks, embedded in tanks or pump stations nearby, or simply gone, hurled out of sight.

Warhorse sat with his back against a building, a crater in the wall with his shoulders at the epicenter. His sides heaved with exhaustion. Blood stained both his hands, some of it his, leaking from split knuckles and some of it from his opponent. His face was bruised and swollen. The battle had destroyed his t-shirt and stripped him of his weapons, leaving him in scuffed and torn jeans and bare feet.

Still, his eyes sparkled with a joy Jingshen envied. It had been centuries since he'd enjoyed being in a fight. From what he could see, Warhorse had been in a knock-down drag-out that was one for the record books. Anchor lay facedown several yards away, her outfit nearly as shredded as Warhorse's. An engine block with a skull-sized dent in it sat beside her, quietly glugging the last of its oil onto the pavement.

"Is she dead?" Jingshen asked.

"Fuck, I sure hope not," Warhorse said. "I owe her a beer at the very least. She's just a professional, you know? Like us."

"Like you," Jingshen said. "I'm leaving the industry."

Warhorse shrugged. "More for the rest of us." He stood, wincing at the numerous bruises and contusions decorating his skin. "Anybody have a pen?"

Kobura held one out to the huge mercenary. He accepted it gratefully and limped over to where Anchor lay. He knelt beside her and checked the pulse in her neck, then smiled at the others.

"She's alive," he said with a smile. "And she is going to have one hell of a headache when she wakes up."

"What are you doing?" Zoe asked.

Warhorse was writing on Anchor's bare arm. "Giving her my number," he said.

Zoe burst out laughing. "You're crushing on her. You go, girl." Her laugh was too loud, too forced.

Jingshen could tell she was close to cracking up completely. The abuses she'd suffered over the past few days would wreck almost anyone's psyche. "We need to leave. Where are the others?"

"I don't think any of the tac team's left. Stinger got spooked during mine and Anchor's fight and bailed. Sniper hasn't taken any more shots. Maybe Pony Girl got him?" Warhorse offered the pen back to Kobura.

"Keep it," she said, amusement playing across her face.

"Killer Queen is . . . dealt with," Jingshen said. "I never saw whomever created the foam."

"Neither did I," Kobura said.

"Then they're still around somewhere. Fuck, I hate loose ends," Warhorse grumbled. "They always come back to bite you. Come on, let's get to my truck before those reinforcements come."

A figure stepped around the corner of the building. Jingshen spun to see a slender, nondescript man holding a trash can like it was a hostage with a knife against it.

The air around the trash can wavered for a moment and then it was Zoe with the knife against her throat and the trash can tottering beside Jingshen.

"X-Change," Warhorse growled.

"Yes, it's me, douchebag," the man said. Zoe struggled in his grasp for a moment until the point of his knife drew a thin trickle of blood from her throat.

"Your struggling. Cut. It. Out." He had gloves and long sleeves protecting his skin, and his black turtleneck stretched up over his lower face as well.

"Let the girl go," Kobura called. "We've got you outnumbered, X-Change."

"That's what you think, losers. Except I'm holding all the cards here. Or at least, I'm holding the wild card. The one that matters. So here's what's gonna happen. I'm gonna take this slit for a walk and you all are gonna wait right there so I don't get creative with my knife. Follow me?"

"You won't get far," Jingshen said. "You should walk away from this. Now. Alone."

X-Change laughed. "Not for what I'm getting paid."

"He is strictly a bottom-feeder," Kobura said softly. "He cannot back up anything he claims. He is probably only here because of availability."

"I heard that," X-Change shouted. "Pick up one of your toys and it'll be mine in a second, bitch."

A red and gold blur flashed past X-Change, sweeping Zoe from his grasp before he could so much as blink.

A moment later, Warhorse hurled the engine block beside him into X-Change. The hunk of metal caught the slender man dead center in his chest and drove him into the wall behind him. Blood splattered as X-Change's torso exploded like a water balloon. The engine block fell to the ground with X-Change following after, mostly cut in half.

Pony Girl skidded to a halt, managing the tricky task of keeping Zoe from falling without actually touching her. She turned to see the human wreckage that had been X-Change and her face went pale. "Jesus Christ," she said in a whisper.

Warhorse stood. "You accept the job, you accept the risk that comes with it. You take care of that sniper?"

Pony Girl raised one of her horseshoes and flicked away something that looked suspiciously like a piece of scalp. "He's not going to be shooting at anyone for a while. At least, not until the swelling goes down."

"Take us to your truck," Kobura said to Warhorse.

The big man nodded. "Follow me. Pony Girl, watch our six."

Pony Girl grumbled something under her breath that Jingshen assumed was something about retirement.

The party crossed the refinery, keeping close to nonfunctional cracking towers and shadowing long pipes between tanks. It was full-on night and only a few isolated orange lights remained in operation, bathing most of the refinery in oppressive darkness. Zoe shrank against Jingshen. He let her wrap her arms around his but took care to only let her touch his coat sleeve. He suspected they weren't done battling for the night. DuraGen wouldn't give up on their prize so easily. There were at least two more parahuman mercenaries they hadn't accounted for in the foam-generator or the flyer Warhorse called Stinger.

The cracking towers gave way to row upon row of storage tanks. "Not far now," Warhorse said softly. "Watch yourself. I'd set a trap here if it was me."

His words proved prophetic, for a twenty-foot wall of foam shot across the gap between two tanks. More walls sealed in the group to the sides and behind, holding them in a lot bordered by huge tanks and masses of foam.

Kobura stepped back into a shadow and vanished right in front of Jingshen's eyes. Stinger arose from behind one of the walls and lanced golden energy bolts into the base of one of the tanks. Sludge sprayed out, stinking of petrochemicals and decay. The fumes made Jingshen dizzy and sick to his stomach.

Warhorse seemed unimpressed. "You think this is going to hold us? Hold *me*?" he bellowed at Stinger.

Stinger smiled down at the mercenary. "Not really, but we know about you, Warhorse. We know you won't back down from a job. Reputation is everything in this industry. You know that better than anyone."

"Just give us the girl and nobody needs to get hurt." A woman sitting atop a throne of foam arose from behind one of the hardening walls. Her legs were crossed primly and her hands rested upon the arms of her throne as if it were made of gold. Her outfit was white with gold trim, and had hardened-foam armor plating protecting her vital points. A crown with cheek plates and stylized horns adorned her head, leaving her regal face uncovered.

"Yeah, what Lady Foam said," added another young man who appeared at the top of the tank Stinger had holed. He wore jeans and a dirty white t-shirt. His head was shaved and an unholy light gleamed in his eyes. His fists were hidden within balls of fire. "Give me a reason. I would love to kill you. I would *love* to kill you," he reiterated, making it sound dirty. The firelight from his hands showed off the contours of his youthful face.

"Shut up, Napalm. Adults are talking," Stinger said. "How about it, Warhorse? I happen to know the Source contracted you to kill the Ghost and there he is. You wouldn't want that to get out, would you? Give us the girl and nobody ever has to know you're a failure and a fraud."

Jingshen winced. Stinger may have thought he was operating from a position of power, but getting on Warhorse's bad side was not a good business decision under any circumstances.

"Come a little closer and say that," Warhorse said quietly. "I'll show you what a failure and a fraud looks like."

"Boys, stop comparing dick sizes already because I'm not impressed," said Lady Foam. "Otherwise I'll just fill all your lungs with foam and wait for you to die, and that's bad for business. Warhorse has a reputation to protect. I don't know why Ghost isn't dead yet except that you must have made some kind of deal. Pony Girl's been out of the hero game for a while and I'm damn sure she's not here in any sort of official capacity. And . . ." Her eyes narrowed. "Where's Kobura?"

"Yeah, where's the chink?" Napalm called. "I wanna see if she smells like egg rolls when I crisp her."

"Napalm, shut the fuck up," Stinger said.

"Kobura, wherever you went, pay attention." Lady Foam made a staircase grow out of one of her walls. "Walk up here, sweetie," she called to Zoe. "And we can all go home."

"N-no!" Zoe cried. "I'm not going anywhere with you."

A blur of foam emerged from another wall to encapsulate Pony Girl up to her knees. "Perhaps we can convince you," Lady Foam said. "Napalm, if the girl doesn't start up my steps, you can cook Pony Girl where she stands."

Napalm leered. "I'm gonna be famous for this." The flames at his fists brightened.

Kobura stepped out of the shadows behind Lady Foam and slit her throat in a quick, decisive motion with the tip of one of her sais.

Chapter Nineteen

September, 1993
Lancaster, California

Warhorse moved before anyone else. As Lady Foam pitched forward from her throne, blood pouring from her throat, Warhorse grabbed Jingshen in both hands and threw him at Napalm. Jingshen didn't even have time to formulate a plan as he found himself hurling through the air.

"Bitch!" Napalm screamed at Kobura and loosed a jet of flame at her. Kobura melted into the shadows again and was gone.

Napalm's flame ignited Lady Foam's throne. The material composing it burned bright and hot, fueled by the pockets of air trapped within. It collapsed into a lattice of ash, sending toxic smoke stinking of plastic into the sky. As Jingshen flew toward him, he swung his flame jet around and just missed Jingshen, singeing the hem of his coat.

The fire from the burning dried foam raced down toward the petrochemical sludge Stinger had released from the holding tank. Warhorse aimed a kick at the foam holding Pony Girl in place, which exploded into dust. Pony Girl sprinted up the foam stairs even as they burned away into nothing, outracing the flames. Warhorse grabbed Zoe and sprang skyward just as the sludge erupted in a massive fireball.

Jingshen rolled across the top of the storage tank as Napalm traced fire toward him, unmindful of his surroundings in his homicidal frenzy.

"Goddammit, Napalm!" Stinger screamed as a gigantic fireball exploded upward. The flying mercenary turned and flew away, apparently deciding no paycheck was worth being roasted alive.

Jingshen grabbed hold of a piece of pipe, softened by Napalm's fire, and wrenched it free. His hand burned black but it would heal. He ducked beneath a jet of flame and smashed the pipe down on Napalm's wrist, shattering it. Napalm howled and his flame cut off. Jingshen followed up with another blow to the side of Napalm's head, then before the man could fall over, drove a foot into his ribs. Napalm flew across the top of the tank to crash against the railing.

"Ghost!" Pony Girl screamed.

He turned to see her pointing frantically toward Warhorse, who lay atop another fuel tank with Zoe beside him. Warhorse wasn't moving and Jingshen was afraid the powerful mercenary might have gotten a bad touch from Zoe's power.

"Help them!" he shouted, then turned to look toward Napalm.

Fire was billowing out from the unconscious man's hands, which was both worrisome and unexpected. Most parahumans couldn't use their powers when they were unconscious, but Napalm's powers seemed to be stuck in *idling mode* even when he'd been knocked out. It was like someone had left the engine running in a car and walked away from it.

And he was sprawled atop a tank that might be full of petrochemical waste.

Pony Girl ran up the adjacent tank and ran Zoe back to the ground, careful to only touch her with her gloved hands. "Go, that way!" she screamed over the roar of the flames, and pointed toward the nearest edge of the refinery.

Kobura stepped out of a shadow atop Jingshen's tank. "Come with me. Quickly. I cannot move Warhorse by myself." She held a hand out to Jingshen.

Not knowing what else to do, he took it.

"This is going to feel weird. Don't let go."

The world dissolved into darkness around Jingshen, flowing into him through every pore like an insidious fog. He barely felt Kobura's small hand clasped around his. He couldn't breathe or move.

Then the fog lifted and Jingshen and Kobura stood in a shadow atop the tank where Warhorse had landed.

"You weren't wrong," Jingshen said as he ran over to Warhorse. "Get out of here. We'll catch up."

Pony Girl appeared beside him. "Is he hurt?"

"I don't know. He's supposed to be damn near invulnerable. I think Zoe's skin touched his, and now he's dealing with the aftereffects."

"What do we do? I can't carry him. I'm not sure both of us could."

"Roll him off the edge. He'll survive the fall. Or he won't. Either way, this tank is going to go along with the rest of the refinery, thanks to that guy."

Pony Girl looked toward the other tank. "Shit. He's gone. I thought you killed him."

Jingshen shrugged. "I thought you were retired."

Faint traceries of dark energy crackled across Warhorse's skin as whatever ability granted to him by Zoe's touch worked itself into his body. The power would either kill him or he would learn to control it, given time. Time, unfortunately, was a luxury they didn't have. Jingshen and Pony Girl rolled the heavy man to the edge of the tank and shoved him beneath the railing. He fell without a sound and cracked the cement below where he hit. Jingshen looked at Pony Girl. "Go." He vaulted over the railing and dropped thirty feet to the ground.

He rolled with the impact and, for once, didn't break anything upon landing. As he came to his feet, he smiled. It was a good omen.

Warhorse sat up and screamed in agony, his hands pressed against his head as if he could crush the pain out of it.

Jingshen and Pony Girl ran over to him.

"Oh goddamn, what the fuck is happening to me?" the huge man cried.

"Zoe has given you a new parahuman ability. Your body is trying to adjust to it," Jingshen said. "You will survive it or you won't. We need to get to your truck. This refinery is about to burn down."

Warhorse's eyes rolled up in his head and he fell back to the cement.

"Well, that's awkward," Pony Girl said. "What's Plan B?"

"Drag him, I guess," Jingshen said.

"Are you kidding? He's got to be over three hundred pounds!"

"You have a better idea? No? Then grab a fucking leg!" Jingshen followed his own directions and raised one of Warhorse's legs to his hip. It was like lifting a tree trunk. He was mad at himself for losing his cool with Pony Girl, who was there strictly as a volunteer. What was that like, doing work not for money, but because it needed to be done? He'd have to reflect on that. Maybe he could try it himself someday. Eventually, he amended, because he had a lengthy engagement with Kobura and Kokorotai to fulfill first.

"I have a better idea." Kobura stepped out of the shadow beside the adjacent tank. "Bring him here, but hurry. The fire is spreading and I'm running out of shade."

Pony Girl sighed and heaved Warhorse's other leg, gasping at the effort. "Oh shit, I hate when I'm right."

They dragged Warhorse across the cement as fire crackled behind them. Jingshen was surprised Kobura hadn't fled the scene altogether, taking Zoe with her and leaving the others to fend for themselves. In the end, that probably would have been a satisfactory and profitable conclusion to the night's activities.

Somewhere behind them, a high-pitched whistle preceded a fifty-five gallon drum launching itself skyward like a rocket, riding a column of flame. The drum arced over the storage tank and crashed to the cement not far from Jingshen and the others. "Holy shit!" Pony Girl shouted as the burnt, twisted steel drum bounced erratically across the concrete.

Fire roared up the side of a cracking tower. Thermal expansion of the piping burst rivets, which shot in all directions like lethal popcorn kernels.

"I hope you know what you're doing!" Pony Girl shouted over the sound of support structures failing. Behind them, the cracking tower folded in on itself, sending a fresh explosion of flames in all directions.

They reached the shadow. Kobura directed them to take Warhorse's hands and then took each of theirs in turn. Heat washed over them just as Kobura took them into the darkness.

* * *

They emerged in the shadow of a large eight-wheeled truck. It was oddly-shaped, with a front that was shaped like a wedge with several protrusions that were almost certainly weapon barrels. It might have begun life as an airport fire truck, but Jingshen could tell it had been upgraded significantly with armor, weapons, and any number of additional dirty tricks. It sat in the darkness along the side of an auxiliary road to the north of the refinery.

Pony Girl fell to her hands and knees, retching. Kobura's shadow transit power seemed to have affected her more than it did Jingshen. He knelt beside her but she waved him off. "I'll be okay," she said between gasps. "Just . . . caught me by surprise. Check on the others."

Jingshen patted her back to reassure her. He was still surprised Kobura had come back for them. Maybe she was more honorable than he'd expected. Zoe huddled against one of the truck tires, her face shadowed by the darkness, clearly exhausted. "Are you all right?" he asked her.

She raised her head slightly. "Yeah. I'm sick of feeling like I'm just baggage, though. I feel like a piece of meat."

Jingshen gave her a wry smile. "One that went through the grinder, I'm sure. It will be over soon. I promise." He turned to Warhorse. Kobura stood over him. The wrinkles in her face were much more evident than they had been earlier. She must have nearly drained herself to transport so many people via her parapower. Warhorse still seemed unconscious, but his skin glowed faintly in the darkness. The illumination showed the cement was completely cracked around him, almost as if someone had taken a hammer and chisel and outlined him. "That's odd," he said. "The cement was cracked around him by the tank as well. I thought it was just from the impact when we rolled him off the side but now I'm not so sure."

"Perhaps it is related to the change in his body brought about by the touchstone," Kobura said. "It bears further investigation, to be sure. However, this is neither the time nor the place. Can you drive this truck?"

Something exploded in the refinery, sending a fireball skyward. If the authorities weren't already on their way, they would be any moment.

Jingshen looked up at the monster. He'd never driven one like it, but he'd operated quite a bit of heavy machinery over the course of his life. "Yes," he said, trying to put as much conviction as possible into one word. The door was locked with a surprisingly low-tech key that Jingshen found in Warhorse's pocket. "Zoe, Kobura, get inside. Pony Girl . . ."

Pony Girl stood up, shaky on her feet. "I know, help you get this heavy fucker into the truck."

They struggled with Warhorse's dead weight, trying to lever him into the middle of the second row of seating. Kobura was all the way across, behind the driver's seat. Zoe sat in the passenger seat, where she wouldn't risk touching anyone inadvertently.

The air around them heated up as fires broke out atop the big tanks closest to them. It would only be a matter of time before they, too, exploded.

"If I survive this . . ." Pony Girl grunted as she fought to get Warhorse's hips off the ground. "I'm going to find out . . . who owned this refinery . . . and kick his ass."

Warhorse mumbled something and shifted as they struggled with him. "Wake up!" Jingshen shouted in his ear. "Time to work!"

Warhorse's eyes flew open and a crack appeared in the concrete beneath his feet, spreading out in a rough circle. The truck, which probably weighed dozens of tons, tilted as concrete beneath it collapsed.

"Get into the damn truck already!" Pony Girl yelled.

Moving with glacial slowness, Warhorse dragged himself into the middle seat. The ground shifted again, tilting the heavy truck further off level. Jingshen was afraid it was about to fall into a sinkhole and ran around the front of the truck. Concrete broke beneath his feet, nearly spilling him into the growing crevasse beside the truck. He jumped and his hands caught the handle beside the door. He flung open the door and pulled himself into the seat.

Cockpit might have been a better description than *driver's seat*, for he immediately felt like he was in a military jet of some kind. He spotted the ignition, jammed the key into it, and twisted.

Two engines roared into life, their basso thrum drowning out the roar of flames across the street. The display panels lit up with a Christmas tree's worth of colored lights and indicators. Two screens lit up in the center console, one showing status of various systems and the other some sort of weapons targeting display.

A brilliant flash to the truck's right preceded Pony Girl's disappearance in a blur just ahead of a powerful shock wave that rocked the truck. One of the big storage tanks had exploded, sending white-hot shrapnel in all directions. One jagged piece stuck a couple inches through the bulletproof Lexan pane in the passenger door.

"*Go!*" Kobura screamed in Jingshen's ear.

Jingshen threw the truck into gear and hammered the accelerator to the floor. The engines shrieked and the tires chirped as they spun on the loose concrete. Then they found traction and the massive truck climbed out of the growing hole around it.

As they pulled away from the side of the road, three more of the giant storage tanks exploded in quick succession, turning the entire refinery into a massive fireball. The shock waves hammered into the truck, hard enough to make it slip and skid like it had hit a patch of ice. Heat washed through the cabin and the glow reflected in the mirrors was like daylight.

Pony Girl appeared beside the passenger door, running alongside the truck. She knocked and Warhorse leaned over to open the latch. The door slid back along its tracks and Pony Girl jumped onto the running board and then climbed into the seat beside the huge mercenary.

"Glad to see you made it," Jingshen said, noticing the singeing on her costume.

"I almost didn't," she said, brushing at the soot. "But you've got other problems."

"What's that?"

"Of course we couldn't be lucky enough that he died in the explosion," Pony Girl said. "It's Napalm."

Chapter Twenty

September, 1993
Lancaster, California

Warhorse's truck lumbered away from the burning refinery as explosion after explosion rent the nighttime sky. A SUV pursued them with Napalm hanging out of the passenger window, firing jet after jet of fire at them. Heat washed through the truck even past its armor and insulation. The ride was rough as the road seemed to be shattering as they passed across it. "Just how heavy is this thing?" Jingshen asked over his shoulder.

Warhorse still had the unnatural glow about his skin, but he had grown more alert and leaned forward. "Not that heavy. Fifty tons spread over eight wheels shouldn't be breaking anything."

"It's him," Kobura said with confidence.

"Excuse me?"

"Something about his new power. He's breaking ground beneath him. It happened at the refinery and now here as well."

"New power?" Warhorse looked at his hands as if for the first time. "What the fuck? I'm glowing."

"Sorry." Zoe bowed her head. "I'm . . . contagious."

A stream of emergency vehicles passed them, going the opposite direction toward the refinery fire, all lights and sirens. Jingshen caught the surprised expression of one fireman in a brief flash before they were gone.

"Whatever it is, you need to figure it out and how to stop it," Pony Girl said, bouncing in her seat as the truck jounced over broken road. "I'm afraid I'll bite through my tongue at this rate."

A rapid pinging from the rear of the truck made Jingshen swerve across all the lanes and then back. "They're also shooting at us."

The truck bounced across broken road, suspension absorbing the lesser irregularities but still bouncing its occupants around. "Whatever you're doing, stop it!" Kobura said to Warhorse.

"I don't know what I'm doing!" he shouted, raising his hands in frustration.

Chunks of concrete flew into the air from the road ahead of the truck, bouncing off the armor plating and cracking the bulletproof panes of the windshield. A jet of superheated plasma from Napalm's hands struck the truck's roof, causing an alarm to start buzzing insistently. One of the systems highlighted on the display panel shifted from green to red. Jingshen didn't have time to check what it was, as he maneuvered the truck through a storm of floating rocks.

"You're levitating them. Something earth- or stone-related," Pony Girl said. "Try to calm down. Focus on smoothing the road ahead of us."

"What are you, a parahuman shrink now?" Warhorse snarled.

"Will you just fucking try it already before you wreck us?" she snarled back, not backing down in the least.

The chasing SUV swerved through the debris left in the truck's wake.

Warhorse raised his hands again, motioning like he was shushing a noisy audience. Whether it was the gesture, the intent behind it, or a simple refocusing of his attention, the road smoothed out and the truck stopped bouncing.

That in turn allowed Jingshen to put more of his attention toward their pursuers. "Weapons," he said aloud.

"Come again?" Kobura asked.

"Warhorse, I saw two turrets on this truck. Can we use them against Napalm?"

Warhorse pointed at the display. Ahead of the truck, a piece of asphalt ripped itself away and flew into the sky like a scared bird. The truck bounced hard, banging Warhorse's head off the ceiling. "Goddammit. Sorry. I'm still trying to figure this shit out. You see that? That was my fifty-cal. Napalm nailed it hard. It's probably melted. All I've got up there now is the snozzle."

For a moment, the only sound in the cabin was the roar of the engines and Zoe's snort of amusement.

"What's a *snozzle?*" Pony Girl asked at last. "Sounds like a kids' TV show."

"It's the penetrating nozzle at the end of the articulated boom. It's not really a weapon. I just kept it installed because, well, I kind of like the idea of a hydraulically driven spear." Warhorse shrugged and the ground shrugged with him. "Goddammit," he said again. "It's going to get real fucking old if this happens every time I move."

Heat washed through the cabin and fire flared across the driver's side door, blackening the Lexan window. A couple components in the cabin shorted out in brief surges of sparks. Jingshen cranked the wheel hard to the left, hoping to run Napalm and his SUV off the road. The driver must have expected the move and braked before the collision.

"Shit, I lost him," Jingshen said. His side mirror had melted in Napalm's attack. Another blast from the pyrokinetic would either punch through the side of the truck or heat the interior so rapidly that everyone but Jingshen would die. "Your snozzle thing. Is it still connected?"

Warhorse's sharp inhalation whistled through his teeth. "It is. I think there's even water in the tank. Right hand joystick."

Zoe reached out and grabbed it. "What do I do?"

Warhorse talked her through the basic operation. "It'll run while we're driving," he said when he finished.

"Don't you have a gun or something up here?" Pony Girl asked.

"No, everything's in the armory. It's not accessible from the cab. It's where the hoses used to be stored."

"Why are you using a fire truck at all?" Kobura asked. "Why not a regular truck, or something full military-spec?"

Warhorse grinned. "Have you *seen* this thing? It's a goddamn tank without the treads. Also, fire trucks tend to not get stopped by police."

"Boys and their toys," Pony Girl grumbled.

"Here comes Napalm again," Jingshen warned. "Hit it!"

Zoe unlimbered the boom, trying to get a sense of how it moved while watching through the camera on the center console. "I can't see anything!" she complained. "Where's the SUV?"

Warhorse slid open a hidden panel on the roof. "I'll guide you," he said, and stood so his head stuck up above the roof.

Zoe's tongue poked out the corner of her mouth as she struggled to interpret Warhorse's bellowed directions into movements of the articulated boom. Jingshen had to keep swerving to avoid blasts from Napalm. If he got the boom, they'd be back to square one. "Hurry up," he urged Zoe. "We're running out of time."

The truck roared up an on-ramp and barreled down the highway, swerving around traffic. Jingshen flipped on the emergency lights, hoping people ahead of them would pull over.

"Down!" Warhorse yelled. "Hard! Water on!"

Zoe thumbed the button to activate the water jet. The truck slowed its headlong rush down the road as engine power shifted to the pumps.

Jingshen looked back over his left shoulder to see the SUV enveloped in a blast of high-pressure water, steam escaping as the force overcame Napalm's natural parahuman ability. The SUV fishtailed left and right as the driver lost traction beneath the relentless spray.

"Right here, you son of a bitch!" Warhorse yelled, and the pavement beneath the SUV ripped free. The SUV vaulted into the air, sending piece of itself in all directions as chunks of asphalt pummeled it under Warhorse's direction. The SUV crashed back to the ground, rolling over and over away from the highway. "Oh shit, *look out!*" Warhorse yelled.

Jingshen looked back forward just in time. He'd nearly run the fire truck off the road watching the SUV's destruction. As he swerved back away from the breakdown lane, the extended boom caught a framework holding an overhead highway sign. The truck jerked and metal shrieked as the boom ripped away from the glancing blow.

Warhorse dropped back into the middle of the back seat and slammed the rooftop hatch shut. "Things are worse."

"What do you mean?" Jingshen asked.

"They have a helicopter."

Golden energy bolts blasted chunks from the road just outside Jingshen's door. He swerved to the right just as a stream of tracer bullets cut through the space the truck had occupied a moment before. "And Stinger," Jingshen said.

Stinger took potshots at them, although it was clear his energy blasts weren't up to the task of penetrating the truck's armor. They could still damage peripheral items not protected within the truck's hull, and he managed to take out a couple of cameras. Likewise, the gunners on the helicopter didn't seem to be doing much damage to the truck, but there was the possibility they had heavier weapons still available.

"I've got a surface-to-air missile launcher in my armory back there, but I can't get to it while the truck's running."

"I can," Pony Girl said.

Jingshen shook his head. "The gunners will pick you off while you're getting in and out."

"You have a better idea?"

"No. I have a stupid idea." He laid it out for them in a couple of terse sentences.

Everybody agreed it was a stupid idea, but they agreed to try it.

Jingshen leaned the seat as far back as he could, stretching to reach the pedals with his legs. Pony Girl clambered over the center console to take the wheel, freeing him. The truck wavered as she took control. "I hope you guys figure this out soon. I have no idea what I'm doing," she said. "Jesus, this thing is big." A passenger car ahead failed to get out of the way and she leaned on the truck's horn.

Warhorse slid the roof hatch open once again and looked at Jingshen. "You're one crazy son of a bitch, Ghost. Good luck."

"Just don't drop me."

Bullets rained down around Jingshen as he climbed onto the roof of the truck, keeping low so he wouldn't be hurled off by any sudden maneuvers. Gunners from either side of the helicopter opened up upon him. None hit him, thanks largely to Pony Girl swerving back and forth at random intervals, but it would only be a matter of seconds before they got their range. Warhorse, unafraid of bullets, stood tall in the hatch. He raised one of his hands toward the roadway and made a fist. Steam rose off his head in the cold air as he sweated with the effort of concentration.

A hunk of asphalt as big as a desk tore free from the passing lane and floated into the air beside the truck. Pieces of rebar dangled beneath it, trailing loose dirt into the passing wind. Before giving himself the chance to second-guess his plan, Jingshen leaped onto it. The floating rock held his weight but it swayed and twisted, like a surfboard on stormy seas. He splayed out his arms and legs to grip it tightly as Warhorse started directing it toward the pursuing helicopter.

The gunners shifted their aim from the truck to the floating asphalt, trying to hit Jingshen. Bullets ricocheted off the material and one creased the side of his head, sending a gush of blood down his neck into the collar of his shirt. He shifted position to put more of the chunk's bulk between him and the gunners, and the asphalt beneath his hands crumbled into fragments. The roadway spread out beneath him, inviting massive road rash, but one of his flailing hands caught a piece of rebar. It cut painfully into his palm but kept him from falling.

In the second half of the Nineteenth Century, he'd been in Australia and assisted an engineer named Hargrave with his man-lift kite trials. It felt the same way, dangling beneath a flying object completely out of his control.

More bullets chewed into the chunk of road and it started to break apart. Jingshen couldn't catch his breath enough to shout to Warhorse, and the mercenary wouldn't have heard him over the helicopter's blades anyway. Warhorse noticed and somehow managed to guide the floating debris faster toward the 'copter. The rebar Jingshen hung upon started to work itself loose and he had no choice but to swing himself through the sky like a trapeze artist.

The chunk of road material struck the helicopter's canopy, shattering against it and breaking some of the cockpit glass. The 'copter jerked in the sky and the pilot angled it to one side.

Jingshen managed to catch hold of one of the skids to hang beneath the helicopter. He knew that whatever else he did, he needed to keep the others safe in the fleeing truck below. The best way to do that would be to keep everyone in the helicopter busy with him. He started swinging himself on the skid, struggling to get one of his legs onto it so he could pull himself up. Warhorse would have been strong enough to do it without needing his legs, but Warhorse could die. Jingshen, as far as he knew, couldn't. His foot bumped off the skid. Almost there. He tried again and hooked it, feeling triumphant at last. Then the wind caught his hat and sent it spinning off into the darkness.

Damn.

Chapter Twenty-One

September, 1993
Lancaster, California

Jingshen pulled himself onto the skid, hugging it to him as the helicopter swept back and forth to give the gunners every chance to fire at Warhorse's truck. Bullets chewed into armor and solid tires. Eventually something would give if Jingshen didn't take action, and his . . . were they his friends? He wasn't the sort to form lasting relationships with people. They tended to take his apparent immortality poorly. It was easier to keep moving, to keep people at arm's length.

Yes, he decided, they were his friends. At least, they were for now, and he would fight to protect them.

The gunner at the door hadn't seen him yet. Jingshen let go of the skid with one hand, holding himself in place with the other hand and his feet. The gunner had his foot out of the 'copter, braced on the skid. He wasn't belted into the 'copter, because henchmen never were. Jingshen locked his hand around the man's ankle and pulled hard, dislodging the man's foot from the skid. The gunner overbalanced and Jingshen swung his legs up and around to wrap around the man's waist. His weight dragged the man completely out of the 'copter and he screamed all the way to the roadway below.

Stinger circled around, firing at Jingshen. Bolts whizzed past him and a couple cracked against the helicopter's body panels, leaving smoking holes where they struck. The pilot instinctively steered the 'copter away from the flying man shooting energy bolts. The sudden motion nearly dislodged Jingshen from his precarious position beneath the skid. He gritted his teeth and pulled his legs back up to wrap around the skid.

Stinger flew toward the front of the canopy, gesticulating angrily at the pilot, probably to warn him about Jingshen. The other gunner appeared in the doorway above Jingshen and lowered his assault rifle. With nowhere to hide and no other options, Jingshen flung himself out and away from the skid, trying to generate momentum with his swing. He went down below the skid, contorting his body to squeeze every bit of extra stretch he could, and let go.

It felt like an eternity as he flew across empty air beneath the helicopter, arms outstretched toward the opposite skid. He was sure he'd muffed it. His fingers would be an inch too short. He'd bark his knuckles instead of grasping the skid. He'd catch it but his grip would fail and he would fall.

Instead, his fingers closed around the skid with all the grace of the proverbial man on the flying trapeze. He clenched his core muscles, pulling himself up and around to slide into the 'copter on his stomach, feet first, heart racing.

Stinger looked appalled. He'd seen Jingshen's maneuver of desperation and clearly couldn't believe it. He pointed and yelled, even though the helicopter's whirling blades drowned out anything the flying merc might have said.

A piece of pavement caught him in the small of the back and he crashed against the canopy. Whether it had been flung by muscles or by Warhorse's newfound power, it had successfully distracted both pilot and Stinger. Jingshen started to get to his feet and a gun butt crashed into the side of his head. He fell and hit the deck hard, stars flashing all around his eyes. Experience had taught him he would heal from a cracked skull or concussion in seconds, but in those seconds the gunner could empty an entire clip into him.

Jingshen kicked up and back and felt his foot connect against something meaty that snapped with the impact. He was pretty sure that had been the gunner's rib. He rolled over and saw the gunner leaning against the edge of the door, gun pointed at the ground in one hand while the other pressed against his side.

"Get rid of him!" the pilot shouted over his shoulder. As if it would help, he took the helicopter into a sharp, spiraling turn that nearly threw Jingshen out the open door. His fingers caught the seat belt from the rear seat and he pulled himself tight against the seat.

The gunner crashed into him, nearly throwing both of them from the cabin. Jingshen drove his free hand into the man's ribs, knowing one was already cracked or broken. The man howled and hit Jingshen across the face with the stock of his rifle.

As the man spun his gun around to fire point-blank, Jingshen tore the auxiliary fire extinguisher from its clips beside the doorframe. He flung it into the man's face. The mercenary's nose burst like a balloon and blood poured from the wound. He staggered back against the opposite doorframe. The pilot went into another sharp turn and Jingshen flew across the cabin to collide with the gunner. The man tripped through the door and fell. As he did, the gun strap looped around Jingshen's wrist and pulled him along. Jingshen managed to grab the bar on the inside of the door to keep from tumbling out into open air.

Bones cracked and split in Jingshen's hand as the strap snapped tight, threatening to sever the hand altogether. The mercenary dangled beneath him with a one-handed death grip on the gun's stock. He flailed and screamed, then screamed again as his hand slipped and he fell away into the darkness.

Jingshen pulled himself up, grimacing at the pain in his injured hand. He turned to face the pilot but before he could change hands to jam the gun against the man's head, Stinger came flying out of the darkness. He fired two energy blasts into Jingshen. The golden bolts punched right through his torso, parboiling the flesh and organs where they struck. Then Stinger barreled into him and body-checked him right out of the helicopter. It happened so fast his body didn't even have time to go into shock.

The world spun crazily as Jingshen whirled through the air, and then his back slammed into a hard surface, well before he expected to impact with the ground. The shock from his injuries hit him immediately thereafter, and faded almost as quickly as his body worked to heal his wounds. He felt faint from hunger and exhaustion but didn't dare give in to the weakness for even a moment. Air still whistled around him and the helicopter was still over his head, a shadow against the sky. He sat up and realized he was sitting on a piece of roadway cement, crumbling at the edges but more or less holding together. It felt like he was sitting on a waterbed. He glanced over the edge and saw the shadow of Warhorse against the fire truck's flashing lights, arms raised. Somehow, the man had gained enough control of his abilities to save Jingshen from falling all the way to the ground.

Not daring to hope, Jingshen waved at him and then pointed at the helicopter. Warhorse must have seen him, for two things happened in short order. First, a turreted spotlight on the truck illuminated, swung around and up to target the helicopter. Second, the cement rose, carrying Jingshen back toward that helicopter. He felt a tug on his wrist and realized the assault rifle strap was still wrapped around it.

The floating cement reached a parallel height with the helicopter's cabin. Jingshen raised the rifle and saw Stinger standing in the opposite door, looking down instead of out at Jingshen on his levitating debris. He fired energy bolts down at the truck. He must have seen the movement out of the corner of his eye and his gaze met Jingshen's in the moment before Jingshen pulled the trigger.

Bullets sprayed across the open door, holing both the helicopter's skin and Stinger's, who took three hits across his torso, all of which penetrated his body armor. The flying mercenary fell out of the 'copter without a sound.

The pilot stood the 'copter on its tail and climbed, accelerating away from Jingshen and the floating concrete.

Jingshen waved at Warhorse to get him to send the chunk of roadway after it, but he didn't seem to be getting any higher. In fact, the cement was dropping— not quickly enough to be considered falling, but certainly at a steady rate. It approached Warhorse's truck and Jingshen could see the tendons in the man's throat standing out like cables as he strained. His hair was drenched with sweat from the effort of using his newfound powers. Jingshen sprang from the cement to land atop the truck and Warhorse let the debris fall. He slumped into the truck through the top hatch.

Jingshen looked around, at last able to do so with his feet on a comparatively stable platform. The truck had left Lancaster behind and was heading east into a stretch of land that had no cross streets or lights suggesting residences. He couldn't hear the helicopter over the roar of the truck's engine but knew it still had to be up there. DuraGen had invested so much in Zoe, first in its research into her unique ability and then into hired guns to bring her back. There was no way they'd just let her go.

He followed Warhorse through the roof hatch. "We've got to get off the road," he said to Pony Girl without preamble. "They're still up there, following us."

"Why off the road?" Pony Girl asked. She'd stripped off her gloves and was gripping the steering wheel with white-knuckled determination.

Jingshen looked at Kobura. "How much would Kokorotai spend attempting to retrieve Zoe before it no longer became cost effective?"

"There is no limit," Kobura said. The admission worried Jingshen. Surely that meant she would eventually renege on their deal. He would have to cross that bridge when he came to it.

"Then we have to assume DuraGen is operating on the same principle. They will not stop coming after her unless we can convince them Zoe is dead."

"What's your plan?" Pony Girl asked over her shoulder.

"Make it look like a booby trap that went wrong."

"That sounds . . . expensive," Warhorse said faintly. He looked exhausted.

Jingshen shrugged. "I hope you're not too attached to this truck."

* * *

Once Jingshen explained the bare-bones outline of his plan to fake Zoe's death, Pony Girl agreed they needed to be away from any civilians. She took the truck over the shoulder and slowed enough so they wouldn't crash into any arroyos or rocks. The fire truck rode on oversize off-road tires and its heavy duty shocks kept the ride smooth.

The truck's radar and infrared systems showed the helicopter was still pursuing them, staying high enough as to stay safe from firearms. "How do they know she's even in this truck?" Warhorse grumbled. "Corporate spies or not, they couldn't have known."

"They must be tracking her somehow," Kobura suggested. "We would do the same."

"Then how come they didn't come after us when we were in that cabin?" Zoe asked. "They must have had enough time to get there."

"The cabin had no power, no phone. They must have lost you then. When we came back to civilization, they started tracking you again. It's technological, whatever it is," Jingshen said.

Zoe's eyes grew wide. "Uh . . . it might be . . . my IUD. They put one in me right after they grabbed me. I figured it was to, you know, make sure I didn't get pregnant and give a baby powers it couldn't control."

Warhorse grabbed a device from a small hatch in the side wall. "May I?" Zoe shrugged. The huge man passed the device across Zoe's hips. It made a squealing sound as it crossed over her center. "Son of a bitch," he muttered. "Good call. She's got a transmitter in her."

"That's perfect," Jingshen said. "We take it out and leave it in the truck. Kobura, you take Zoe and shadow-walk a safe distance away. Then we blow up the truck with the transmitter in it. Zoe's in the wind and we can all move on."

Pony Girl coughed to cover up a bitter laugh. "You don't know the first thing about IUDs, do you? I had one for awhile. It takes tools. I'm guessing you don't have forceps or a speculum or anything like that in your toy box, Warhorse."

"I believe I can transport Zoe without the IUD," Kobura said. "I have a fine enough control over my ability. Now that I know it is there, I can . . . leave it behind."

"I'm more concerned about the part where we blow up my truck," Warhorse said. "This thing cost me more than a million dollars."

Jingshen shrugged. "Put it on my tab."

Chapter Twenty-Two

September, 1993
Lancaster, California

Pony Girl killed the truck's engine and they coasted to a stop in the middle of a deserted plain, surrounded by windblown scrub grass and sand-scoured flat rocks. Warhorse leaned forward and turned off all the exterior and cabin lights, plunging them all into darkness lit only by the rising half-moon, low over the distant shadowy mountains to the east.

The truck's scope showed the helicopter hovering overhead, probably to report in their position. "I contracted with Gate to drop me off in the area," Warhorse said as he rummaged through his cabin bins. "I'm sure DuraGen is going to use her to send in their next wave."

"At least we know they didn't use Medium to track Zoe," Jingshen said.

"We don't know that," Warhorse countered.

"True, but the fewer people outside of the organizations who know of her existence, the better. They had a technological solution in place." Jingshen accepted a brick of plastic explosives from Warhorse, placed it under his seat, and armed the detonator.

"I think you guys are all nuts," was Pony Girl's contribution. "At this point, I'm sticking around purely because it's like watching a car crash in slow motion."

"Um, aren't all car crashes in slow motion for you?" Zoe asked.

Pony Girl laughed. "I guess they are, at that."

Jingshen took another detonator from Warhorse's stash. "Got any tape?"

Warhorse passed him a roll of duct tape. Jingshen opened his shirt, activated the detonator, and taped it to his chest.

"What's that for?" Zoe asked.

"Insurance."

"For what?"

"For whatever I need it to be."

Warhorse said, "Kobura, now would be the best time to find out if you can move Zoe without taking her tracker too."

Kobura nodded. She reached out to touch Zoe's jacket, careful not to touch the young woman's skin.

"If you can't do it, bring her back and we'll figure out something else. If they can track her, this is the safest place for her," Jingshen said.

Kobura smiled at him, her teeth white in the darkness. She reminded Jingshen of Lewis Carroll's Cheshire Cat, only the Cat had seemed less predatory. "Don't tell me my job, Ghost. Remember, you work for me now." She backed into the darkest part of the truck's interior and Zoe faded away with her.

Jingshen peered into the front seat. A small T-shaped object sat upon it, festooned with a trio of flickering red LED lights.

Kobura reappeared without Zoe. "Did it work?"

Jingshen nodded. "So it would seem. Where's Zoe?"

"Safe."

"She'd better be safe *and free*," he said, emphasizing the latter.

"That was our agreement. She's a couple miles away from here, near the road but out of sight. She's safe."

Pony Girl cleared her throat. "I hate to interrupt your important business-related discussion, but I think we're about to have company." She pointed at a shimmering distortion in the air not far from the front of the truck.

Warhorse leaned forward to get a better look. "That's Gate's power. It's time to go."

"Take me where you took Zoe," Pony Girl said. "Right now."

Kobura nodded. "Of course. Gentlemen?"

Warhorse yawned. "I'm wore the fuck out. This new power I've got drains me like nothing I've ever felt. I could sleep for two days."

"I'll stay behind," Jingshen said. "Someone has to set off the detonators."

"Why you?" Warhorse asked.

"Because I'll survive even if I'm in the middle of the explosion." He grimaced. "I've *been* blown up before."

"Goddamn, dude. How long did it take you to come back from that?" Warhorse asked with genuine curiosity.

"Awhile," Jingshen said. Flickers appeared in Gate's window as figures emerged from it. "Go. Now."

Kobura disappeared with Warhorse and Pony Girl, leaving Jingshen alone in the truck's cabin.

The figures who'd come through the gate approached the truck. In the faint moonlight, Jingshen could see their SWAT-style tactical armor and helmets. They had targeting lasers that glistened red in the dusty air and their goggles had a faint greenish glow within them. Jingshen realized too late the flaw in his plan. The moment one of them opened the fire truck's cabin, they would realize Zoe wasn't in it. They might put the psychic tracker Medium into play to find her. Somehow Jingshen had to convince them Zoe was in it without them actually seeing her.

Then he saw the tall shadow carrying a long bladed weapon and knew how he could pull off that particular con. He armed the detonator and slipped it into his pocket. He wished he still had his hat.

He opened the back door to a chorus of rifles cocking and a spray of targeting lasers forming a swirling crimson blossom on his chest. He kept his hands raised as he stepped out of the truck. "I want to make a deal," he announced.

"You!" gasped a harsh, feminine voice.

Jingshen smiled. "Hello, Bishop."

"Light him up!" said one of the troopers.

"Hold your fire!" Bishop screamed over the top of him. Her naginata crackled and spat purple-white electricity. "Anyone shoots that motherfucker gets split in half the hard way."

Nobody took a shot, and there was a lengthy, uncomfortable silence until one of the troopers called, "So, uh, what's your deal?"

Bishop's head snapped around to scream at who had spoken, but with all their faces covered, it was hard to tell. And technically, Jingshen supposed, he hadn't done anything to earn her wrath.

"Simple. I walk away. When I'm clear, you can have what's left of the girl."

"What do you mean, *what's left?*" asked another trooper, voice full of suspicion.

Jingshen shrugged. "It's been a difficult few days."

"She better be alive."

"She is. So that's the deal. I walk, and she's yours. My heart stops or you open the door and the truck goes boom. It's wired to explode." Jingshen opened his shirt to show the detonator taped to his chest. A couple of the troopers stepped back involuntarily as if the very act of displaying it would get them killed.

"How do we know she's even in there?" asked the first trooper.

Jingshen shrugged again. "I figure you're tracking her. It's the only way you guys could manage to keep showing up. You tell me if she's in there." He spoke as nonchalantly as possible. This was the entire ploy. If they believed Zoe was in the truck, Jingshen could safely detonate it. If they were tracking her through some other method, like using a parahuman ability that focused on something besides her IUD transmitter, they'd be back to square one. On the other hand, Jingshen thought, if they were tracking her psychically, they wouldn't be hanging around outside Warhorse's truck. No, they had to suspect she was in it or they'd have departed already.

His theory was confirmed a moment later when another trooper gave him a thumbs-up.

It was going to work.

Now he just needed to sell it.

"So I walk away, and when I'm safe I disarm the bomb and you can take your package. I see anybody sneaking around me . . . or above me . . . I blow it. Deal?" Jingshen pointedly ignored the seething Bishop and spoke to the DuraGen trooper who seemed to be in charge.

"Agreed," the trooper said immediately. "Get out of here, Ghost. You're free to go."

"The fuck he is," Bishop shouted. "That bastard killed my brother!"

"Your brother was trying to kill me," Jingshen retorted. "I'm just better at it than he was."

"You son of a bitch!" Bishop's hand slapped downward and she whipped a pistol from its holster to level at him.

"Stand down, Bishop!" the trooper yelled, sounding fearful. "That's an order!"

Bishop whirled and put a bullet through the trooper's faceplate.

The other troopers reacted with professional speed, turning their guns away from Jingshen and firing at Bishop. She moved with inhuman speed and grace, and their bullets whistled through empty air. Jingshen threw himself to the ground and watched as Bishop danced around the troopers, shooting some and slicing through others with her crackling naginata. In a matter of seconds she dispatched the entire strike team. Then she turned to face Jingshen, sides heaving and blood trickling down one arm where a bullet had blown out a chunk of meat. "Get up," she said.

Jingshen stood. "DuraGen isn't going to be happy with you for this."

"I don't fucking care."

"The Source cares. They'll come after you."

Bishop laughed. "Just like they came after you, and here you are. You're like a goddamn cockroach, Ghost." She lowered her head and said through clenched teeth, "And I'm going to kill you."

Jingshen took a fighting stance. "Better than you have tried." He knew he was outmatched against the parahuman mercenary, and there would be no buying her off the way he'd bought off Warhorse.

Bishop screamed a wordless battle cry of fury and charged in at him, whipping her naginata back and forth in a blur.

Jingshen went on full defense immediately, ducking and dodging as the crackling blade slashed and stabbed at him. He stepped on one of the trooper corpses and lost his footing. His fall saved him from being bisected by Bishop's attack. Ozone crackled around him, filling his nose with its acrid stink. The blade came down across his wrist and his left hand went flying, smoking from the electrical energy, adding the sickly stench of burnt flesh to the air. He rolled away to avoid taking a worse injury as Bishop tried to chop off one of his legs.

He scrambled beneath Warhorse's truck, his wrist shooting pain up his arm with every motion.

Bishop's cruel hand closed around one of his ankles. She was strong, but not inhumanly so. She pulled and Jingshen kicked back into her face with his other foot. Her nose crunched with the impact and her grip slipped loose. He hooked his arms on the truck's suspension, trying to ignore the pain of his severed hand as he pulled himself along the undercarriage. He emerged toward the truck's rear and found ladder rungs bolted to the sheet metal. Working one-handed, he started to climb.

Bishop stepped around the front of the truck, a pistol with a giant bore clutched in her free hand. She fired twice at Jingshen, missing both times because her eyes were streaming from the pain of her broken nose. Blood ran down either side of her mouth, giving her a crimson goatee. "*Gho-o-o-ost!*" she screamed, and ran up the front slope of the truck.

Jingshen looked up from the ladder to see Bishop glaring down at him, her naginata crackling with electricity. The naginata looped down at him and he threw himself backward from the truck, twisting in midair as he did so. He dragged the armed detonator from his pocket with his remaining hand. He landed on his back, knocking the wind out of himself.

Bishop raised her naginata over her head and leaped, intent upon driving the blade down through him. He couldn't dodge or even breathe, but he could move his thumb.

He detonated the truck.

Chapter Twenty-Three

September, 1993
Lancaster, California

Jingshen opened his eyes to see a towering fist of flame reaching into the sky. His entire body ached from the shock wave's impact. He'd been so close to the explosion he was lucky not to have been vaporized. The truck itself appeared to have shaped the explosion up and out so the worst of it passed above his prone position on the ground.

There was no sign of Bishop. She must have been incinerated in the blast. He took a deep, shuddering breath. It couldn't have happened to a nicer psychopath.

"*Shinjirarenai!*" Kobura said softly behind him.

"I don't believe it either, yet here I am." Jingshen sat up and looked at her. "I need a vacation. Somewhere in a nice prison cell, with only medical experiments to look forward to."

"I believe that can be arranged." She took him into the shadows with her.

They emerged from the darkness into a stand of cedars, their fragrance replacing the stink of gunpowder and explosives. Jingshen saw a faint but steady green light through the trees. He overheard snatches of conversation, even though he couldn't make out the details between the whispering breeze through treetops and the gentle hiss of nearby highway traffic.

"Everything is handled?" Kobura asked Jingshen as they walked toward the light.

"As best as I could," he replied. "I can't say for certain that DuraGen will stop looking for Zoe, but there should be pretty strong evidence that she died in the truck explosion."

"The best you can is all we can ever hope for," Kobura said. "I appreciate your efforts. I give you my personal guarantee that Kokorotai will not mistreat you."

Jingshen shrugged, even though she might not be able to see it in the darkness. Or maybe she could, given her affinity for the shadows.

They stepped out from the trees to find Pony Girl pacing a bare spot in the wild grass. Warhorse leaned against a large rock, and Zoe sat nearby with her chin resting on her hands. A single green glowstick sat between them all.

"Ghost!" Pony Girl said as she saw them. "I was thinking the worst."

"Were you in that explosion?" Zoe asked. "What was that like?"

Jingshen stopped and thought about it for a moment. "It was loud."

"And expensive," Warhorse said. "While you've been off blowing up my shit, I've been doing some invoicing for you. Between my time, materials used, and incidentals, I figure you're on the hook for . . . let's call it four point five mill."

Pony Girl stopped her pacing. "Four and a half million dollars? Are you high? You told him three million back in the refinery, which I still think is highway robbery."

"Actually, I told him two million. He offered three for expanded services, which I accepted and you all witnessed. Not that we could go to a court of law with this, but it is enforceable according to California laws." Warhorse smiled, showing his teeth. "I have numerous attorneys on retainer."

"I blew up his truck," Jingshen said softly.

Warhorse pointed at him. "Exactly. You blew up my truck, which represented a sizable capital investment in my company. I also was put at severe risk through contact with your charge."

"You got new powers out of the deal," Pony Girl argued. "Seems to me you came out ahead."

"Ah, but we don't know if there are side effects, or there will be side effects later on. I could conceivably have expensive medical care in my future directly related to this business engagement. Therefore, four point five is where it's at."

"You goddamn soldiers of fortune—" Pony Girl began.

"Pony Girl," Jingshen said.

"—and your insufferable, obnoxious—"

"Faith," Jingshen said, loud enough that Pony Girl stopped. "I'll pay it. He earned it."

Pony Girl shut her mouth.

"So, uh, yeah, that's settled, then," Warhorse said awkwardly into the silence. Clearly he'd expected to have to argue more.

Pony Girl turned to Zoe. "You sure you want me to leave you in the charge of these assholes?"

Zoe smiled. "I'll be fine. I'm not staying with them, anyway. I'd shake your hand, but . . . yeah. Thanks, I guess."

"Take care of yourself, Zoe," Pony Girl said. "This world will do its damnedest to break you down and you have to fight every step of the way. You ever need help, get hold of Juice in Just Cause. He knows how to reach me."

"I thought you were retired," Warhorse said with a chuckle. "I heard that somewhere."

Pony Girl crossed her arms. "I *am* retired. And being retired, I can choose to do whatever the fuck I want to do. Right now, I'm going to find a clean hotel with a soft bed and room service. Have a nice meal. Have a bath. Have a nap. Then I'm going to go home to my daughter." She looked around at each of the others. "Maybe if any of you have homes, you should go there as well."

She nodded at Jingshen, sharing the look of recognition reserved for soldiers who've gone to war together. Or maybe he'd just imagined it, for she was gone a heartbeat later.

Zoe stood. "Guess I'll go, too."

Kobura stepped forward. "I will take you wherever you wish to go."

Zoe shook her head. "Nope. Not this time. No offense, but I think it's best if you don't know where I'm going."

Kobura nodded. "That is probably for the best. I wish you well. I, too, offer you any assistance you may need in the future. I may be contacted through any Kokorotai office."

Zoe snorted. "Yeah, don't hold your breath. I'm done being a lab monkey." She looked over at Jingshen. "Hey, Jones, you mind walking a girl down to the roadside, in case there are bears or some shit in the woods here?"

"There are no bears here, but yes, I'll escort you." Jingshen walked over to stand beside her.

"Make sure you come back," Kobura said softly. "Or I will send Warhorse to *bring you*."

Warhorse cracked his knuckles. "And you best believe I will enjoy that task, Ghost."

"I will be back shortly," Jingshen said. "I promise."

* * *

"You look weird without your hat," Zoe said as she picked her way through the trees toward the steady stream of headlights down the hill. "I've barely seen you without it."

Jingshen shrugged, even though she couldn't see it in the darkness. "I've been told it suits me. I'll have to find another one."

They reached the edge of the trees. Zoe stopped before stepping out where drivers could see her. "Hey, I never thanked you."

"Yes, you did. Many times."

"Yeah, well, anyone can *say* thanks. It's different when you say it and you *mean* it. Thank you. For everything you did when you didn't have to. For everything you did for free. I know that's kind of tough for someone like you. Thank you, Jingshen."

He smiled. "You can call me Chinese Indiana Jones. Nobody else gets to do that."

She brushed his lips with hers, the gentlest of busses that barely raised a tingle of discomfort. "Not until you get another hat." She stepped out onto the dirt shoulder and raised her thumb.

Jingshen watched until she was picked up. It only took a few minutes. She was a young woman hitchhiking alone. A beat-up pickup truck pulled over and the figure behind the wheel gestured for her to get in. She did so without hesitating, or even looking back. She could take care of herself. Any man who decided to try to take advantage of her would likely find himself dissolving into sludge or spontaneously combusting. The truck pulled away from the roadside, taking Zoe with it. The driver forgot to switch off his turn signal and Jingshen watched it until it went around a curve and was gone.

He returned to Warhorse and Kobura. "'Bout time you came back," Warhorse said. "You have a quickie in the woods or something?"

Jingshen didn't dignify the jibe with a response.

"Hey," Warhorse said suddenly. "My cash is gone."

A thought occurred to Jingshen and he checked his own pockets. "Mine as well. I didn't have very much left, though."

"I had ten fucking grand." A look of disgust crossed Warhorse's face. "Son of a bitch. She stole it. Right out from under my goddamn nose, that devious bitch!"

For a moment, the only sound was the wind in the trees. Then Jingshen snorted with sudden amusement. Kobura covered her mouth but not before a titter escaped. Warhorse looked at the two of them and burst out in an explosion of laughter.

Epilogue

October, 1993
Yokohama, Kanagawa Prefecture, Japan

The tea was very hot, but it was very good. It had a flavor that reminded Jingshen of the first cut grass of the spring, with just a hint of smoky earthiness. He closed his eyes and let the steaming vapor fill his sinuses, imagining the mountainside where it was harvested, eighty-eight days after the Lunar New Year.

He heard her sit in the chair across the table but didn't open his eyes. He hadn't quite finished enjoying his tea.

"You look like a man in the throes of pleasure," Kobura said.

He opened his eyes and met her gaze. "It's been a long time since I had good tea."

She smiled. "Americans make terrible tea."

He poured some into a second cup for her. "Please."

She raised the clay cup in both hands, holding it before her nose to inhale the heady fragrances. She sipped it and smiled. "Delicious."

He said nothing and drank his own tea.

"I brought you something, Ghost." Kobura set a book on the table before him. It was bound on the right and titled with gorgeous calligraphy. His Japanese was rusty as he hadn't been to the island since the early Nineteenth Century, but it was improving every day. "*Hagakure*, by Yamamoto Tsunetomo."

"I thought you might enjoy having your own copy."

He bowed his head. "Thank you. It is very thoughtful of you."

"It's time to go," she said at last. "They're waiting."

"They can wait until I finish my tea," Jingshen said. "Surely they'd consider that proper."

Kobura nodded. "It's very good tea. I will vouch for it."

They drank their tea in silence until the pot was empty and the sun sat low on the horizon, a smoky red casting long shadows across the teahouse floor. At last, Jingshen set down his cup and picked up his book. "I'm ready."

Kobura took his hand and led him to the back of the teahouse. "I promise, you will be treated very well."

Jingshen said, "I believe you."

Together, they went into the darkness.

Chinatown Ghost

A Just Cause Universe Story

Originally published in The Good Fight 5: The Golden Age anthology (2019), this story is Jingshen's first appearance in the Just Cause Universe.

November, 1948
New York City, NY

A lesser man might have stayed indoors on a night with a frigid wind carrying stinging sleet. Or perhaps a smarter man might have, Adrian thought. He crouched on the fire escape of a tenement, cold wetness seeping through his headscarf, and watched the street through Army surplus binoculars. He might not be a lesser man, but he was willing to entertain the idea that he was being stupid in his heroism.

He hadn't intended originally to become a costumed hero, like the members of the team known as American Justice. They had returned to America as war heroes, first for their efforts in Germany and the in Pacific. Adrian was rich, fit, and bored. He had a gift for archery, and had lobbied for its inclusion in the canceled '44 and then the '48 Summer Olympics in London. Despite his efforts, the Committee had passed with the excuse that it was too soon after the War to introduce an event that hadn't been included for a quarter of a century. Disappointed, Adrian had thrown himself into his training with no clear idea what to do with it.

In '46, American Justice had debuted in New York, and everything changed. The veteran heroes wore costumes, hid their faces behind masks, and fought crime with fantastic abilities far beyond those of normal men. They were called parahumans, and they rooted out criminals wherever they could be found.

Adrian read everything he could about the team. One wall of his basement workshop was plastered with articles and magazine covers. He imagined what it would be like, fighting crime as a masked hero. Then it occurred to him there was no reason he couldn't do exactly that. He had the resources in a sizable inheritance from his parents who died in a boating accident shortly after his nineteenth birthday. He had the skill with a bow to perform shots that rivaled the legend of Robin Hood. Someone who had trained with him at the club said he was like a surgeon with a broadhead. From there had been a short stretch to call himself Dr. Danger and start patrolling the streets and rooftops of Manhattan. Perhaps it was a young, rich man's fantasy, but he knew he had made a difference. He had saved lives.

He was crouching on a fire escape in the sleet that evening with intent to save more lives.

Someone had been grabbing prostitutes off the streets. Four had disappeared in the past week and a half, approximately the same time the weather had turned and fewer people had been out at night. The police weren't keen to follow up on the disappearances of women of ill repute, and American Justice was busy doing its own thing. That left Manhattan's masked archer to pick up the slack. A friend of the fourth missing woman had spotted him in an alley and called to him for help. When he arrived, she poured out her tale of terror amid a flood of tears and exhortations for him to find her friend. Word spread throughout the community of streetwalkers that they were being hunted, and barely any women at all were trying to work in the chilly, wet weather. Those who were clustered together, careful not to be caught anywhere alone and careful about which johns they went with and which they sent packing.

Adrian had gone to his usual haunts, information sources he'd developed over the past half a year. Pawnshops. Seedy bars that catered to a lower-class clientele. A massage parlor in Queens. A bookie in the Bowery.

Nothing.

Nobody had heard anything about prostitutes being kidnapped. No bodies had turned up, which suggested the women might still be alive, which in turn suggested that someone had a reason for keeping them alive. Whatever the reason, Adrian was certain it was a situation they would gladly abandon given the chance. It galled him that he couldn't find even a hint of what might have happened. It was like they had disappeared off the face of the world.

That was why he monitored the lone streetwalker as she stood under the awning of a closed watch-repair shop. She was near enough to a streetlight that a passing driver might see her and take a fancy, but far enough away not to be obvious about it. For three nights, he'd been staking her out, well aware of the irony of his own spying behavior. As easily as Adrian found her, the kidnappers might do so as well. He hoped no harm would come to her, but if it did, he would be ready with his tools of the trade.

In the summer, when he'd begun his adventuring, he'd picked a swashbuckling-style outfit because he thought it gave him a suitably dashing look to match his *nom de guerre*. He wore pirate boots with the tops folded down, tight-fitting trousers, a loose blouse with his quiver strapped over it, and a scarf tied over the top half of his head and face, leaving only his eyes visible. Now that the weather had turned, he'd added a greatcoat and an old-fashioned tricorne hat. It wasn't the warmest outfit he could have worn, but it made what he felt was a reasonable accommodation to comfort while retaining his overall swashbuckling look. Icy water trickled off the brim of his hat and still found its way inside the turned-up collar of the coat. He wished he could pop into an all-night diner for a cup of soup or hot coffee.

He wondered who would break first, him or the streetwalker below. She had her arms wrapped around herself with a coat that looked uncomfortably thin for the weather. Go home, he silently implored her. Safer for you there. She reached into her purse and pulled something out—perhaps a couple of coins—then glanced in the direction of the pay phone on the corner. It looked like she was about to give up for the night and call for a ride.

At that moment, a nondescript sedan pulled up to the curb alongside her, engine rumbling and wipers slapping away accumulated sleet. The streetwalker went into business mode, bending over to speak to the driver and opening her coat a little to show off her cleavage. The sedan's rear doors opened and two men emerged, wearing long dark coats and hats pulled low. Adrian's pulse quickened and it took everything he had not to leap to the screaming woman's defense as they shoved her into the back seat.

Adrian stuck an arrow between his teeth and went over the side of the fire escape, sliding down a cord he'd tied earlier for just such a quick descent. He landed in a puddle in the alley below, splattering slush everywhere as he whipped his bow off his back. He nocked the arrow, drew, and fired it at the departing car's taillights. The arrow was one of his own design. A spring rode right behind the arrowhead. Behind it was a small battery-operated transmitter that would operate for half an hour before it ran out of power. It was an ungainly arrow, prone sometimes to flying off course or other times the transmitter would shatter on impact despite the shock absorber. This time, he saw the arrow punch into the car's sheet metal, just above the bumper. The car neither slowed nor stopped, suggesting the driver must have thought the bang of impact was either a backfire or a pothole. It turned a corner and disappeared.

Adrian sprinted through the sleet for his own car, a new Mercury with the latest factory options and a few he'd added himself. He dug in his pocket, found the key, and slipped inside behind the wheel. He started the engine and opened the glove box. Instead of gloves or documents, he had installed an armature with his transmitter tracker. Wires ran from it back into the glove box. He switched it on and waited impatiently for the device to warm up. Adrian shivered in the ice cold air from the vents, realizing how wet he'd gotten crouching on the fire escape. He needed a better cold-weather outfit—something insulated and waterproof.

His tracker featured a ring of eight lights corresponding to the cardinal directions. Two glowed to life, pointing in the approximate direction of the transmitter. It wasn't a perfect system, but it was the best he could manage with his basic understanding of electronics. He pulled away from the curb, the wipers adding rhythm to the basso rumble and treble hiss of tires on wet pavement. He hoped his makeshift transmitter wouldn't fail due to the weather and drove faster than was probably prudent given the conditions. In a few minutes, he spotted the taillights of his prey. Instead of trusting the tracker, stayed a block back and crept along so as not to raise suspicions. Between the weather and the late hour, the streets were mostly empty, making his pursuit easier.

Adrian kept the target car in view and occasionally switched off his headlights to make it appear as if he had disappeared. The target car rolled into Chinatown and Adrian grimaced. No wonder there hadn't been any sign of the women who'd disappeared. Chinatown was a black hole, full of gangs and secrets and lies, and very, very few women. American immigration laws for

Chinese were highly restrictive, and almost all of those who did manage to make their way through Ellis Island or other centers were male. Adrian frowned as he considered the likely fate for women being kidnapped off the streets and brought into Chinatown. Sex slavery was something *nice* people didn't talk about, but *nice* people didn't normally deal with the kind of criminal scum that Adrian fought on a daily basis.

Despite the lateness of the hour, the street still glowed with neon and flickering lanterns in windows. Adrian knew his car would be even easier to see and pulled over to park behind a delivery sedan with flowing, hand-lettered pinyin characters on its rear doors. He sat there with the car idling, watching as the other car went three blocks farther, then made a left turn. He advanced slowly, nosing the car out into the intersection before making the same turn. The other car had vanished, and Adrian kept one eye on his tracker and the other on the road as he cruised up the street. When the lights changed, he made a note of the building in question. It was a nondescript tenement amid all the other closely packed buildings. He continued onward for another block, turned left again, and parked the car.

Keeping his hat pulled low over his headscarf and coat collar turned up, he slipped into a narrow alley nearby. It was too tight for a car, almost too tight for two men to have passed each other without turning sideways. He slung his quiver, quickly assembled his bow, and strung it. Ready for action, he moved through the walkway toward the building where the target car had disappeared. Overflowing trash cans competed for space with stacks of wooden crates and boxes, making it difficult to pass through the alley without knocking something over. Adrian briefly considered climbing up to the rooftops, but this part of town offered no convenient fire escapes.

The path between the buildings was dark and narrow and wound around like a river meandering through a box canyon. Adrian found the building where the transmitter had led him. What he'd thought was a tenement was an old carriage house instead. He listened at a door leading into the alley but heard nothing except splattering sleet splattering down. He tested the handle to see if it might be unlocked. As it started to twist, he sensed motion behind him and started to turn.

A hard blow crashed against his skull and he spun into darkness.

* * *

Adrian awakened to throbbing pain in his head. Before he even opened his eyes, he reached up to gingerly feel the hard lump behind his ear. It was tender and his headscarf didn't appear to have dulled the blow in the least. He realized after a moment that he was still wearing the headscarf, although his hat and coat didn't appear to still be on his person. He was lying on a thin mattress set on a floor. The tiny skittering sounds of cockroaches were all too familiar to him from some of the terrible places his crusade had brought him over the past six months. He cracked his eyes open, resisting the temptation to leap to his feet in an unfamiliar location.

A flickering naked bulb overhead cast a dim light through the room. Years of water damage and tobacco smoke stained the ceiling. From his position, Adrian saw a window with the shade drawn and the glow of a red neon light flashing behind it. A lamp sitting on a small table underneath the window was switched off. Beside the table, a shadowy figure sat in a wooden chair with arms crossed and face hidden by the brim of a hat pulled low.

"You're awake," the man said in a heavily accented voice. Adrian pegged him as Chinese, although to be fair it wasn't a wild assumption given his most recent location. "You should not be here, *bairen.*"

Careful to keep his hands in plain sight, Adrian gingerly sat up, feeling his head throb with every motion. The mattress, like everything else in the room, was filthy. His skin crawled the way the roaches skittered around the edges of the floor. He saw his coat and hat sitting on another chair in the corner, along with his quiver and his bow. He glanced at the man by the window and back at his equipment, wondering if he could get to it before the man shot him or otherwise attacked. Maybe on his best day he could, but not when he was still woozy from a blow to the head.

"You would not make it," the man said as if reading Adrian's mind.

"Fine," Adrian retorted. "You didn't kill me or unmask me, so you have some other agenda. Why am I here? And where is *here*, anyway?"

"Chinatown, of course," the man said. "You were about to make a big mistake."

"And who are you?" Adrian's tone was challenging, but he didn't feel the bravado he was trying to display. In all the months of his adventuring, this was the first time he'd found himself in this kind of predicament.

"Nobody special."

"I'm not calling you that. What's your name?"

"Jingshen. And you are Dr. Danger. You should not be here."

"You already said that."

Jingshen raised his head enough for Adrian to see the light reflecting off the man's dark eyes. His face was crisscrossed by a network of fine white lines in the man's natural skin tone. They looked like scars, but if they were, Jingshen must have suffered a horrific injury. Adrian had once seen a mobster after he'd been flung through a plate glass window by Strongman of American Justice. That man hadn't had as many cuts as Jingshen must have. "Do you speak Cantonese?"

"No."

"You do not read it, either." Jingshen didn't make it a question.

"No."

"You have no *shungyu*."

"I don't know what that means."

"Reputation. Prestige. You might call it *cachet*."

"Aren't we a walking thesaurus? Look, I've got a mission to fulfill, and you've delayed me long enough. I'm going to take my bow and walk out of here."

Jingshen stood. He wasn't as tall as Adrian, but his movements had a fluid grace that made Adrian nervous. "No, you are not."

So it would be a fight, then. Adrian had been in any number of scraps since he'd begun his career. Most guys didn't know anything about the rudiments of boxing, which he'd studied and practiced, and tended toward brawling instead. The problem with being trained in a specific style of fighting was that training tended to assume one's opponent followed a similar style. Adrian had learned quickly that although knowing how to fight was all well and good, what really mattered was knowing how to win a fight quickly. That was one reason he liked archery; he could win most fights before he ever had to get up close and personal with someone.

He raised his fists and took a step toward Jingshen. The other man twisted around, springing into the air, and kicked. The next thing Adrian knew he was lying on his back on the floor, gasping for breath. He coughed and rolled over, trying to get back onto his feet.

"Stay down, white man."

"No!" Still fighting to get air, Adrian struggled up and forward, lunging for Jingshen.

Jingshen slapped his charge aside and drove an elbow into the back of Adrian's head. He crashed to the floor again. "Stay. Down."

Adrian groaned and got to his hands and knees. He was close to the chair in which Jingshen had sat. He grabbed it by its legs and swung it around.

Jingshen caught the chair, pulled it from Adrian's hands as easily as if it had been an intentional handoff, and wound up sitting in it facing Adrian. When Adrian tried to follow up with another attack, Jingshen slapped his fist out of the way without even getting up from the chair. Suddenly his fist floated only a half inch from Adrian's nose. "Are you done?"

Adrian leaped back, and the fuzziness in his brain cleared. He realized Jingshen had thoroughly beaten him and probably could have killed him outright at any time. Instead, the Chinese man had held back. He lowered his head and his fists. "Yes, for now."

"Take your bow and go back to your people. Stay out of Chinatown."

Adrian went over to the corner where his gear was stashed. He shrugged his shoulders into the coat and slung the quiver and bow over his shoulder. He didn't even consider trying for a sneak attack after seeing the speed and ruthless efficiency Jingshen had used to defeat him. "Women have been kidnapped. Stolen from the streets. I followed a car here. I'm trying to save them."

"You can't," Jingshen said.

"Do you know where they are?" Adrian rounded upon the smaller man, careful to keep his intensity under control.

Jingshen looked away.

"You do know!" Adrian clenched his fists, aching to beat the information from Jingshen and knowing he couldn't. "Tell me. Tell me where to find them."

"It is not for you to help." Jingshen sounded miserable suddenly, and Adrian wondered what the man was holding back from him.

"Are you in cahoots with them? Are you defending the kidnappers? Because karate wizard or not, I will fight you until you tell me what I want to know."

Jingshen's mouth fell open. "Karate?" He paused, then laughed. "Oh. Oh, no. Not karate. Not this time." He sobered. "You should not have come here. The Tongs would see you cut to pieces."

"Not if I see them first. There's not a gangster alive that can outrun an arrow."

"You would kill them?"

"It's not my first choice. I don't want to start a war. I just want to save those poor prostitutes before they are . . ." Adrian stopped as he considered what the women already did for a living. "Well, it doesn't matter who they are. I'd try to save them regardless. So you need to stand aside and let me do my job. Keep knocking me down and I'll keep getting back up."

Jingshen nodded. "I believe you would. I . . . did not expect you to be an honorable man. There are not many here in this city, in this time."

"Do you know where to find these missing women?"

"Not for certain, but I have an idea."

"Will you tell me?"

"No . . ." Jingshen adjusted his hat to ride lower on his face, obscuring it in shadow. "But I will take you."

* * *

The sleet had turned to snow and it was starting to build up on the street. Patches of white reflected the harsh orange and red neon prevalent in the local signs, none of which Adrian could read. He'd begun to think Jingshen was right about him being in over his head, but that was part and parcel of being a hero.

Jingshen was far more than he seemed, and Adrian was burning with questions that he feared might forever go unanswered. The Chinese man had left his coat behind in favor of a tight black sweater. He had clips attached to the back of his suspenders and had placed a thirty-inch baton wrapped in black electrical tape into each clip. Clearly, the man's training extended beyond mere karate—or whatever it was. Maybe he could teach Adrian a thing or two about infighting. The more he pursued his justice crusade, the more he realized he couldn't always stand off at a distance and shoot arrows.

"Where are we going?" Adrian asked.

"To ask the right person the right questions." Jingshen paused under an awning and removed his hat to shake the water off it. His hair stuck out in all directions. Seeing his face clearly for the first time made Adrian stare. The man was younger than he'd

257

expected, perhaps even younger than Adrian. His eyes, though . . . they had the shadows of a man haunted by the things he'd seen; the sort of things that aged a man far faster than time.

"Okay, I'm following your lead."

The two men crossed the street, passed through a narrow alley, and wound up at a door with pinyin characters scrawled in paint that had run before it dried. A sharp, vinegary smell emerged from building. Jingshen stopped at the door. "Expect to fight lackeys before we reach the man we must speak to. Try not to kill them. Restraint will reflect favorably upon you."

Adrian nodded, feeling his pulse quicken.

Jingshen rapped on the door in a quick, syncopated pattern. A moment later, a small panel in the door slid aside and a rough voice spoke Chinese from a darkened room beyond. Jingshen replied in kind. The man on the other side uttered a curt laugh and slammed the panel shut.

Jingshen moved in a blur and wedged one of his sticks into the panel. The man on the far side made a curious grunt which terminated suddenly as Jingshen shoved the stick into what Adrian imagined was the other man's face. He heard the sound of a body slumping to the floor behind the door.

"How are we supposed to get in now?" he asked.

"They will open the door." Jingshen levered the panel open with his stick and shouted something in Chinese through the hole.

Adrian heard indistinct shouting in response. He drew a ball-tip arrow from his quiver and nocked it to the string. Ball-tips could break bones and knock out opponents without killing them, and he suspected questioning would play an important part in the next phase of his mission. He stepped a few feet back from the door, giving himself enough time to fire an arrow and draw another before someone closed with him. "How many, do you think?"

"Not many. Five or six."

"Five or six," Adrian muttered. "That's *not many*?"

The shouting reached the door and Adrian heard the sound of locks being released. The door was thrown open.

The first man out clutched a decades-old Tommy gun. Before he could pull the trigger, Adrian loosed his arrow, catching the man in the center of his forehead. The blow might have cracked his skull but probably didn't kill him. Nevertheless, he went down as efficiently as if he'd been shot with something lethal.

The next two men fell under a barrage of blows from Jingshen's sticks. They whistled through the air, carving visible trails through the falling snow as they struck wrists, elbows, necks. Their weapons, a pair of broad-bladed knives and a revolver, clattered to the pavement.

Adrian shot another ball-tip beneath Jingshen's raised arms, catching the next man in his sternum. He gasped as the arrow knocked his wind out, then fell in the doorway. Jingshen glanced back at him and nodded. "Only four, it appears. Come, we'll go in and ask our questions."

Adrian kicked aside the fallen weapons so they wouldn't be in easy reach of anyone who awakened prematurely. He retrieved what arrows were still usable. "What is this place?"

"Hip Sing Tong."

"I don't know what that means." Adrian followed Jingshen into the building. The vinegar smell intensified and a cloying smoke drifted through the air.

"Heroin."

Adrian stopped in the middle of the hall. "This is a . . . an opium den?"

Jingshen snorted. "Opium is a drug for old men. Heroin is where young men make their dollars now."

"It's made here?"

"Made, packaged, distributed."

"And you've done nothing to stop it, even though you knew?"

Jingshen turned to face him. "What would you have me do, *bairen*? I am just one man."

"So am I."

"You will not destroy this place."

"Why not?" Adrian challenged. "Will you stop me? It's the right thing to do, and I think you know it. You're not as aloof as you pretend to be."

"Tonight, you are seeking your missing streetwalkers. Hsing Shou will know where they are."

"And he'll just tell us if we ask nicely and don't take a torch to his drugs?"

"Something like that."

A footstep down the hall made both men freeze in the darkness. Adrian's blood pounded in his ears and he reached for an arrow, barely daring to breathe.

Jingshen smashed his open palm into Adrian's chest, knocking him backward as the light and thunder of a machine gun filled the hallway. In the flickering flash from the barrel, Adrian saw Jingshen's body shudder as bullet after bullet smashed into him. "No!" Adrian cried. He yanked an arrow from the quiver, selecting it by the pattern of its fletching without having to look. He dragged the arrowhead against the hallway wall, igniting it like a strike-anywhere match. He raised the flaming arrow to his bow and sent it flying up the hall in barely a second. Instead of blowing out the flames at the tip, the wind of the arrow's passage dragged the fire along the shaft, which was coated with a flammable resin. The firebrand buried itself in the chest of the man with the machine gun. He fell back against the far wall, dropping his gun and staring in mute shock at the flaming arrow sticking out from his ribs.

"Jingshen!" Adrian knelt by the other man.

Jingshen grabbed his arm. "I am . . . fine. Give me a moment." He rolled onto his hands and knees and grunted. With a sound like gravel falling, bullets rained down from the Chinese man's torso to clatter on the floor. He coughed once and spat out a final bloody bullet.

"You . . . you're one of them! A parahuman."

"I don't know what I am." Jingshen stood. "But I do know that I hate being shot. It hurts." He looked up the hall where the gunman had died with the flaming arrow still burning against his chest. "That was unwise."

"I didn't have much time to think about it. For all I knew, you were dead." Adrian glared at Jingshen. "You could have told me you're bulletproof."

Angry voices sounded further down the hall, shouting in Chinese.

Jingshen shouted something back and the voices stopped.

"What did you say?"

"I said we are here to speak to Hsing Shou. If they allow us passage to do that, we will leave when we are finished."

"What if they don't?"

Jingshen nodded toward Adrian's quiver. "Then I hope you have enough arrows."

* * *

In cowboy boots with silver spurs, Hsing Shou looked like he'd stepped out of a dime store Western novel. A pistol rode in a Kansas loop on one hip, angled for a cross-body draw. His leather vest was fringed at the bottom and he peeked out from beneath a dusty bowler hat. He smirked at Jingshen and Adrian as they stood before him. He hadn't required them to surrender their weapons; clearly he felt protected well enough with the dozen men standing behind and to either side of him, armed to the teeth and muttering.

"Jingshen. You bring a foreigner here. Into my house. You kill my men. I am disappointed." Hsing Shou spoke in heavily accented but understandable English. He must have been doing so for Adrian's benefit, to make it clear he had nothing to hide. "I thought we had an understanding, you and I."

Adrian glanced sharply at Jingshen but the man's face was impassive. "We have nothing."

"Foreigner?" Adrian asked. "Last I checked, Chinatown is still in New York."

"You are a foreigner here, *bairen.* As far as you are concerned, you are in China now, and you are trespassing." Hsing Shou laughed. "I could kill you now and that would be the last anyone heard of Dr. Danger."

"I'm looking for some missing women. I tracked the car that took them here to Chinatown," Adrian said. "I'm betting you know where they are."

Jingshen sighed at Adrian's lack of diplomacy.

"We are not permitted to import our women," Hsing Shou said. "Therefore we must use yours."

One of Hsing Shou's men apparently translated what he said and several of them laughed.

"Prostitutes or not, they have dignity. They have the right not to be enslaved. Or raped. Now where are they?" Adrian clenched his fists, aching to put an arrow right into Hsing Shou's smug face.

"What makes you think you have any power here at all, *bairen*? One word from me and my men will kill you where you stand."

"They may kill him, but you cannot kill me," Jingshen said. "Better than you have tried and failed. I will keep coming until you are all dead and then I will find another Hip Sing man to tell me where the women are."

For a minute, nobody said anything. The tension made it feel like the entire room was vibrating. At last, Hsing Shou smiled and lowered his head. "Of course. *Tangrenjie Gui* has found his voice at last. We have always known this day was coming. Very well. Perhaps we can come to an . . . arrangement."

"What arrangement?" Adrian asked, suspicion making his voice hoarse.

"If I tell you where to find your white whores, you will take them and leave Chinatown. I never want you to set foot within its boundaries again, Dr. Danger. If you do so, your life is forfeit. You cannot hide behind *Tangrenjie Gui* forever. You will be hunted down and killed. Chinatown is mine, *bairen*. Those who enter it live or die at my decree." Hsing Shou grinned. "Decide quickly. My dogs are anxious to be let out to play."

Adrian glanced at Jingshen, but his face was an impassive mask beneath the shadow of his hat brim. "Yes, I can live with that."

Hsing Shou motioned to one of his men, who bent down and listened to his boss whisper to him. The man tucked his pistol into his waistband and left out the back of the room. "Very well. I have sent instructions ahead to have the women released and you will be led to a place where you can retrieve them." He spread his hands in mocking generosity. "Go in peace, my friends."

A gaunt man with a thin mustache and a large overcoat stepped forward, a pistol clutched in one eager hand. He spoke in curt Chinese and Jingshen responded with a single syllable.

"We are to follow him," Jingshen said softly.

"They're going to kill us," Adrian muttered.

"They will try."

"I'm not bulletproof."

"Then don't get shot." Jingshen's mouth twitched in a momentary half-smile. Or perhaps it had just been a trick of the light as the men went down the hallway.

* * *

Hsing Shou had left Jingshen his sticks and Adrian his bow and arrows. Adrian wondered if it was to lull them into a false sense of security or to make their approaching deaths seem somehow more honorable. Regardless, he was grateful for the weight of his quiver against his back. He only wished it were heavier with arrows. Hsing Shou seemed like the kind of man who had resources to waste on excess, and that likely extended to the hit squad awaiting them in their eventual destination.

The thin man led them to a doorway into a courtyard that stank of the garbage piled around the edges, highlighted by a growing white blanket of snow. He pointed to a door across from them.

Adrian and Jingshen stepped out into the new fallen snow, making dark tracks as their boots sank into the black mud below. "They must think we are fools to go along with this," Jingshen muttered.

"Wiser men than us would have stayed home tonight, warm and dry."

"And yet here we are, neither warm nor dry."

"Two fools," Adrian agreed. "They'll take us when we reach the middle."

"Dr. Danger!" Hsing Shou's voice echoed across the courtyard from somewhere behind them. "I am almost ashamed to kill a fool such as you. Almost." He laughed and Adrian *moved.*

He spun around in a crouch, already setting a ball-tip arrow to string as an object the size of a baseball arced toward them through the snow. Adrian's vision narrowed to a tunnel, making a straight line between the tip of his arrow and the incoming grenade. He loosed his arrow and it sped straight and true, catching the grenade dead center. The heavy ball-tip deflected the explosive away from its intended course to explode against the wall of Hsing Shou's heroin production facility. Shrapnel peppered him but his coat absorbed the worst of it. Part of the wall behind him collapsed and screams of pain emerged from behind it.

Guns erupted around them and Adrian ran slipping and sliding through the snow to crash into a pile of garbage against a wall. He saw a muzzle flash in a second floor window and a bullet creased his side, stinging like he'd been attacked by a vicious cat. He shot an arrow into that window and a man tumbled out, clutching helplessly at the shaft coming out of his throat.

Jingshen seemed to be everywhere at once. His sticks flashed through the snow and he leaped into the path of oncoming bullets like a tiger charging at a spear to slay the hunter holding it. Adrian rolled aside as bullets from a Tommy gun on full auto chewed into the mud. A frog-crotch arrow lanced out and sliced the support spar of an awning. It collapsed onto the gunmen beneath and they cursed and shouted in

Chinese as they tried to extricate themselves. Jingshen was on them in a moment, his sticks whistling and beating a rapid Gene Krupa tattoo on the indistinct shapes beneath the canvas.

Fire burned through Adrian's leg as a bullet lodged in the meaty part of his thigh and he lost his balance. He still shot an arrow through the chest of the man who'd fired at him and pinned him to the wall like a butterfly in a display case. Flames licked at the side of the heroin building. Adrian suspected it might burn up completely before the nearest fire department managed to get through the storm to help.

Jingshen hauled him to his feet. "I told you not to get shot," he chided, pummeling a man who charged at them with a sword.

With no time to reach an arrow, Adrian used his bow like a staff to deflect the blow of another man with a long knife. The blade caught on the wood and stuck for a moment, allowing Adrian to drive a solid right into the man's face, breaking teeth and bone. Behind him, Jingshen fought in a flurry of hand to hand, kicking and swinging his sticks. More men charged in, armed with knives and hatchets. Adrian ducked beneath a hatchet blow and Jingshen's foot lanced over his head, catching the assailant on the side of his jaw and sending him spinning away.

Adrian grabbed an arrow from his quiver and pounded it down into the foot of a knife-wielder, who howled in sudden agony. He grabbed the man and spun him into another hatchet-man and both went down. Jingshen drove his sticks down tip first into the backs of each man's neck with sounds like gunshots.

And just like that, the battle was ended. Adrian and Jingshen stared at each other, sides heaving in exhaustion. Jingshen looked like he'd absorbed an armada's worth of bullets. The bits of lead rained down from him as his body rejected them. "Are you . . . all right?" Adrian gasped, suddenly feeling the pain from his wounds.

"I told you . . . not to . . . get shot." Jingshen sounded amused, finding a spark of joy despite the carnage around them. "Now what?"

One of the men Adrian had shot groaned, the arrow still sticking from a spot just to the left of his aorta. Only by the grace of a half inch was he still alive to feel the pain the arrow had inflicted.

"You missed," Jinshen said.

Adrian snorted. "I'd like to say I winged him on purpose, but that would be a lie. Hey . . ." He addressed the wounded man lying on the snow. "You speak English?"

Jingshen asked him a question in Chinese. The man coughed out a weak response. "He does not speak English. I will translate for you until he dies. He does not have long."

"Ask him where the women are." Adrian fervently hoped they hadn't been in the building behind him, now engulfed in flames. He could hear sirens in the distance as someone must have finally gotten through to a fire brigade.

Jingshen listened to the man's response, interspersed with coughing jags and bloody foam leaking from his mouth. "There," he said at last, pointing across the courtyard. "That is the brothel."

"Is it defended?"

"Not as well as it would have been before this." Jingshen motioned to the courtyard.

"Tell them we're coming in, and we'll destroy anyone who gets in our way." Adrian looked down at the man with the arrow in his chest, realized he'd died, and stood. His fingers ached from the cold, but not so much he couldn't put one of his few remaining arrows to the string.

Jingshen took his sticks in both hands once more and issued his warning as they approached the door at the far end of the courtyard. It opened as they reached it and both men tensed. Instead of the attack they expected, an old man made himself visible in the doorway and then held it open for them. He bowed his head and whispered something in Chinese. "He says nobody inside will harm us. He hopes we will extend the same courtesy," Jingshen said.

"Do you believe him?"

"I do."

They entered the narrow hallway, Jingshen taking the lead and keeping one shoulder to the wall so Adrian had a clear shot past him if needed. A few men stepped to the doorways of the tiny rooms so they could be seen and bowed their heads as the first man had. "Why are they doing this?"

"They do not wish to offend or anger us. They are afraid of us."

"They should be." After the combat in the courtyard, Adrian was finding it difficult to keep his temper up when he was confronted over and over by men not wishing to fight. "Ask them where the women are, and tell them we're taking them and leaving."

"They are in the room at the end of the hall," Jingshen said after a brief conversation with one of the other men. "They are . . . they have been given heroin to make them . . . docile."

One of the men looked up from his position of contrition and said something directly to Adrian in Chinese. His expression was haunted and Adrian couldn't even guess as to what he'd said. "Well?" he asked Jingshen.

"He asks you not to take their livelihood away. He says Hsing Shou will punish them."

There was the anger Adrian had been struggling to maintain. He felt his pulse pounding as the enormity of what he'd been asked struck him full force. These men . . . these inhumane monsters . . . they'd rather see women drugged up and abused until death rather than look for new employment. "Get out," Adrian said in a thick, rage-choked voice.

"What?" Jingshen asked.

"Tell them to get out. All of them. Anyone left inside this building is going to die in it after I get the women out of here."

Jingshen raised his head enough that Adrian could see the faint surprise on his face. He studied Adrian for a moment, perhaps to determine whether he was serious. Then he relayed Adrian's warning to the men in the hall. They all left their rooms and filed out, moving with a nervous haste, as if Adrian's fury pushed them out like rowboats ahead of a wave.

Adrian and Jingshen found six women, five Caucasian and one Chinese, sprawled on cots in a roach-infested room that stank of vomit and feces. All the women were dirty and stank of sweat and abuse except for the one whom Adrian had seen kidnapped. Half were naked or mostly naked while the others wore stained cotton shifts. They had needle marks on their arms and legs, and were so dead to their surroundings that they didn't even react when roaches ran across their bare flesh.

"Help me get them out of here, for God's sake!" Adrian's voice was rough and he had to clench his teeth to keep from breaking down into tears at the sight of such human misery. It was the first time in his experience as a costumed hero where he'd encountered such depravity. He hoped it would be the last time, but feared it would only get worse as he kept up his crusade.

The Chinese woman and one of the Americans were so thin they were looked like bags of loose bones wrapped in sore-covered skin. Adrian and Jingshen each lifted one into their arms and went out the same side door the men had left through. The pain from his wounds made Adrian wince with every step and he wished he had the ability to heal as Jingshen did. "There," Adrian said, nodding at a delivery van with a faded picture of a chicken on the side. "We'll put them all in the back. Make them comfortable, and I'll take them to the hospital."

Jingshen wrenched open the van's rear door with one of his sticks. Chicken droppings stained the van's floorboards, but a tarpaulin was rolled up beside one of the fender wells. They spread it out, covering the worst of the mess. "I will bring out the others," Jingshen said. "Stay here, make sure no harm comes to them. Can you start the motor?"

Adrian nodded. He'd hot-wired cars before. He would have to come back for his own car later . . . assuming it didn't get stolen in the meantime.

It took him a few long minutes to find the right wires beneath the van's cracked dashboard. As Jingshen brought out the last woman, he managed to get the engine to crank over and shudder to life amid a cloud of smoke. Jingshen shut the van's door. Adrian engaged the emergency brake and got out, leaving the engine running. He extended his hand to the Chinese man. "Thank you," he said. "I couldn't have done this without you."

"You are a good man," Jingshen said. "It was my honor to help. Be a better fighter, though. You cannot always shoot arrows."

"Maybe you could teach me some fundamentals."

"Perhaps." Jingshen paused. "Will you stay away from Chinatown?"

"Perhaps," Adrian replied. "Seems like you could do a fine job protecting this area yourself. Maybe I'll only come by if you need help. Somehow, I don't think you'll need much." He paused. "Oh, there is one more thing." He reached into the van and withdrew his bow and a single arrow with a heavy, cylindrical tip.

"What will you do?"

"Shoot an arrow." Adrian aimed the arrow at the door from which they had emerged and let it fly. The arrow, packed from tip to tail with gelignite, pierced the darkness. A moment later, a brilliant, hot explosion rent the air as the explosive erupted. The front half of the building blew apart into flaming splinters.

Jingshen's eyes were as wide as the full moon as he stared at the devastation Adrian had wrought, and then turned his eyes to Adrian.

Adrian gave him a grim smile.

Jingshen smiled back. "Perhaps shooting one arrow is not so bad. Farewell, Dr. Danger."

"Make it Adrian. You ever need me, leave a message at Frank's on Second Avenue. They know how to reach me."

"What does *Adrian* mean?"

"It means *from Adria*. Not very interesting. What does *Jingshen* mean?"

"Spirit. Like one's essence."

"Spirit also means *ghost*. The Chinatown Ghost has a nice, heroic ring to it."

"Perhaps." Jingshen shook Adrian's hand and then faded into the shadows.

Adrian put the van into gear and drove far faster than he should have toward the hospital, precious cargo in the back. He smiled to himself, in spite of his cold, wet clothes. In spite of the aching bullet wound. In spite of the stench the chickens had left behind. He didn't always win when he put on the mask . . . but sometimes he did.

ABOUT THE AUTHOR

Ian Thomas Healy dabbles in many different genres. He's a multiple participant and winner of National Novel Writing Month. He created the popular ongoing superhero series, the *Just Cause Universe*, and is also the creator of the *Writing Better Action Through Cinematic Techniques* workshop, which helps writers to improve their action scenes.

When not writing, which is rare, he enjoys watching hockey, reading comic books (and serious books, too), and living in the great state of Colorado, which he shares with his wife, children, house-pets, and approximately five million other people.

Visit *www.ianthealy.com* for more information.

www.ingramcontent.com/pod-product-compliance
Lightning Source LLC
Chambersburg PA
CBHW031609240626
47153CB00002B/695